I0451604

barry crashes his future big wheel

To the old friend who planted a beautiful seed into my frustrated heart

My tongue was really quite quick when I drew salary as a loan lumper. It all came about so fast, being a very good student with the numbers and then, just like that, the only calculation was how to not dam the river for a moment with any sensible math. I sat back and my tongue spat yesses to the borrowers and bosses and bond buyers, and those yesses had a dollar figure for more people than I can comprehend.

When I came to, not quite twenty-five years old, well, the words began originating from a different place. It took many lean years, which are mostly for another day, before I felt that I was truly part of an even more involved currency.

Craziest thing about the loan lumping was that it was not so dialed-up like the fifty-somethings in the office, they were always going all yahoo up in my space, talking about how way-back-when they were just out of college and loan lumping everything in sight. But still, I was clipping along in the next-generation loan lump, more conscientious they said, and the general mood around there was that good years were ahead. Then I kind of went crazy over a woman, and the loan lumping became stupid to me very quickly, because, to keep it simple, I preferred to make her laugh by making fun of the loan lumping, instead of doing loan lumps.

So, in order to keep my special colleague entertained, I had to find new and creative ways to avoid any loan lumping. It got pretty intense, all the work I was doing to not do any work while at work. I had to cut my days short, big time. The old-timers, I think they considered it all a phase and tried to hand me more interesting loan lumps, to pull me out of it. It was flammable material to me. I knew deep down that I could never support her happiness, could never keep myself happy, by playing it straight with the loan lumping.

Her laughs, for awhile they were uninhibited and sometimes even dug up a rogue snort which made her bashful, and made for perfect moments. Then gradually, they began to seem like her best way to regard my feelings, and then, warning that she could not regard my feelings much longer. I knew I was in trouble on many fronts.

By the time I announced my resignation to the loan lumping commission, I could barely speak. My tongue was completely spent. They still, unbelievable, they still wanted me to stay, almost as if they would pay me full salary to show my face for twenty minutes a week and ink my signature on a few of the worst loan lumps. But in a single trip around the sun, I had gone from knowing everything and was down to knowing only one thing: I had to leave. As I sat in front of the commission and tried to find some explanation why I could not continue to waltz in on occasion to sign a loan lump, my lower back was very tight and I could not blame the chair, it was a very decent chair for sure. All I could do to relieve the knot in my lower back was to scream: "I WANT ALL THE CHOCOLATE! ALL THE CHOCOLATE! I WANT IT!" The commission gathered themselves and then went through the explanations of how loan lump was the best place to get all the chocolate, and I'd listen until my back tightened again and, once again, "I WANT ALL THE CHOCOLATE!" Well Barry, would you like to take unpaid leave for three months and then come right back to your position and salary? "I WANT ALL THE CHOCOLATE!" How about being paid as an independent contractor? "I WANT ALL THE CHOCOLATE!" Sabbatical? Transfer? "I WANT ALL THE CHOCOLATE!" And so on. You get the idea.

Well, I wish I could tell you that it was an isolated incident, and I walked out the door to have crazy fun adventures about the globe, and whenever I arrived in a new place, someone tossed me some super chips with a smile, letting me in on the secret beach made of graham cracker sand where my totally original loan lump dance weaved some licorice hammocks. Has anyone seen those yet, licorice hammocks?

I got into a run of odd jobs around Chicago, walking dogs, driving the caged golf cart which everyone tried to hit at the practice range, cross-checking the cross-checks of petition signatures for judicial chairs, hauling unmarked gravestones across state lines, playing chicken with one of those turkey fryers, selling cutlery, caretaking for adults, fundraising for children, and so on. A lot of the time I was just doing my best to keep my mouth shut and go unnoticed, because the moment someone observed me thinking, or whatever, they had to step in and check on my business there, like I might make off with that caged cart and all of the practice balls to start my own range in the middle of nowhere. But anyway, whenever it came to the big talk instead of the task at hand, my back tightened and my outburst came again. So the vicious cycle had its grips on me for many years.

Everyone I had known from before only asked when I was going to return to the loan lumping. I was able to give them responses which were maybe better than the screaming.

What was clear regarding work was not as simple with the hanging out and such. I did not belong in the artiste neighborhood, or the one which was the artiste neighborhood before that, or down by the river where you had to showcase your esteem with footwear. So I continued, on occasion, visiting football barn and syrah cottage. At football barn I could let out frustrations into the nebulous space up above the wooden beams, and at syrah cottage, well, it seemed that a lot of women were disappointed in the guys who they worked with and such, so I thought maybe I might be so lucky to meet someone; that was kind of tough for me. Anyway, I don't know, maybe I kept going back to football barn and syrah cottage over the years to check on my progress.

Things finally began to turn around on that day when I needed a new phone battery. I did not want a new phone because my phone had funhouse viewer, and I could peer through it times, mostly at crowds of people, all elongated and out of proportion, to lighten up my mood. But funhouse viewer was no longer featured, I don't know, maybe too many of us were spending time peering through funhouse viewer instead of being prolific. So I visited the, sorry, connec....tittyvity counter for a new battery and went all berserk that battery replacement was no option, and told them I'd keep my phone for the very last gasp of charge for funhouse viewer, oh boy, I'd clamp the jumper cables from a good coupe and onto that phone to funhouse the shit out of the sidewalk for a flash before it blew to smithereens.

Anyway, I needed a bonus juice after all of that talking. Now, there was only slight indication of this from the street, but at the rear end of the long hallway, past the connec...tittyvity counters on both sides, the space opened up into a big room that had the typical coolers and shelves of snacks and beverages around the outside, but then in the center there was a wraparound bar with maybe twenty stools, and a sign hanging up front which said, "Please wait patiently for full service if you desire a seat." I sat and took it all in. There was a small roped-off area at the head of the bar where anyone who wanted to be in and out could scan out after grabbing what they needed from along the walls. The two video screens were both showing nature, one of them seeming to be through the eyes of a bird and the other through eyes of a fish. There was no mirror in the center of the oval, just open space above the schmootzies and super chips. Ten or a dozen guys were in stools, a few groups of three, some loners, if their appearance was made to show off anything it was practicality. I took it all in without worry of the time passing before the steward, whom I later came to know as Karim, the owner, greeted me as if I had already passed some sort of test. There was little going back from there. martbar was my spot.

Over time, I became familiar with a number of the guys around there, coming to learn that almost all of them had a usual time of day for martbar, and I could count on seeing professor and silver fox and captain strum in the early evening, the coliseum trough master and maybe even free willy somewhat later at night. Ron though, you never knew when Ron would be in. I think, from the number of guys I saw approaching him with this or that kind of business, I think he had to keep his visits unpredictable so those with the so-so offers could not wait around for him. My best guess for why Ron took a liking to me was that sometimes I asked questions just for the sake of thought, and Ron kind of stared off like he was completely at peace for a moment, knowing he did not owe me an answer and could savor the nugget for a bit. Come to think of it, Karim did that quite a bit for me. I mean, Ron said things which made me think too but he usually wanted a response.

Anyway, Ron and I came to know each other over time, became what you could call friends if it did not matter that we only saw each other at martbar. So when my summer gig on the street festival circuit, yeah, that one, it was pretty much four months of fences and stages, up on Thursday and then down on Sunday, taking money for tickets in the time between, over and over again, set it all up and then tear it all down and then three days later repeat the entire process under one-half mile away, fences everywhere, like, don't worry folks those fences are coming to your street really soon, we promise, and then they did for three full days of money for tickets and, ahem, music and dancing, extremely festival music and dancing, and I was on tour with the carnival but only logged a total of five or six miles the whole summer to set up the fences and stages on twenty different blocks, and not even a foreman or stage hand with skills, but rather I was a guy handing over a bracket or a wrench and chuckling on cue, waiting for my own quiet weekend to rest up for another very familiar go-round. By the end of the season my brilliant idea to shout out at the coordinators was to erect more fences inside of the fences, and with each successive fence inside of the fence we could give out fewer tickets per dollar, and we would get huge raises from all of the extra money from all of the VIP sections. The coordinators just stared at me after that one like it was against the law to even suggest it.

But anyway. When that gig was up Ron told me he'd set me up for an interview with this guy Gehri he knew, who owned tanning bed and also Asian Pita next to it. I was all for tanning bed. Gehri made a pass over my resume and complimented me for not using any bogus taglines, and I was more than ready to not move any heavy objects around. The interview was about five minutes long. Gehri seemed to be drawing my attention to his cuff links as he asked what I was looking for, and I did not have to scream for my lower back, instead replying calmly that I was simply tired of fences. Gehri shrugged and his brows moved the deep lines on his forehead, his sole response. So it was, fourteen years removed from the loan lump and I got the counter next to the front window at tanning bed.

I feel as if I loosened up through the winter at tanning bed, becoming comfortable with the familiar faces and with the absence of parts and labor. Still though, no assistant necessary to manage the social schedule. I believe there were a few awkward first dates at syrah cottage, that one sold-out concert where I followed the security guard into the restroom to pay my way in, and also some real progress with the chili.

It was during the blossom of artificial shamrocks when cobra and I were sitting next to each other with our bonus juices, not a whole lot to say to one another, and we were near the little-roped off area where those just passing through could scan out, and she stepped up with a pint of ice cream that matched her sweater, ear buds in, and cobra, you know, sometimes the silence goes too long and then he broke it by leaning in and making a comment about the lady's body, and I kind of said, yeah, I know, because, yeah, there was an energy to her, this dash of mysterious zeal which made her unique and whispered that she had not completely resigned to the machines, but I was not going to get into all of that with cobra, and instead said, well sure, but check out her flavor in ice cream, that's a good one, and also what might be the occasion for the ice cream, it seemed like an occasion and not just a routine snack especially at that time of year, so yeah, I was just doing my best to get cobra to see the attraction differently or talk about it differently, especially since the woman had the earbuds in, and even if she did not, I doubt I would have mustered a hello, as simple as it now sounds. Anyway, I still do not know if she heard me or not, or could tell by a glance over, but suddenly I looked away from cobra and had these intense eyes upon me and a stern pop out of the earbuds, and at that very instant when time froze, I bit my tongue to halt an accurate recount of everything that was said because I did not want any more attention towards cobra's comment, and also could not immediately think of a way to be honest about it while leaving that part out, so the eyes were wide and earbuds out, and my lower back sure could yank the laces from each end fast. It was on its way, no stopping it. The disruption in the suddenly frozen martbar was melted off a moment later by the return of rustle and chatter, and a few seconds after that I was able to raise my head again to one sweet chuckle, giving way to a smile which made me feel warm and just a bit understood.

I had just yelled out my baby Barry thing to a speech therapist.

Thea worked mostly with a large handful of preteens in the school district. She intiated our conversation with clear focus on my impediment, sitting with a leg crossed over in the stool which cobra had quickly abandoned. I made sure to only ask questions about her work with the kids, as much as I wanted to make the reason she was there into something different. So we talked. Thea would engage me on this extremely personable level and then excuse herself into thought, I knew she was being professional and respected that with an ease which I believe was owing to experience moreso than age. She did not seem too bothered that the origins of my condition were far different than she had encountered. It was all quite complicated from the very beginning. I had never done too well with attempts to start much of anything off simple.

Our sessions began out in the meadow, near the cluster of white wooden birdhouses, while the dandelions were all yellow and there were patches of them thick enough to make everything golden when I blurred my eyes. Thea had me take off shoes. So I stood barefoot and wiggled my toes into the soil until they felt right, facing the horizon of water while she sat for a moment in the fold-out chair and looked over her notebook. Thea wanted me to work on my balance. I had long legs and was of a lanky build, and it was difficult for me to stand on one foot for long without needing to waver and flail erratically in order to hold it. She stood up and kicked off her sandals. Her toes were nicely lacquered with a pastel blue. She smoothed out a little patch of the wild shag five feet or so away.

"Okay, keep the left leg straight and raise it to the side, like this." She swung hers up, and probably stopped short of the limits to not be too much a showoff, then wavered it about for a few seconds, effortlessly. I followed suit.

"Now the right." Thea abbreviated her demonstration, then locked her fingers together and threw her palms to the sky, her long sleeve tee rising to expose a sliver of her belly. I turned away and got back to this balance stuff quick.

"Okay, now keep your left leg straight and raise it behind you. Use your arms, they'll help you balance." I had no range on this one and as I returned my left foot to the earth Thea stepped back with a pensive look. I grimaced while peering up at the rich white texturing of clouds inching from the north and slowly unfurling their inner charcoal.

"Is one leg stronger than the other?"

"That was the strong leg, unfortunately."

"Don't be so hard on yourself Barry. That's probably a difficult one for a lot of guys. Ummm……..how about this. Raise onto your toes and extend your arms straight up, then try to move them slowly, behind you, like this……"

I said to myself, again, this is a kind professional who is dedicating time to cure my lonely condition out of nothing but the goodness of her heart, and maybe a doctoral thesis if it all worked. But that spot in my back was beginning to feel the conflict. I got into the suggested pose a little too impatiently and stumbled out of it a few seconds later.

It was hard to say how much she knew, so I just guessed that she knew everything, and went from there. I did not say anything of my lower back after I had lost that pose, but immediately thereafter Thea returned to her chair and instructed me to perform some abdominal and hamstring stretches. I became quite embarrassed over my hamstring stretches. My hamstrings were bad. Thea asked me to do the toe touch one for a fifteen count and I couldn't quite get to the ankle bones.

"Wait…..Barry…..that was a fifteen count? It seemed like four or five to me….."

"No, no……1234567……like that, to fifteen."

"Oh, no….we're not doing the multiplication races in math class Barry. You have to breathe. Slow. In…….."

I had a hundred thoughts which ran all over the place while her lungs were full. "……..and out." That's one. Okay, let's not even worry about stretching for now. Just get your shoulders back and breathe."

"Okay." I was ashamed. I had always, of course, felt as if I was breathing correctly, because I had not gone blue. I closed my eyes and drew in the cool breeze until scents of the lake whispered as if it were moving within me. And, for a moment, I was gone, in the best way. But then I remembered I was supposed to be counting and I was back making a conscious effort to not count too fast, which meant I was counting fast.

After some time of breathing and stretching and what not, I supposed that maybe I was relaxed but then started wondering if I should invite Thea to the martbar afterwards, and those considerations churned up thoughts that if I was really relaxed I would have just said, let's go to martbar with no doubt that Thea wanted some ice cream. Yeah, I was a ways from that.

Thea stood from her chair and flung one of her legs around for a few seconds, cutting out tiny circles with her pointed toes. She checked the time and I knew ours was about through for the afternoon. "Let's try one more balance exercise Barry. Bring your left knee up, and keep your shoulders back, and breathe, the way we discussed. Really do your best to let that tension out with your breathing."
"Okay, I'm ready."
I turned towards the water and listened to the ensemble of the young leaves becoming full for their one season. I brought my knee up slowly, steadily, it all felt coordinated and good. I adjusted my arms to catch the breeze and let it hold me aloft, proud and esteemed. But I was not ready. Because then Thea took a few easy barefoot steps towards me, and the relationship with nature became much more complicated. I met her eyes

very briefly, then felt the knot as I looked back to the sky. She took another step, and even though there was no contact I could feel her breast against my right arm, I swore. The tension grew. Her breath opposed the wind and it was too beautiful for that knot to take. I brought my knee up further, but it was too late. "I WANT ALL THE CHOCOLATE!! CHOCOLATE I WANT IT!" Two dogs barked in the distance. A jogger fifty yards off did a one-eighty turn and clipped back in the other direction. I fell to the grass and threw my arms around my knees and set my head down to pick at a few blades. "Hey, hey, Barry......." She bent over a bit and rubbed my shoulder. "This is gonna take a little time, but you're doing fine, we'll get there. Don't be so hard on yourself."

"Thanks." I kept my head down though. "I'll keep working on this stuff before our next session."

"I know you will. I'll drop you off if you'll carry this chair back to the car."

"Oh, it's okay, you don't........"

"BARRY! Take the ride!"

"Alright, okay...." I chuckled for a moment and this made Thea smile. We threw on our shoes and I took a brief peek at the lake before walking kind of loose across the meadow so Thea knew once again that I was relaxed and cool.

"Brianne! How was lunch today?" Brianne often came by several times a week, but certainly every Thursday after a dragonfruit margarita and lunch at Asian Pita.

"Oh, Barry, when are you gonna listen to me and use that discount over there, honey? Edamame falafel, oooh, baby, I'll be singing that song under the bright lights. I'm sure you were a dear and warmed up the Vortex for me?"

"You know I don't even need to tell Andrés and he takes care of it. He probably brought an ice water when he set the bed."

A wistful look came over Brianne. Nothing unusual. "Isn't he the best? I MUST keep him in mind when I make my famous tree ornaments."

Brianne made quite a thing over the handmade and personalized tree ornaments. "I don't know….maybe a gift certificate for him."

"Barry don't you worry your prudish head over that. I play to my audience with *some acclaim*."

"Oh I know. I just had to keep mine out in the kitchen where it could remind me more of a mushroom."

"That was only your first one honey…..mmm, time for me to lie down and dream of that follow up."

"Ha ha, okay."

Brianne blew me a kiss as if about to board a cruise liner, then began singing a pop song and gyrating towards the back.

I got back into my puzzle and alternated standing on one foot, then the other, really feeling the progress and thinking about myself as a real slackline kind of guy. Then Cheryl stormed in for what must have been an emergency visit before a date or something.

"Barry I need the Vortex for a half hour." Once, when Cheryl was rapping her fingernails on the counter, I told her she might be a natural on a piano, really, but that did nothing to slow the habit.

"The Vortex is taken for another forty-five minutes Cheryl, this time on Thursdays probably for at least the next decade."

"Well…..uh….." This was not going to be fun. "……I *need* that Vortex. Isn't there *something* you can do? Look at these lines!" She moved some fabric off of her shoulder. Hooray.

"Bronzeville and Everglades are both available." The rooms and beds were mostly unique color schemes and musical compilations. The beds themselves were pretty much the same, other than slight differences in bulb configuration and glass temperament; just enough for a big story about desired look and feel. Really, I was a bit surprised that when my skin paled through the winter that Gehri did not come by and tell me I needed to do some time. Then again, I had only seen Gehri twice since our interview, one of those instances a few hours before the surprise health inspection, where Andrés did not flinch for a second over having both tanning bed and Asian Pita sewn up tight. Anyway, I mostly tried to feel out visitors' preferences for the music, staying away from the hocus pocus over the bulbs. But that Vortex, it beat me, that was the one some people just went bonkers for. The walls all done up with a digital rendering of Sedona, and supposedly people had found these energy vortices in Sedona where the core of the earth made your chest tingle or something. So I knew that Cheryl was going to freak a bit, because at some point she read that 'the customer is always right' and decided right then and there not much further knowledge of any sort to be necessary. If I could go way back in time and take an eraser to one quote…….

"HMMMM….." She swiped at her phone with a frustrated motion. "……..I *could* pick up my dry

cleaning and have my brows tweezed and then circle back…….but it would be such an inconvenience…..”
“The jazz in Bronzeville is untangling traffic jams right now. A guy came out of there an hour ago like a……tadpole swimming out of a saxophone.”
Here came the decision-face. “Well……OOOkay. It’s not the same rate as the Vortex, is it?”
“Flat rate across the board Cheryl.”
“Could you let it run for an extra five minutes, just for good measure? I’m not sure I have my adjustments timed right in the strange environment.”
“I suppose.” I hated myself for this. But I could get over it quick if she was away from the counter.

One of the best things about martbar was that Karim dealt with such a variety of everything that he did not even seem to have a popular concept of cool in his mind, let alone any care of how to protect it. I really think he only judged impatience and senseless talking. But, like, if you went to syrah cottage or football barn the stewards were so worn into what was normal that if you weren’t there for that exact reason it was like you just came in for directions back to the door and must buy one item for them to point at it. At football barn I could maybe think, oh, it was late afternoon on a Wednesday in the off-season, maybe they were playing decent music and some random group needed a fourth for the mini-shuffleboard. Then I would go in and the steward had his back turned to display the tagline with attitude, a sweatband around his forearm, and he was staring at a large numbered man running around orange cones as the stopwatch ticked and was compared at various intervals to various others, and this was on all of the televisions with the sound on the loudspeakers, and the steward's two pals at the bar who were probably doing bullets for free were making their own commentaries over the cone running, and then the steward wiped his brow after two more cone runnings and stomped over like something bad happened if his arms touched against his sides, and then threw the championship softball paws wide onto the wood and said HOW MANY CHICKEN WINGS FOR YA? And if I hesitated or anything maybe he would clarify that Wednesdays were for combine and chicken wings, and get really impatient to run back to his pals. Then the dozen wings took like a year to arrive, literally I swear, even if I was staring at the stopwatch for the cones the entire while. So then just on the other side of a street with a bus route was syrah cottage, maybe it was a little more sociable, and I had put on a decent pair of shoes, but it was closed for a private event and I could see though the bay window all the neutral colors of corporation and everyone doing the interdepartmental thing with the gigantic stemware in their hands.

martbar had a posting right above the fire capacity sign. Not available for private events. You never showed at martbar to see it closed for a totally original wedding or some kind of convention after-party. No natural light, no private events, no exceptions, no apologies. That's martbar all right.

Ron had his usual: a couple of jerky sticks and a bonus juice. He always lined up the jerky sticks carefully and spaced them about an inch apart on the mat, and one time I asked Ron if that was out of habit from working with the fluorescent bulbs for so many years. He went silent and I couldn't tell if he irked at me for asking or irked at everyone else for never asking. Today he was chatting a bit with some others, to my right, as I watched dolphin drone. He did a lot of work around the area and seemed to know anyone in martbar who had too many keys for the chain to fit in their pocket. Sometimes I guessed Ron was just being kind and listening to me talk of the goings-on around tanning bed while he nodded with this look on his face where I could not tell if he was fascinated by what I was saying or just totally miffed that I was sitting there talking about it at all. That was the thing about Ron. He seemed really simple and straightforward in a lot of ways, but then also had these quiet, removed looks where it was like if he so much as nodded his head or said 'yeah, I know', then he was committed to let me in on the legend of batman or something.

He had been talking to what looked like a father-son duo of some sort for a few minutes when the conversation suddenly led him to go for his first jerky stick. This was quite the production. He surveyed the three by rolling each one between thumb and forefinger, ran them cigar-style beneath his nose, set them back down carefully. Finally, he chose one and bit into the center of the stick instead of an end. Then he said to the two guys, "You're quoting me a price as if I never heard what happened at that café during its first rainstorm". End of discussion. They both stuffed hands back into their hoodie pockets, sheepishly, and went down the bar. Ron turned and threw his palms up, kind of like, hey Barry, sometimes you gotta be a dick like that. Then he cut in on my dolphin drone, fine by me. "These reefs here always seem to be light on fish. I don't know if I hope that it's just the drone chasing them off or not." "There's a shark nearby for sure. Dolphin drone will find it. I'm betting on hammerhead."

"All of the video in the oceans, it's always looking for the sharks. Who walks out to go to the store and hopes that they bump into an assassin along the way?" Damn that Ron, he knew with a glimpse when I was staring at a screen and filling in blanks with my ego. "I mean, it's still nice to look at the reef and stuff……"

"Does it tell you where this is in the world?"

"There's a little scramble code they show every few minutes. If I hold up my phone and tell them where I'm at, they'll tell me where dolphin drone is."

"Do you do that?"

"No way. They might send a shark after me." I made that comment as a joke, and then thought about it for a moment.

Ron did too, maybe. He uncrossed his arms, pulling a hand free to fiddle habitually with one of the top buttons of his daily flannel. The other forearm remained just below the sternum as if there was a shelf. I was glad Ron did not have his sleeves rolled up; the sight of his forearms made me feel like I could only leg out infield singles. "Don't try to appease its appetite with my jerky sticks okay?"

"Are you kidding? Whatever it might look like I'd take my chances with something else."

Down the bar, Karim, he had the slightest sign when he was frustrated with patrons, always a brief two finger rub along the outside of his brow.

"Are you a shark to those two guys who just walked off?"

"They keep plenty busy. Plus it's not as if a shark swims around all day saying to itself, 'yes, I'm a shark'. It's just searching for food, same as every other fish."

"A lot of them though, they go a really long time between meals. I'd think at some point right after they get a seal….maybe they chill out and take it all in for awhile."

"Their ancestors could probably afford to do much more of that."

That one came at me kind of heavy. We were silent for a long moment.

"So….back to sharks on land though. Do you know what you'd try to feed one if it showed?"

"I'm too old for a shark to want much from me Barry. I've already generated almost all of the fat I'm going to in this life. You though….." When he dipped his head to the near shoulder; that was the only time when the excess skin about his cheek and chin folded.

"I don't see much reason for one to come for me."

Oh boy. It was jerky time. Ron did his thing, and I tried to look away while also trying not to look away too much. Finally, he finished with his bite after all of the what-to-do. "You could consider that you've been inside of its guts for some time, and it doesn't want you to slip out."

"So I'd have to scurry through while it's opened up for something else?"

I was not going to get an answer there. That was another thing about Ron. He had a mustache. It was partly grey just about the same as his hair around the ears, and even though it was thick all the way out to each corner of his mouth it kind of seemed like he sneezed one morning long ago and there it was, all at once like it sprouted from a single vine out of each nostril. Anyway, sometimes Ron turned towards me for an instant and the mustache spoke between the lines and said no further questions.

I was at least twenty minutes early to meet Thea at our spot, and laid down on my back, holding my breath on several occasions until I became kinda freaked that it was already a done deal and I would remain frozen and lucid but unable to tell Thea where I was. This breathing stuff really was okay. I was practicing it at times when I caught myself going for some connec....tittyvity for no reason. Balancing too. It was the simplest practice that ever required my full concentration.

The lakefront was a tad odd in my opinion. After crossing over the exercise superhighway, a lot of the time there was barely anyone out there in the afternoons. So much wide open space for people to meet and do whatever weird stuff they wished, but not many did much more than let the dog sniff around, or step up to the top of the terraces and snap a photo to show the world that they were not the type to stop exploring at the parking lot a hundred yards back.

I turned and saw Thea in the distance making way across the meadow, then turned away quick as if I just arrived myself, being extra chill. She was wearing a flowery sundress and despite all of my breathing and balance practice I instantly reconsidered how long I could avoid the screaming.

"Barry! I'm so glad to be out here. What a day. Ugh. How are you?"

I leapt to my feet to say, "I'm good. Yeah! It's been a good day."

"Okay! I thought up a few new exercises, we can work those in with the routine. I had little romeo messaging during our entire session. How am I supposed to help a kid's speech impediment if he's doing fine with girls without having to even speak?!? Sorry, sorry, let's get to work. Maybe a quick glass of wine afterwards?"

"Ohh….." For some stupid reason I paused for a second as if I had other offers to consider……"yeah, definitely, cool. I've been practicing quite a bit for this. For these exercises, practicing for that."

"Awesome. Let's start off with a little stretching. Ahh, this sun! Isn't it perfect?"

Thea led me through a few stretches of the hip flexors, after telling me exactly where the hip flexors were. Oh yeah, I forgot to say earlier, she had leggings on down past her knees, so this wasn't all quite looking like some photography shoot in a Dutch tulip field. After that we did hamstrings again. "You ARE making progress."

"I have a lot of faith that the work will pay off."

"Keep doing it, stretch!" Her enthusiasm on this day was so great, and I loved it, and hoped it would continue this way, not just some fervor during the two weeks of spring. But I did not worry over it too much. I was waving one leg up in the air, feeling the sun flood all tributaries to my starving cheek with warmth, feeling like I'd learn to fly in no time flat with Thea showing me how and cheering me on.

Thea was especially active too. She did a few of the exercises right along with me. Then she stepped back and off to the side to dance around for a bit. Within a minute this bulk widget salesman had climbed down out of a tree or blown recess from his own bootcamp to walk up and stock compliment her, then stood and waited for her to ask how many pushups he could do or something. I knew Thea had it under control but still had to break my pose and just look at him like he was gonna have to come up with a much better line than that. Then I did some extra weird stretch, for the hell of it.

"Okay, Barry, wow, you're doing great. This is fun! Let's go for one last balance exercise." I nodded with enthusiasm, making a slight effort to conceal that I would have done that with a suggestion of any sort. "Let's try this: raise the left leg straight out to your side, and after you've got it up as far as possible, then arch your left arm over and bend to your right." Thea was demonstrating as she talked. It was graceful and pretty. First, I decided to turn so that the wind, not quite blustery but more than just a sweat tickler on the temples, it was blowing directly at my left side. I did not know any better but it felt best there. Then I dug my right foot into an ideal contour of earth and set my shoulders back with a long breath. It was time. I pointed the left toe as best I could as it left the ground. Every time I thought it was up as far as could be, I took a big breath and that seemed to allow for a bit more elevation. And when my balance felt a little shaky I found myself moving my hands and cupping them towards the breeze, making myself into a pretty awesome pirate ship. Thea was somewhere behind me. I got nervous for a second that she would startle me from back there, and felt my balance waver, then cleared the worry and sailed some more. A moment later she walked around to my front, her blue eyes all big and round with one hand cupped around her chin. "Okay left arm over now Barry." She said it real quiet and calm like a memorable goodnight. I stretched the left arm over. "You can keep going Barry." A few coils of strawberry hair jumped as she gave a little nod. Suddenly there was another moving part to account for. It seemed to change the weight of my head. I did not know if it was lighter or heavier, but I felt even more balanced and pretty sure nothing was on display. "Take another breath sweetie." I did so. Some muscles had been shaking like mad for a bit but then the rest of me was a new level of calm. I looked at Thea and our eyes met for just an instant, as I was sure she could hear my wishes for her to please walk over to me now. She made a slow lap all the way around me. Everything about me was a euphoric mess of anticipation. Then, it happened. Thea grabbed her bag from the grass, threw it over her shoulder, and started toward the car without so much as a look in my direction. I held the pose as best I could, thinking maybe she was bluffing, but it was not five seconds before the knot asserted itself. I dropped myself to the grass and squatted, reaching my arms forward, in attempt to untie it, but it was of no use. "DON'T TAKE AWAY MY CHOCOLATE! BRING BACK MY

CHOCOLATE!" Ohhh boy. I sat down and stared at a distant point in the field, stunned.

Thea hustled back over. "Barry, honey, you never told me about that one."
"I never knew about that one."
She parked right next to me, crossed her legs, and pressed her palms together in concentration. "It was.....have you.....um......said the chocolate rant when someone has walked away?"
"No. I don't think.......no, definitely not."
"Okay, okay. Hey, hey, don't worry, look at all of the progress you've made with this! We're out on a limb, trying something experimental, there's gonna be a few surprises here and there."
"What if I.....what if I.....am just becoming someone who......screams different things.....no matter what happens."
"Whoa, whoah. Do you know what kind of stress you had your body under there? It was incredible! I am seriously stunned at your progress. So don't act like we were just standing around chewing gum when I tailed off."
"Yeah, okay."
We stared ahead quietly for a little bit, my posture coming out of a slump pretty quick. Then Thea nudged me with her elbow. "Full disclosure Barry: I saw your shorts. You DEVIL!" She shoved me over and I fell onto my shoulder in the grass. I started laughing about it, surprising myself. Then Thea let out this accidental hee haw, and the damn broke. We both lost it good, totally falling apart in the tall grass for a few minutes. We weren't really even looking at each other or anything.

Both of us were laughing in our own space, yet, together. It was nice.

"You're sure I can wear shorts into syrah cottage?"
"When you're with me, you can."
"Oh, do you keep a 'signature vintage' in the cellar?" I didn't even know what that might have meant, it just sounded like the best way to ask if she was gonna do the double-kiss on the cheek with the owner, while I stood three feet behind in my dumb shorts.
"Noooo. Smartass! What I meant was you're coming in with me to a wine bar. As in, we're coming here because you're a good listener, not to show off your clothes. If you went in alone, yes, you're right, no shorts."
"Oh, okay, I see." I felt as if Thea was speaking for women in general about this, and not just herself. It was like she had told me a secret, and it felt good even if everybody else already knew. But still, if coming from home I would have at least thrown on some damn jeans. I mean, come on.

We took a high table in a little nook which buffered away the din from a large group in the main room. It looked as if we were supposed to believe we were in Maine, congratulating ourselves on all of our life choices. "Barry I hope you know how nice it is to work with you, especially after another day of wondering what I can do for, and with, the kids."
"Oh, yeah, I like it too. You make me want to be better." Thea's shoulders sunk a bit and her head fell to the side, like she just saw a penguin. "You're so sweet!"

"Ahh. I'm just sayin'……..I know this is a good thing, even if I'm a little afraid of screaming different."

"I think you'll be fine. That was a pretty rare instance today."

I hoped not. I kind of wanted to do poses all the time with her nearby. I wondered if she knew by my silence that if I spoke right then, I would be saying too much.

"Your hips and sides might be kind of sore for a few days."

"I'll manage." The stool had armrests. A nice feature for reclining back for a second, dude style, enough said about toughing out the hip soreness. The steward arrived from behind me. Thea listened to him as he said something about France and it was tough to say if he was trying to sell a bottle or insinuating he and Thea take holiday there. So I reclined a little further from the picture, like, that's okay, I'm dude style in shorts because I stretch for her. Thea already had our glasses picked out and eventually closed off the fairy tale at that polite point which expressed lack of interest but also appreciation of the effort. She really was something, this Thea.

"My brother Elliot thinks I should return to school, *again*, and earn a doctorate. He's not giving me cheap advice either, even told me he's in a place where he can help with the tuition. I just…….I don't know Barry, I have a masters degree and here I am, two years in, taking care of kids whose speech is fed up into a massive analysis and comes back as some type of outlier, and I work with them according to statistics fed up and then back down. The only leeway for me is the personable touch I can use to make them believe that it's unique attention for a unique situation. But something in these kids, I can see it, deep down, something in them is numb because they know…..they smell that company line behind it, and it hurts. It eats away at everything I got into this for. So I wonder if I go for a doctorate, do I end up at one of the institutes where the statistics and normalized ranges are set, spend years fighting for this tiny change in the program so whomever steps into the position I have now can have more impact? I don't even know if I'd be making a change for the kids or for who has my old job…….or if either would even notice….."

"Wow……yeah……I don't know…..when I took off from the loan lump, at first I was all crazy about grad school, and went after those practice tests for admission nonstop for a few weeks, and then, nothing big happened to make me see it but all of the sudden I just saw myself after it all, this vision of me, thirty feet away from my old cubicle, in one of the offices. And that was the end of me thinking of grad school. But that was different……I had big problems with myself and didn't feel I could face them at loan lump. I know you don't have those problems with yourself."

"That's nice of you to say…..but……."

I let her pause finish. "No, Thea, really, I sucked. Bad."

"Because of the job?"

"Because I never knew before I fell in love for the first time."

"Oh, Barry…..we all feel that at times when we're in love baby."

"Well…..maybe some of us….fall for someone who protects us from that……and then some of us fall for someone who…..knows to hang back while you expose…..all of it."

We went quiet and I rubbed my thumb and forefinger on the stem of the glass. For some reason I remembered right then that we weren't on a date-date, or whatever. I wasn't all sad, unless you considered it sad whenever taking a moment to adjust to the reality of everything.

syrah cottage had an anchor on the wall. I didn't know what it was about the anchor on the wall that was really making me bothered. I mean, I'd seen anchors on the walls before, yeah, you could be sure I had seen plenty of wall anchors in my day, and from the first one it always seemed like a note from the owner that nothing on the walls had anything to do with his or her life. But maybe I was missing something, and there was this language amongst people who liked the hotels by the sea quite a bit, and when at syrah cottage they needed to look over at the wall anchor for some support, you know, pull up for awhile there high-riser, let the water move around you for a second. I didn't think this wall anchor was saying that to me, no, I was on the move with my stretching and breathing, oh wow, that sounded a little nuts, but sometimes at syrah cottage I lost my identity for a little bit and maybe I needed to look at the anchor on the wall and make sure it wasn't speaking to me, because it wasn't like it was the anchor that the owners dropped into a warm sunny key and by the time they pulled it back up there were pearls hanging everywhere and they said, let's go to Chicago and open syrah cottage, no, that was the thing, it was just something bought out of a stack of a hundred, and I didn't know why they couldn't just put in dolphin drone, and I would be at martbar if not having such a good time with, oh wow, "THEA! Hey, sorry......um, wall anchors......."

She was laughing and covering her face with both hands. "You maniac! You drank almost your entire glass in one gulp!"

"What?" Oh, look at that.

"Just remember why I said you were good to wear shorts here, drifter."

"I'm all ears."

"Do you need another glass for this? The restroom first?"

"Nooo....."

"You are one curious bird. We're all even on walkaways for the day now, eh?"

"Yep." I liked that.

"Thanks for sharing that, by the way."

"Oh, sure."

"I didn't mean to be all whiny; especially when you......" Thea caught herself, but I could tell where she was about to go.

"It's okay. tanning bed is also a place for the leaders of tomorrow."

I could sense her shaking off the urge to inquire about what else I might do. Thankfully. "I wouldn't mind being called doctor."

"I'll call you doctor."

"Don't you try to replace my dreams with that easy charm now....."

"Oh, nah, I meant.....with how much you're helping me......it would probably make for an okay thesis, what you're doing for me, you know, speech therapy through stretching for a middling basket case......they might even make a new institute for you for something like that."

I said as much kind of sure that Thea had already thought about thesis idea, to some degree. But it was apparent she had not. Sometimes I overestimated how many things others had thought about, and forgot that they, well, had other things to do.

"Don't get me thinking about that too much now. I'll start making up progress in my head; the real strides are plenty great."

"Okay. Just so you know I'm not too worried over being something of an academic subject."

Thea grinned. It seemed more appreciative than opportunistic.

She got to talking about a few of her kids, weaving herself in and out of individual tales and collective frustrations, dabbing in touches of bureaucratic buffoonery and a few of the strange things she witnessed others eating in the lounge. I was listening attentively, for the most part, but also drifting into thoughts that would possibly get me into trouble. Everything Thea said was plenty interesting, it was just that, well, when you haven't been into trouble in too long, thoughts of it seem to sneak into everything and with great frequency.

The worry always set in just a bit when Kid Tippy rolled in that he was gonna turn his headcam around and put me on the spot with his livefeed. Sometimes I pictured him narrating and framing his entrance as he skated down the block, a moment later opening the door and saying, 'here he is, Barry, everyone!', and I would be live in front of — you know, definitely overstated in several manners, but still—his viewers, and I would either say something very dumb, or, worse yet, try so hard to not say something very dumb that I had a tantrum, and then went viral for the impediment I was trying to beat, and then walked down the street for everyone to say, 'Barry, give me the line!', and all I could do was go along with it and maybe print some tee shirts and hope I sold enough to retire to a remote tropical place where no one cared about that stuff, find a seat at open-air martbar to start a better version of the story, the only problem being that Kid Tippy would be skating right behind me, and we'd be shouting back and forth about an appropriate percentage for him, back and forth until the end of time on the petty side of the decimal points, all of this even though we had checked away the rights to a connec…..tittyvity provider, and they owned the tee shirt license and sent us little golden exposure star stickers to show off in public like military decorations, only everyone else on the street was staring at livefeed anyway, so, yeah.

Anyway, Kid Tippy just came in. The routine was that I just held out a pair of goggles and he snared them as he skated past, on his way to Bronzeville. We never spoke. He was always narrating in front of the camera…."TRSB! Consciousness expansion. Rolling thunder, WPW, indigenous, hop onto my city bus, no traffic signals. Just hit the nine-two for the day, HM, suckers!" I handed off the goggles, real smooth exchange, well done again, Barry. Kid Tippy held them to his face and continued. "Institute of technology, radiant, byk, we will burst into the light, burn many things, obin, the establishment……." I heard his heel brake squeal against the hardwood and knew he was pulling into Bronzeville.

I didn't know if he unlaced his skates in there or not. That was one of the things. About a week before Kid Tippy ever came in, Gehri dropped a paper in front of me, and he was really straight about it, just short and firm and like owners of all kinds knew the perfect moment to catch me, but he just said he needed me to sign a declaration that I would not ever watch Kid Tippy's livefeed while employed at tanning bed. So I signed right away and didn't think of it a bit until, the following week, some guy I'd never seen before rolled in on livefeed and only yelled 'goggles!', and then yelled it again after only, like, two seconds at most, and I got those goggles out and I am pretty sure that he understood with our very brief eye contact that I would in the future have the goggles out and he would most certainly not scream like that again. But he was already down the hall and I was worrying that he had just pulled a free tan and word would spread big about pulling free tans, and I doubted it would cause too big of a land rush to tanning bed, but if Cheryl heard about someone else pulling a free tan, well, you'd probably see me on a bad hair day, walking in to ominous bass notes while the screen punched in 'defendant' real heavy, one letter at a time. That's when I remembered the paper that I had signed for Gehri, and placed name and face. Anyway, it was kind of nice to have a real excuse, for once, why you couldn't keep up with someone's livefeed. It itched every so often to be all sly, and smarter than Gehri, by sneaking a look at this livefeed, even if I wouldn't want to catch it when Kid Tippy was in the bed; that would make me feel a little dirty about it all. Also, Gehri had bothered to go out and find a sheet of paper for it. So it must have been pretty important.

It was just one of those #ETT mornings, that was for sure. I was only thirty feet off on my stroll to martbar when I nearly tripped on one of the nicefoam royal blue hashtags that were all over the sidewalks on #ETT. The nicefoam royal blue hashtags had one cheer adjective on them, and the children had morning play on #ETT and they would all run around on the sidewalks to collect a few nicefoam royal blue hashtags, which did not roll into the streets or cause any ouchies or booboos as a ball could, and every child that posted with #ETT for morning play would at least be able to grab one or two cheer adjectives. One of the connec…..tittyvity companies bought the nicefoam and there would be a few streets shut down and everyone stayed out of the way and let the children chase around the hashtags #ETT. Sometimes when I was on my way to martbar on #ETT, I felt a bit like being a scrooge and picking up one or two, you know, kind of roiling up the system and making the game a bit tougher on the children, but then when I got to thinking about it, wondered if maybe the streets were flooded with so many nicefoam royal blue hashtags on one #ETT that the children would bore of it and not show next #ETT and instead play another game. But it had been going on since………..well, on the first #ETT the children were already out for morning play while I walked to martbar, and two different children on that walk had run up close to me and stopped and stared all eerie at me while dropping their nicefoams, and I moved along wordless after very brief pause but then so many minutes later came to the mob of people outside martbar, and it must have been a parent of one of the children who was watching livefeed, and she yelled, THAT'S HIM, HE WENT NEAR MY BABY AT MORNING PLAY, and like, a hundred people all jumped in my face and barked names at me, and the knot in my back did not come on or anything. I just walked right through like I could not hear a thing, and they yelled more names and that I had to explain myself, but I just walked through all unfazed past the connec....tittyvity counter and into martbar, stared at dolphin drone, and sat there to see that no one had followed me in to yell more, maybe because they did not want to lose their spot in line or something. But anyway, from then on, I made sure to check the #ETT and walk over to martbar before morning play.

So that was a while back, I supposed. The adults were all out in front on this #ETT, in line for rollout at the connec....tittyvity counter. It was hard to not know when #ETT was coming up, because for two days or so before, this pop singer with a ton of swagger would follow you around like lifecoach, perched atop an escalator with arms crossed, 'rollllllOUTTT', out front the bank leaning way back pointing both fingers at you, 'rollllOUTTT', or hurdling in awesome sneakers over two lanes of traffic, 'rollllOUTTT', and you'd see it and hear it everywhere and know #ETT was coming.

The adults were calm and quiet, as usual, in the line down the sidewalk. Quite a few were taking photos of the street or the wall, and the sun had not made way over the buildings yet, but they would go in for megapixel and then come back out with the upgrade and take a similar photo but by then the sun had drawn the street into all this contrast of light, and shadows reached up and out into all these lively abstract shapes, and then if you went to #ETT you'd probably see a few before and after photos with a caption of #LOOK WHAT MEGAPIXEL DID. There really was quite a difference. So yeah, today's rollout was megapixel. There was also celebrity, and after that accessory. Then another megapixel, and so on.

Here was the thing, though. Opposite the connec….tittyvity counter and on the left side of the hallway as you entered was the jewelry counter. The two jewelry guys, man, they were ready, they knew how to catch people at that very moment when they did not know if conquest was just before or just behind them. The one with the necktie always somewhere in between comedy and fashion, he was, literally, a magician. There were phones and stones and watches and gold all sliding out of his cuffs and lapels and other people's ears and handbags, and he talked without moving his lips, all monotone, but within thirty seconds he had like three of his guest's devices mixed in with his own and all of the sudden the guest was immersed in this funnel cloud of devices and gems coming and going, and the thing was, you always could remember which card was yours but never knew how many others you got to get all excited and see until yours came back around. So it was. Diamonds coming and going out of handkerchiefs, watches from one wrist to another, one of those antique squiggly cords stretching and contracting, somehow attached to a phone which then disappeared into the center of the funnel cloud, or a sock, where it redressed in private to a new case by the time the squiggly cord blew out its spirals again. This whole, well, magical, no better word than magical, production and experience going down while thirty or forty people shuffled by in each direction, none the wiser, occupied with their devices and not bumping into anyone. It was almost like he was replicating some kind of entire industry with his own two hands, even if I was not sure he could possibly only have that many. Either way, he was very impressive and I hoped one day he would sit at martbar and maybe pull a jar of macadamia nuts from thin air, or something like that.

So after the magician had blurred everything up for the guest, turned it all into all this four-way mix-and-match of questions, answers, what the guest had, and what they wanted, the guest was all hypnotized and nodding, like, 'do I have gold trim on your watch why yes I want those stones they're mine', the magician raised his voice from a mumble for the first time, sort of, 'hey, we have a grand prize winner', and his partner was right there to take over and speak in very simple facts about parts and labor and maybe most important how long the guest would have to leave their device, catching them in this daze of physical experience which allowed them to let go for a few hours and maybe even go try to pass the miracle along. And the magician would drift through his loose suit like sleepwalk down the counter and draw in the next person who was closest to being there by accident.

martbar was quiet. I sat and ordered a bonus juice from Karim and thought about seeing Thea again.

There were quite a few times when I was alone and restless and there was no entertainment which could settle me. So it was cool to be working on balance and stuff, surprising myself with some new postures which seemed to open up possibilities for comfort with others. All of the slow moves rarely got totally out of control where, by the time I laid down flat on the floor, I was saying to myself, 'well, Barry you have been gifted. There is only one thing to do and that is continue to work towards becoming a ballerina'. Most of the time it was more realistic dreams, like Thea and I both doing our own weird stuff at opposite ends of the room until, at some point, some song made us both drift into the center and look up, like, 'whoah, hey there!' And even if we weren't quite doing the same thing in the center of the room, we were drawing a tad closer and that was cool.

I was thinking about all that as I walked towards the line of mature trees which made a bit of a U-shape in separation of forest and meadow, and they were the first trees to really catch the lake breezes, so the leaves up high were always swaying, and I couldn't identify what type of trees they were but if I listened close enough for a moment the sounds of the different leaves became separate as they fluttered against each other. Sometimes it felt like nature just sat around and waited for me to stop talking to myself, and then cued up a nice little number when it finally had an audience.

All of the leaves were in full harmony when Thea called all frantic and frustrated telling me she couldn't make it out there today and she'd make it up to me on another day and we'd figure that out very soon okay bye. I was immediately worried that something wasn't right with Thea.

I turned away from the trees as I could not hear the leaves as well anymore, and found myself bumbling with my head down towards the water. That was what happened, I supposed. You got a tad low and went to stare at the lake.

The water always seemed to be moving in several directions. The lake went on forever as an ocean did, but the ocean always had at least tiny waves crashing into lines of foam which gurgled up all slow and fast at the same time. The ocean seemed to help you back to the sand if you went for a dip, seemed to tell you in a very kind and fun way that it was not to be trifled with. This lake, though, it was full of little peaks which rose up and ducked under, moved to the left and right, danced towards the wall and tailed back away, and one little peak bumped into another little peak, they rose up a bit higher for a second, but the thing was, after they did this, after the two peaks melded into one, you could never tell if they bounced off one another, or went through one another. So you could not tell which little peak was which, moving along. It was a tricky lake; that was for sure.

I removed my shoes and started up with some of the balancing and stretching and kept facing the water, knowing Thea was not watching so not really concerned if anyone else passing happened to be. After a few minutes I found myself doing something kind of cool. While hoisting one leg up in the air, I was moving my arms around for balance, as usual. Then I realized that I was letting my hands wave around all slow and languid, no tension in my wrists, mimicking the movements of the water, and it seemed to be helping me balance better, but even if not, it was very enjoyable to follow along to what the lake was doing.

"Play that number again!"
Wait, what? I had just finished a pose and then thought, damn, there is a stranger hollering at me and I'm making believe it is Thea's voice. I turned to see. It was Thea, alright. I was feeling too many things right then. Kind of like when your sports team just won but it was only because of a bogus call by the refs.
"Well….hey. Thanks for making it? Is everything okay?"
"Sure! Just a meeting that went longer than it had to and then a lane closure. How are you?"
"Oh, yeah……good. Damn Thea, it sounded like, well, I don't know but something bad happened, on the phone."
"Nah. Hey, sorry I told you I couldn't make it. I knew I was running late and just had the idea to tell you I couldn't make it at all."
"But…..why?"
"I thought I'd take the opportunity to see if you'd stay out here and practice, or immediately run off to that,

hmm, martbar. So I'm pretty damn happy to see you out here Barry." She was happy, I could tell.

"Well yeah, you know I've been working at it. But I thought something was really wrong there."

"Sorry to worry you Barry. It probably sounded that way because I'm a bad liar."

Uh-oh. I had to turn away and mull over that for a moment. It was one of those scary things people said that they certainly thought to be true. And it always seemed like this demand for trust at the wrong time to be asking for it. So I faced the lake and waved my arms about to the water, to calm myself, because I knew she was truly helping me and wanted the best for me, and there I was getting ahead of myself and wondering if twenty years later she'd tell me that she was double-agent. Following a trail of logic into the future could be a real pain in the ass at times, but it was probably the only reason there was any future at all.

"Barry?"

"I'm here.....just getting the weird thoughts out of my system....."

"You know I'm all ears if you want to talk."

I turned back to Thea. She had sat on the terrace and had one foot just a bit off the ground, so she could dangle her sandal about in concentration. Of course she looked very pretty, but there was an academic separation to her, I could see the roots of her curiosity a bit clearer. I did not know if that was because of a difference in her, or in me. I also did not know how to like her less, only how to pretend to because of the circumstances.

"Nah, let's do some exercises. You good with staying down here by the water for today?"

"For sure. Hey, Barry……." Her voice had fallen an

octave. I made some kind of face to encourage her to keep going. "I hope I didn't cross a line with that call, please forgive me if I did. You respond so well every time I push you a bit, and after a day of not being able to challenge the kids with much, I might have gotten carried away with that one."

"Oh, don't worry about that. It's just, I know you're looking out for me with this stuff, and then I was worried you might need a little looking out for something else that was going on."

"You're nice."

"I'm trying."

"I don't think trying has anything to do with it."

"Well, either way, let's try to do some work, yeah? I mean, you could probably use a stretch yourself, right?"

"Yes I could." An appreciative smile lit up Thea's face. At that moment I became comfortable that she needed me just a bit, too, and that was a nice feeling.

My balance was way off. It was a weird frustration all of the sudden, like I knew I'd learned some stuff but when it wasn't working I did not know one thing, or a single step, for an attempted fix. The sudden lack of coordination reminded me of ping pong with ZaZa. Some of the evenings at the truck rental after a day of the loan lumping, ZaZa and I would get into a rhythm, and he made this goofy little 'boop' sound when the ball came off his paddle, so the ball bouncing on the table and knocking on the paddles and his 'boops' all melded into a trance, and we were competing but at the same time when this began to go down it was better to simply keep the rhythm than try something aggressive to win the point, and the thump-tick-boop-tick-thump-tick-boop, its pace would ebb and flow and I almost felt like I could close my eyes and lose myself completely in those sounds and have the paddle in the right place to keep the rally going. Then the next time ZaZa and I hit the truck rental, maybe something at the loan lump irked me more than usual, but it seemed that the ball was always in the net after one 'boop' or we were constantly fishing it out from beneath the rolls of bubble wrap or over by Maya the Rottweiler on her bean bag. There just wasn't much myself or ZaZa could do about it all, some days it was there, and others not.

Thea was watching me though, possibly she could observe something amiss in technique. She did not say anything for a bit, but I knew she was churning thoughts. So after awhile I slowly walked over to the terrace and sat down, while Thea did something that was probably yoga and definitely graceful. She eventually abandoned the pose which either gave her the idea, or the calm, to carry it out.

"Is anything sore or do you have a kink in a leg muscle?"

"No….I don't know what it is."

"Okay. Okay. There are days when it's not there. Let's go back to one of the basics, your left leg straight back. I'm going to stand in front of you."

"Sure."

Thea sifted over. Her hair, it could probably go quiet for a week in the woods and then all of the sudden float the warm flower bouquet as if the bathroom mirror was all fogged. Her brow was crinkled a touch and sometimes she tucked her upper lip beneath her lower teeth for a second. Her eyes, straight ahead, burned into my collarbone, and all told Thea had the look of a gymnast just about to sprint off towards that little launch board. I was very still, and tingling.

"Alright Barry. I want you to have your arms straight and set your palms on my shoulders." Thea's voice was low. Something told me she thought this a touch risky.

"Okay." I did as she said, telling myself, it's not a shoulder rub Barry, just set them flat, which felt a bit clinical but I'd survive.

"Now you can start raising your leg, and then I'll begin to squat little by little, while you lift that leg back and your shoulders come forward."

"Sure." Thea kept her eyes focused straight ahead, not meeting mine. It really was quite the glare. I did not need her shoulders much at first, but given my clumsiness of the day, it was comforting. I began to raise my leg back further. Thea began to bend her knees while her arms were folded against her torso.

"Do your best to keep your head up, eyes forward, Barry. Don't drop your head." Her whisper voice was just a bit grainy, and whisper orders were not something I heard too often. I kept going, and Thea continued to drop her squat. I was pretty much staring just over her head and taking in all the letters near the tail of the alphabet, sloshing every which way in the lake.

"Try to keep your arms straight out and let yourself go further back on that right leg."

I did so, and kept my head up, but pretty soon my left leg was far enough up, and Thea was deep into a stoop, and it felt like my weight was going to shift forward through my hands and shove Thea down onto the cement. Now, thinking back, I could have simply brought my left leg down, stood up, and thanked Thea for the support. So all that was on my mind at that moment was to not push Thea over onto the cement, but also to not let my hands off of her shoulders. It simply felt natural and obvious to drop my head. Well, who knew what a difference that would make. I had been peering off at the water and suddenly there was a lot happening on land. Thea's rhythmic breaths tickled my ear as she held her squat, and her knees were flared out to the sides. Her shorts had ridden up a bit and her thigh muscles twitched. I think I tried to match her breathing, because the sound of it, the warm brush of it, was the pulse of my flooded head. "Keep it up Barry." Thea's tank top was ruffled, and her toes wiggled all pretty on the cement. I noticed that my hands had closed about the warm cusps of her shoulders as wafts of her hair and breath and body made for this wild medley that was only for this moment. "You're doing great." But it was getting to be too much. Thea's thighs shaking and her stomach rolling slow in constant motion, the scents, her breath, even her toes, it was too much to handle. The knot in my back began to speak. For whatever reason, I decided right then and there that no fucking way was I going to scream. My head got all hot and fuzzy as the pain took over, and it was like all of the pleasant things about Thea were still right there, but rearranged, like her thighs were breathing, her toes about to whisper encouragement, like I was lying on the ground and she was walking in circles above me, and I bit my lip and told myself again not to scream, the water sloshed above my head and Thea rowed up in a canoe, then she was underwater too and moving upward while I dragged along by her shoulders, and then my head popped up above the water, and suddenly I was very very close to where her shorts had wedged up over the curve of her thighs. It would be tough to state the distance any better than saying it felt like I had been freefalling in a dream and opened my eyes to all khaki and stitching. I collapsed. I hit the pavement and my back was out.

"BARRY!"

"Oh…..it'll be okay." I mumbled and stayed motionless. Thea sat down next to me and put a hand on my shoulder.

"What happened?"

"I didn't want to scream. So the knot, it went…..it went. That was nice, though, Thea. Really nice."

"You can't move!"

"Give me a minute….." I stared at the water and it let me tell myself that nothing hurt. I thought I heard Thea sniffling, like she was trying not to cry, and supposed it was best not to turn and look at her for a little bit.

"Maybe we could go up into the grass, and I could lie down up there."

"Can you move?"

"Sure." It was a chore though, that was for certain. After struggling to my feet, I had to sit down on the levels of the terrace, then drag my legs up and around, hoist myself up, then do it again, for all five levels.

"Oh…..sorry, it looks like I marked up your shoulders." Thea curled her head for a brief peek. "Would you just worry about your back? Please?"

"Okay, grass….."

I sank onto my front side and planted my cheek into the earth. Thea sat cannonball-style, with her knees up and arms around them.

"He left to do humanitarian work in Bolivia." I heard this and processed it into something weird in my sleep, then opened my eyes and began to process it while awake. I had no idea how long I'd been out. "Of course it's one of those things where you say it's just a year; we'll make it work......" For some reason I felt it better if I just kept my head where it was and nodded, instead of turning to her. "......but it's over. There's gotta be some kind of reliable math to it, you know, you can say it's just a year if you've been married for ten. When you just start talking about moving in together, and then instead someone goes to Bolivia for a year......no.......we're still talking, but we're not saying anything. It's......it's over."

I was glad she was talking even if very confused as to why. So it was probably good that I was crippled and had no crazy energy to say something like, 'won't you be my cufi?'

"And the way he made *me* feel *guilty* for wanting him to stay, *ooooh*, I could barely get a word in without him acting like I was *literally* taking food out of Bolivian children's hands. I just wanted to hear it straight. It wasn't as if when we met he came right out and said, by the way, Thea, my biggest desire is to be a superhero in South America. Then almost two years later he can walk away whistling as long as he's thinking about Bolivia. I swear it probably gets to be late at night and half of the Americans in the program come out and admit the first reason they're down there is that they couldn't break off a relationship like an adult."

It went quiet for a minute. I measured up some words. "Well it seems the more I respect someone the more I'm afraid of disappointing them."

"That's very thoughtful Barry. But there's a certain time where respect is shown in the tough conversations. Apparently I was alone in thinking we had come to that certain time."

I craned my head around to look at her for the first time, again. I could do this when Thea was showing frustration and be pretty sure I wouldn't say anything all huge and silly about always being there to paste her toothbrush. When she was showing sadness, no way, I had to look off to make sure I'd keep my mouth shut. "Maybe he'll wake up and come back really soon." My back didn't like me for that one. I had formed an image of the guy, carrying a nifty thermos.

"That would involve him admitting to be wrong about something."

"Oh."

I looked on ahead, the blades of grass over my sightline kind of like a miniature bushwhacking I'd have to do to go anywhere. It sounded as if Thea was drumming her heels into the ground. For some reason, I considered that it might have been dark outside already at this time, several weeks back when we began meeting. I kind of wanted to ask Thea if something crazy had just happened in her relationship, you know, that night we met at martbar. I didn't think I was afraid to ask, it was more like this kind of mentality that I had tried to shed, like I was just a doormat if Thea had come into martbar during a boarding call at the airport. That thinking just got me to be all cranky and closed off, so it was better to accept that I was meant to meet people when they were a little stirred up.

"Barry?"

"Present."

"Do you just hate me sometimes? When you're not working or practicing your exercises, do you hate me for a minute or two? Does that boil up at the snap of a finger every so often?"

"Oh, no. No way. I love.......our time together.......why would you think that?"

"I suppose it's.......well, this balancing of forces that I guess I believe exists......I've been on both sides......and now, for me, the anger comes on and I'm cursing him and calling him names in my mind. The other day I was chopping a green pepper and before I knew it I kept cutting until it was mostly mush, and then I swept the knife across and tried to fling the entire pile into the trash a few feet away. Most of it ended up on the floor. So, I just worry that if someone is causing me to feel that way, then I must be passing a little of it off on someone else. I worry that I'm doing that to you."

"Please don't. You know, I'm fine. For sure."

"Well, I worry about that too. That you're always fine, until you're not."

"Ahh. This is good for me. Even when I don't know what it is."

We rescinded into our own spaces for a minute. The feeling of the comfortable silence gradually melted in the broiler, into uncomfortable. It was a very profound feeling. "Thea....."

"Yes?"

"I'm not too good with the advice, but you can use his name, you know."

"Thanks Barry. But I feel better when I don't."

"Okay."

Karim had recommended a few spoonfuls of elk antler powder from martbar's reserve collection when I told him about my back. Now I usually stayed away from the reserve collection, it was a little steep for my budget, plus Ron said it was all just cooking spices mixed with last year's ground up prescriptions, and that Karim knew a pharmacist who had to unload after the corporate housing left his neighborhood and sales went to hell. And it was probably dead true but the only catch being Ron also had zero idea if last year's prescriptions had the elk antler powder or not. I mean, portions had probably been switched in and out of this and that in steady rotation over the years, they were always making the stuff a little better than last time because it was easier to find others who were just a tad bent on it. So, who knew. It was all a blur. I had once tried to figure it out for a bit in my spare hours at tanning bed, after Brianne had come in and said, 'Barry, you're smart, look at this line of my painkillers they switch up every nine months, the names all look like what the space explorers tell me they've named their dildos. *Boooooo*ring!' And so Brianne hit send all dramatically before strutting into Vortex, and the text felt important even if only because Brianne had been thinking of something to keep me entertained while standing around up there. I stared at ixi4doo, odi5iox, xiodio6, and do7oxii for awhile, tried plugging them all into both a Roman numeral converter and a family tree, and became very frustrated by the evidence of sinister pattern. An hour later, Brianne sauntered forward with the hat and sunglasses on, and I said I'd need another week to figure it all out, but it sure appeared that Brianne had zero idea or remembrance of what in the hell I was talking about.

Anyway, elk antler extract or not, I needed to be able to do some exercises for Thea in a few days. Otherwise she might get to talking about her ex and stuff. Karim did a nice presentation of the powder for me, as well as any onlookers curious about the reserve collection.

I wasn't sure if any of it had a purpose, but it was cool to see Karim gyrating around as if his favorite song was playing in his head. He didn't get to unwind all that much.

I supposed I drank my bonus juice a little quicker since the powder was dissolved into it. When it settled in after two passes over the same coral reef, my back felt better and everything else felt worse. Thinking about doing some exercises was my only reprieve from being low. So I packed it up at martbar and decided to go and see if I could get in for a tune up, while the powder held the hood open for awhile.

About every three weeks or so, when I opened up tanning bed with a wave of my fingers over the back door sensor, I would make way up the narrow hallway with the neighborhood art on the walls in between the doors to the beds, and just as I came to the lighting panel where the corridor opened to the desk on the left, it was certainly that I sensed the absence before I even saw it out of the corner of my eye. The wide leather chair with the nice armrests was gone again. When it was not on loan, it was angled to the corner of the reception alcove to the right, facing the glass front or whoever might be sitting in the less desirable maroon plastic chair, which looked as if it had been designed by depriving a bulldog of water and then molding its tongue. You see, this was why I showed up to tanning bed early, even if most times I ended up standing there saying to myself, damn, I got to tanning bed early. Stuff like this came up and I had to go over to the Asian Pita and bring the chair back. Or at least I thought it was what I should do. It wasn't like 'bring the chair back' was in the description manual just beneath 'greet customers courteously'. Also, there was no description manual. Tanning bed opened at four and closed at eleven. That much was for sure.

The chair was always in the same place over at Asian Pita. It made its own end at the big round table. Gehri usually helped Andrés carry it over before some big shot meeting where Gehri only got to sit at your typical Asian Pita chair. To my knowledge I had never seen the guy who sat in the big chair. Andrés gave me stunted descriptions of him, here and there, 'Shoes. Long shoes white', and, 'maybe very young he punchedindenose, the nose, it flat', one time, 'he no take off the hat today. No taking it off. The hat.' But the thing was, these breakfast meetings were the one and only table which Andrés ever waited upon. No one else was even permitted in the room. So I knew he was being kind of wise and throwing me a nugget here and there, without abusing Gehri's trust.

On this day, after I found Andrés going back and forth with the kitchen in Spanish, and we twisted the chair through the two front doors, set it down and I gave Andrés a look he knew as invitation to share whatever he'd like, Andrés kind of giggled and said, 'oh man', and as he did this his shoulders rose up to his ears as he shook his head. This was always how he bought a few seconds to think of what to tell me, or to act as if he hadn't decided hours ago. "Okay, okay." Andrés came set, into his usual slight hunch forward. "Two ladies today. Four guys. One guy, he bringing, uh, how you say.........they going with the cheeseborger......."

"He brought a cheeseburger?"

"No no. He bring.....they verday and....no good, no good......" Andrés scrunched his mouth to indicate a foul taste. ".....Looking like coins.......on a cheeseborger. Cut......."

"Fresh mozzarella? Orrr, radishes?...............Avocado? Pepperoni?"

"No. MAN." Andrés always did this one quick, head down, shake, to fend off frustration with communicating. "Avocado. Phhh. Like coins......one, two, trey, four. On the cheeseborger. No avocado!"

"There's always avocado on burgers. It's good! What are you talking, like those barbeque poppers? Andrés you gotta quit eating at those places. This guy brought *barbeque poppers?*"

"What? Shiiittt. No this guy no bringing the barbycoo peppers."

"Poppers."

"He no bringing the peppers or papas. He bringing.....they verday.....they green. Not peppers."

"Ohh, sorry dude. Cucumber!"

"They no cucommbers. The other guy, he probably bringing the cucommber!" Andrés laughed his giggly laugh and squinted and rubbed his eyes once over. Then I laughed too, because it was contagious. "Okay. Okay. So the guy bringing. He cuts chop chop chop. Then the first guy...." Andrés motioned to his right side……."he taste"…..He scrunched his mouth again……."he taste and he nod yes. The lady with the big watch, she taste and nod………then Gehri, then Gehri……coffee, coffee, yes, yes, no coffee, tea……..Gehri nodding yes. The other lady then, she wait, she grab the phone instead, waiting, waiting, coffee, coffee……..finally she taste and nod. Big chair, he rubbing the beard after he taste. Rubbing, rubbing. Two minutes rubbing."

"No…."

"YEAH. Then he no nod. No nodding. And he say, 'no coffee. Tea.' And me, I going for tea but he say, he say, 'no thank you Andrés' and he looking at me then looking at everybody and, and, he doing this, he doing this….." Andrés raised his index finger and shook it a bit. "…..then he say, 'no coffee. Tea. Then they all going, leaving."

Like I said, sometimes it was good to show up at tanning bed a little early.

I was poking back into martbar….yeah, I know, martbar again, but just in the case that you're wondering about football barn, I read the crawler along the front and it was day four of sled pushing. And then I passed by the connec….tittyvity counter, it was a slow day, and was thinking about all of the people who might be in martbar and what I may have missed since being there last and if someone might fill me in and what else what else there was something else too for sure, and I wasn't really paying attention to anything along the connec….tittyvity counter, but then, POW, the magician whisked open the one side of his unbuttoned coat, and it caught the corner of my eye and made me stagger even though I didn't see anything inside, I staggered as if he was pulling me into his little universe, and then I came to and he was gone, already floating in the opposite direction, towards the front, and I had attempted in the flash to catch a facial expression, but did not.

Anyway, by the time I sat down, I was done lying to myself and wondering about much of anything and could admit, that yeah, yeah I was back for another spoonful of the elk antler powder. When I left a few days prior and broke into some poses and such, the back started tingling and talking to me kind of stern about pushing it a little bit, like I could do more good for it while it was still on the mend.

Karim didn't grab this specifically shaped glass cylinder from a cabinet the last time. The last time he didn't hold a box match up high and then shift all his weight forward into a whipping wrist fling to the other extended hand, to strike the match as if it was the last guitar note for all of damn time. There was no mixing in an ounce or so of water, while humming some random tune, and then setting the cylinder over a burner until wisps of smoke began to rise. I got a bit nervous that he thought I had ordered something else, even more expensive. Karim began dancing while the vapors made paisleys, and I tell ya, it really was kind of pleasant when he was gyrating around back there. I mean, sometimes you'd be in a stool and a steward began dancing a bit, and it seemed to mean that it was either closing time or he or she was just totally sick of everyone's dumb face, because the shoulders and hips and such were all jerking about like the steward was trying different saws to cut down a tree. But Karim was just feeling good, it was obvious. After a few minutes, he pulled the cylinder off of the burner, removed the lid, and inhaled the vapors. He tapped the damp powder out, into my bonus juice, exhaled the smoke very gradually above my head, and said, "Hints of raspberry, excellent for cramps." And Karim nodded officiously, and just like that he was back to being all low-key and serious.

The bonus juice was down to a gurgle of the last drops through a straw, and mostly I was just waiting to go home and exercise, when a guy I had never seen before pulled up in the stool to my right and ordered some super chips from Karim, real matter-of-factly like why would anyone have anything but the super chips ever. Then again most guys who came into martbar were really sure of themselves when it came to their snacks. I gave the gent a brief and friendly nod when he sat; his forehead was long and face really square throughout, his eyes not set back much and chin kind of one with the neck. That's when I said to myself, the powder is taking hold, I just noticed way too much of a stranger's face with one glance. But I did remember it making an impression before he turned back a minute later, and asked, 'So, how are you?' Really attentive and odd. Now, I was well sick of people asking that and then carrying on with orders or what not before even allowing you a second to respond. This though, it almost felt as if he'd stare all wide-eyed until I talked. Like, a bit spooky, but not at all intrusive and probably no cares if I just said, 'not bad', and went back to

dolphin drone. And, I suppose he caught me at a strange moment and I might have given the fellow a little more than he bargained for. "Well, I think my hamstrings are almost loose enough to where I won't scream even if Thea really catches me by surprise, so I'm going to do some exercises while this stuff from the reserve collection has my lower back relaxed, but of course there is the question of whether the exercises are just a waste of time and effort, maybe this stuff is all I need to avoid the screaming, although my best guess is there is some ideal combination of hamstring stretching and elk antler powder for it all, you know, balance, mind and body, of course, but is it really elk antler powder? Does anyone know for sure? Maybe the magician will tell me eventually...........or some crazy dude will take the powder consistently and then go out in the woods during the elk mating season and get in the middle of a joust and take some antlers right in the kisser and then give us all the thumbs-up on livefeed, like, yep, same stuff......but I'm not that crazy dude."
"You're sure about that?"
"Yeah, no, not much time to get away from tanning bed and go into the woods, plus the bonus juice doesn't travel too well, you know. Tents, those are always kind of a weird setup........"
"I'd bet you could figure it out." He furled his lip a tad and nodded.
"Sorry I'm rambling."
"No, please, talk away....." And he meant it. I swear the guy meant it. I had no idea how curious he was, I could have been sparking up his brain good or just firing little pebbles of words that made just enough of a peck on his face to keep all of his expressions firing, I had no idea, but I will say this. He had enough curiosity to sit

there and inspire me to talk, and that was rare in people, and damn, you just don't know how bad you needed to go for a bit until somebody great like that nudged you a touch to spill for a minute.

"Probably I could figure it out but it still might be tough to take an antler right in the kisser and not scream for some xiodio6 or oodi8ix, and then be on livefeed telling everyone that the antlers weren't good enough, they'd all be watching and yelling that I just needed to take a bear claw in the lap or something, yeah, that'd be no good....."

"Or you could simply go out there and relax for a few days, enjoy being away from it all……."

"Yeah, as long as I didn't miss one of my sessions with Thea, I wouldn't want to miss a session with Thea. And I suppose I could do my exercises in the woods to be better for Thea……."

"Sounds like you've got a plan, buddy."

"I better go do my exercises while the powder is going strong, yeah………wow, ha ha, it's going alright……..hey thanks for listening, really." I did my best to show real appreciation, and I think he was happy that I didn't ask him to be a lifetime friend or anything.

"I'm sure you do the same thing at times."

"Yeah." But I walked off kind of doubting that. It all sounded easy enough in theory, the listening stuff, but it took practice, and if I was that guy I would have done something like sneak a real quick peek at dolphin drone, or gone fidgety, and the talking would have ended there.

I passed the connec….tittyvity counter on the way out and walked slow and relaxed, gazing upwards a touch, in hopes that the magician might decide to catch me. He was probably gone for the night. Yeah, it was strange to hope that a magician was going to give me answers about something. The whole idea of magic was that nobody could know what was happening. But that was the thing. I mean, I remembered when I was younger I would get all hunched forward and do an eagle stare at the cards, and that guy at the Sunday brunch, Tony Racine, yeah, Tony Racine, he might have taken a glance at me and decided to save a better routine for someone who wasn't so damn sure they could burn a hole through the deck like a superhero.

The street was kind of alive, there was a warm breeze carousing down the avenue and everyone strolled as if they had an ice cream, even if only a few actually did. I leaned back against the wind and strutted really cool, to show off my good posture. The lights moved and flashed back and forth in three dimensions, and I blurred my eyes enough to make up a video game of my own life, for a moment. It was not long before it was interrupted by two men in suspenders drawing the pistols on each other, so I reached into my pocket and turned off my phone before the name and network dropped from the sky in big block letters. I didn't need all of that, because, strangely enough, I felt like being seen myself. That was a new thing for me.

The night got a bit strange, that was for sure. I mean, even more so than just doing a pirouette, if that was even the right word, pirouette, but you get the idea. I had planned on going to sleep after taking it all down a notch with some breathing. Even after getting a little nuts with the poses and stuff, it was still best to rest up for tanning bed the next day. So I was on my back and really still for awhile, but there were a lot of thoughts dancing around above me and I was chasing those thoughts around one by one, no really, it was like I could feel myself physically chasing those thoughts while I lied still as all hell, and man, it was weird. Who knows how long I was off on that wavy carousel of reaching limbs and also these, like, I don't know, little tingling patches here and there, as if for a minute there were strawberries on my left calf ripe for picking, and then the next thing I knew, the right shoulder was in soft soil with the roots and the earthworms. But when I finally began rising, or sinking, back to surface thoughts of that decent night of sleep I had planned, I kind of knew that was not happening. And all of the sudden I was on the street, its desolation the only time I could tell, feeling everything hang still, even the buildings having dropped their shoulders after the last living room light went out. To the martbar!

I swear Karim had another one teed up for me before I could even decline a stool. He was really dancing this time, Karim was, he looked like a damn condor caught in a complicated updraft, with long wings all over the place. There was an unfamiliar man with all of his face absconded by beard and glasses sitting opposite with his little drum, tapping the canvas softly with his fingers. Something in the room was moving his hands but I doubt anyone would ever know what. martbar was lit differently; it was all colored running lights making frames around people's gestures now. Karim laughed with a couple, three stools down, maybe old friends, who had dressed for something other than martbar some time ago. Karim didn't laugh enough. No one laughed enough.

The spatial oddities continued as I drank the fortified bonus juice without having much idea how close or far away I was from the social moment. That was, until I realized that I was trying to stretch my oblique muscles, instead of taking a seat. And it seemed as if not a second later Karim stepped away from his friends and squared himself to me and looked at me all straight-faced, his stubble shadow heavier from the past few hours and this blue lighting catching the furrow of his brow, and I stood there for what seemed like forever not knowing if he was gonna stun me again with an odd dance, or introduce me to the others, but he gave me one defined nod, I guess one of those nods where you're sure that someone knows what's best for you, and I nodded back, but kind of smile chuckling while I did, because I was like, damn Karim, you know I should be getting back to my exercises, you are wise, but of course smile chuckling while realizing at the very same moment that he may well have just been supportive and trusting about whatever ideas I already had, and then really cool again by walking off before I went all goofy with some kind of thank you where I fumbled up any words and made like ten stupid faces. So I was off, once more. I made long and deliberate tip-toe steps, with my arms raised up like loose wings, past the, I remember thinking that it might have been gone, connec…., connec…., nope, still had it, connec….tittyvity counter, like I was a cat burglar stepping through the grid, and I supposed it could have been a bit of a show for one or two people who might have been looking through the change in light and up the three stairs into the hallway. It felt lucid and proper, that little tip-toe, both just for me and my thoughts and as the best thank you for leaving a place feeling good, for anyone who may have been watching.

I zigged and zagged all the way between the parallel parked cars on each side of the two-lane street, and the autos were a black-and-white photograph spliced into the bottom of a hot neon blur twisting and flashing into distant faces, which might have been in my imagination. What was certainly in my imagination was all of the extreme stuff I was doing on top of the cars and up along the sides of the buildings. Gnarly backside squeaks of third-floor windows, running four-legged up over doorways, super flying from one streetlamp to the next, oh Barry, oh Barry, you can't win *every event* of the radgames and then do a double-cartwheel into jab kick that knocks over an *entire row* of fifteen occupied port-o-potties, next time just thank the nice commentators and tell them how you owe it to the bonus juice. Yeah, it was that kind of evening. I know I wasn't doing the inverted aerials over the roofs of good coupes, or throwing thunderbolts across the block, but I'm pretty sure I was doing some balancing in the middle of the street, so you didn't have to worry over my good health or anything like that.

There was a high-rise up the block where they were working on new balcony rails. Eight tradesmen, all in formation, four wide around the bend of two separate floors, about twenty stories up, each of them seemed to have the drills and jackhammers going at once, now maybe it was how it all echoed and amplified from way up there, but that was how it sounded, loud drills and jackhammers at the same time. I wondered how loose and unreliable the balcony railings had to have been, to bother with replacing them. I mean, you wouldn't think that they had to withstand, say, a two-hundred seventy pound man doing a bull charge out of the condominium after his football team lost in the final seconds, you wouldn't think that someone shopping for a condo would be checking water pressure and then also making sure they could be all dramatic and charge at the railing when the football game went sour, like, really, they could just die after that one. But who knows. It could have been all cosmetic, the new railings, it could have been that. Owners probably did want to be down on the sidewalk and count twenty up and then three over, then double check the count and make sure they didn't lose it, and then nod in approval, yes, that's definitely the one, the outside of their home was looking good.

Anyway, it was all very noisy. And it made my senses all acute to the other noise too as I made way towards the lake. The traffic was sitting as still as the dead heat. There were polluters honking. The front gate of the schoolyard wall motored open and the kids were ushered and rushed quickly with their heads down into awaiting vehicles, while two men in black suits and sunglasses made me into a suspect of some sort. Up ahead, the cars were all jammed and curled around, like two interlocking gears for both entrance to and exit from Lakeshore. I could feel frustration oozing out of the cabins and into the humidity, almost like everyone would prefer to be surprised by the same old gridlock because that was better than knowing all day what was ahead. I made it through the underpass. There was a dangerous crossing ahead, and then I was home free. The exercise superhighway, you see, it was very crowded, and people did not take a side step or slow for anything because that ruined all the optimums on their fitness trackers. The bikers all had shirts for minimum drag and the joggers' shoes always looked under a month old. They all clipped along in the stifling heat. They were all kind of racing, maybe, and halfway trying to appear stylish while looking and being looked at as if they were collecting the low-gluten porno for later. All of it must have been pretty healthy.

I took the mulched path which wound beneath the tree canopy. The sunlight came through in sporadic patches and made patterns on the ground and the weeds, shapes emerging in both the positive and negative space. The leaves and the birds were quiet. Everything was quiet, except for the soft and crunchy steps on the mulch, like walking on a quality snack. I was probably early and did not expect to see Thea just yet as the shade dissipated into scattered pieces on the ground, shadows of leaves raked off into the corner by the unrelenting heat. The horizon, it was a blur, hazy, the definitive line between water and sky smudged by an antique feint pink eraser. I spun around to see if Thea was on her way from the lot, did not see her, and then kept moving towards the lake.

I could see it sweating as I hopped down the terrace. No ripples, no rolls, no tiny pecks from the sun. If it was even breathing then its smooth belly rose and fell too slowly to notice. I stepped across the cement flat to the serrated edge. Now, you could go out there to that spot and look down every day for the rest of your life and know that the water would never be exactly the same. But there might be only once when it looks at you with such a clear invitation to love it forever. The rocks, the big rocks just beneath the surface, a lot of the time they couldn't be seen at all, and then other days appeared only to demonstrate how easily they could smash your ribs. The rocks were glowing on this day, though. They looked like Arizona, underwater, as it was so many millions of years ago, according to Ron. Prairies of corded algae stretched up and waved languid at the sun. Every crag and nook of the stones was all textured and shadowed. The skin of the water was cracked into unique platelets, and I could only tell this by the feint refracted outline of a cobblestone street onto the tan boulders underneath. I mean, there was just so much going on down there, not all the rainbow coral and weird shaped fish like dolphin drone, but that was kind of tourism pretty, and this, well, it was home, this bed of rocks just past the cement and iron wall, only a few minutes from my apartment, they had been there all along, but not really, and now the water had gone still to bare those rocks with this beautiful whispering plea to touch them, like they were each keys of an instrument which would certainly make only beautiful sounds as long as they were stroked with a little care.

There was no one else in sight and I caught myself about to remove my shorts as if I had a swimsuit on underneath. I turned back and looked for Thea and could not wait for Thea to see this too, and marvel at it, and we'd swim and play and frolic on the rocks all of the time forever and that would be life, at home. Suddenly I was spinning in circles like a devious kid had tied a chew treat to my tail because I wanted to get in so badly and also wanted to wait for Thea and we'd go down the ladder together into this timeless little universe below. Every second was an hour and I was terrified of a sudden wind or convoy of stupid power boats making it all dangerous and invisible again.

"Thea! Thea! Come down here! HA HA IT'S AMAZING YOU GOTTA COME DOWN HERE!!" Her hair, it moved a bit with her steps and it already looked like how it might all splayed out underwater.
"Okay, okay……I'm right here Barry….."
"I know I know, but oh man this is cool!"
Thea stepped down the terrace all casual and slow in her sandals, kind of this cool one-legged squat to ease her other foot down. "Barry if there is something terrifying and gross in the water please tell me now."
"NO! No no no…….it's beautiful. So beautiful." I turned to the water and then back to Thea again, frantic, electric, needing all the beauty to be in the same place. She took a deliberate step towards me, that hip kind of forward and starting a slow motion of her shoulders falling back and then her palm brushing over her hair, with a little concern. "How are you doing Barry? Everything good?"
"Yes! Yes! Never mind that anyway…..look at this look at this….." I held my arm out, not to touch her but rather just a welcome to paradise gesture.
"Oh. You can see the rocks today. That's nice."

"The rocks? You can see civilizations, continents, abysses, the past, the future, it's the greatest thing ever let's get in!"

"The water?"

"Of course!"

"Barry I didn't bring a suit."

"Well, um, what you've got on, you know, underneath, that's kind of like a bikini, yeah?"

"You're too funny. No Barry, the unmentionables are not kind of like a bikini, sorry to break the news to ya."

"But there's nobody out here, anywhere! I almost took my damn shorts off by accident! Hey, I can go in and then turn my head until you're underwater, I mean, look at all of the space out here, it's a miniature mountain range! I can be, like, fifty feet away. Now, from fifty feet your, um, unmentionables they're pretty much like a bikini from fifty feet away, for sure."

"You guys, you guys! No they're not pretty much like a bikini no matter how far you or anyone else may be away. They're underwear Barry. I know there's a million photos a minute going up of women in lingerie, or without, but mine is personal, private. I'm not comfortable using it as a swimsuit."

"But this is, like, it's not a pool, it's not even earth, or it's a lot of the earth, I don't know, but it looks way too comfortable to even think for a second about what you're wearing………right?"

"Barry, I'm sorry, but let me spare you of the sales pitch, as cute as it is. That water is cold and I wouldn't be swimming even if I had my suit."

"Cold? Those rocks, they're on fire! They look like something out of a volcano and I'm a little scared they're going to burn me, but no way the water is cold, no way……"

"The water is seventy-one degrees, I saw it earlier today. That's coooold *water* for a leisurely swim. For me, at least. But you should go, check it out. I'm happy to watch or do some exercises right here."

"Well, okay…..but you might change your mind in a bit."

"We'll see. Have fun, and be careful okay?" With that, Thea removed her sandals, sat on the edge of the wall, and let her legs dangle.

The ladder rungs became slimy and slick with algae as I took the first few steps below, and I had thoughts for a second that maybe it wasn't anything too special, maybe I'd just seen Karim one too many times of late. I looked down at the rock just behind the ladder, maybe three feet below water. I released my hands and feet at once and drifted back, and then down, until my feet came into contact with, like, a million tiny little bumps in the stone, and each of them trickled all the way through me, and my feet, they were alive, they were receptive to touch for the first time ever after so many years of being these dull boards that only stank up socks and ached in the heels by the end of the day at tanning bed. I stood still, mouth agape. I gradually turned my stunned face to Thea, who gave one of those smiles like she was happy for me and also wondering what in the hell was going on. I turned around to infinity and waved my arms forward and back, and it was like all of these little muscles around the joints that no one ever showed off or talked about, they all sang out like they'd long ago given up hope of ever being rescued. I had my fingers spread and tendons of the water wound between them, it was alive, every last ounce of it alive with the diverse history of its travels.

"I'M IN OUTER SPACE! THIS IS OUTER SPACE!"
I lifted my feet and stroked with my arms until I could
straighten my legs again on the next imperfect tabletop.
It was another new balance, once again foreign touch
with total wilderness. This boulder was slanted and its
high side just a foot or so under, so I cusped my hands
around that edge and then let my legs drift up until I
was horizontal and staring into the crevice where a lone
nine-inch flopper sifted over the bottom, ten or so feet
down. Then I pushed with one arm to swing my legs
together to one side, and, then back to the other, and,
damn, something in my sides just blew right open, just
like that, those muscles feeling a foot longer. I didn't
know if I was mimicking fish, or ducks, or gulls, or had
become a bit of each, but when I turned back to the wall,
and Thea sitting with that serious curious of hers, arms
braced straight on the cement, anyway, the wall and the
land, they were only fifteen feet away, but I knew I was
going to break myself wide open and shake out all of the
nonsense a thousand times over before I even thought of
going back over that wall. There were no limits. To
anything. I could float or plank or kick at any body
angle, feeling that stone electrify my hands and feet, and
there was just nobody who ever said it was all too much
of this or too little of that, or too weird or not impressive
enough, I had never heard a peep from any of the very
few people who had ever been on those rocks, and I'd
finally won one, because there was nothing besides the
water, the rocks, and me, and the urge of several
lifetimes to just do what felt good. I planted my feet
again and turned to Thea, and I was almost in tears as I
pleaded again, "You have to come in here. It's too
good......you *have* to."

"Maybe next time. I'm happy seeing how great it is for you."

"Thea there might not be a next time, you know, the wind will come back and this will be gone, who knows how long until it's like this again, I'll go down there and look the other way just please slip on in......."

"Not today Barry, not today........keep going. Are you cold?"

"NOOO no no. These rocks are hot! Oh, oh.......look at this one......" I sat myself on a rock which jutted upwards and through the skin of the water, then laid on my back and wiggled until it was digging into a muscle back there and the gentle swish of the water moved the spot in circles around the stationary knuckles of the boulder. "It's a free back massage, it's free everything! Free!" However, there was too much else going on for me to park on a nub for long. So I wandered from one to another, touching some with a hand and others with my feet, doing stretches while halfway under, catapulting myself sideways over a gorge only to spring off the next one shaped like Iowa into a double-move, no way, this Barry cat just cleared the Rockies in one fell swoop, landed on *one hand* in Nevada, then sprung California, pockets stuffed with the heavy chips, ladies and gentlemen Barry has just discovered a new Pacific Island while dominating radgames, it is full of mangoes and blue kangaroos, but he's already off to the moon it appears, maybe he's just stopping by to plant a bonus juice flag.....you just don't know what that Barry is gonna do next unless you see the schedule for tanning bed......

I turned and came to, seeing that I was a few hundred feet from Thea, and began the trip back to see if that was a few planets too. The land, it all looked like a boring knockoff of the dolphin drone, only a few people in sight, walking horizontal along the infinite cement staircase. Thea waved at me. I was through with trying to get her into the water that day, only wanting to be a little closer to her and maybe splash a little bit of magic over the side. The wall, it was a little tough on the eyes. It was just such a stark and grave reminder of all too much that happened once it claimed jurisdiction. Suddenly I wished for thousands of people to rush to the shoreline so I could try to show them the sense in all the weirdness. I drifted closer to the wall, found a high edge of a rock to clutch with my hands, bent one leg back to raise the foot in the air, then brought it down with all my might. The top of my foot broke through the water and it made a very deep and loud THOOOMP against the iron serrations, almost as if I had broken a vacuum seal which allowed the whole damn lake to speak. It was a crazy cool sound. So I stayed and kicked out my best drum solo ever until my legs were finished. "Thea! Was that a nice drum solo or what? Oh, that was fun!"

She shook her head, smiling. "You're too much. Why don't you warm up for a few minutes? Please? You've been in there for close to an hour."

"Oooooookay….." I did a few more sweet moves through an archipelago of planets, extra slow spins, because there was time. As I neared the ladder, Thea stood and backed up a step. She appeared worried. I was about to say something, then reconsidered. I grabbed onto a rung and let my feet follow. Then I remained still on the ladder for awhile. I didn't know why, but I was still and staring at the yellow rungs and rusted out big iron bolts in the wall. I peeked up and could not see Thea from that angle. Finally, I climbed, and felt my weight change profoundly with each inch of leaving the water.

Thea was ten feet or so away from the edge with hands on her hips. Curls of her hair were sticking along her temples. I stood up very slowly. I was shaking like mad. I didn't know if I was cold or exhausted or what, but I was shaking terribly. Thea's eyes were wide, to where I couldn't see anything else if I tried. I took a short step, not even the length of my foot, and was wobbling all the way through, legs, hips, shoulders, a hunched over stagger. Thea was a statue with all the whites of her eyes. I slid the other foot forward a few inches, and I suppose I was kind of unconscious and moving towards her. Again, I was wavering everywhere just trying to keep my feet planted. After a few more very abbreviated and laborious steps, I began to raise my right arm, gradually, my elbow halfway bent, and had to readjust my balance as if I was dragging a shelf along. Thea's eyes remained fixed. I took another step. My arm raised a little more. As I neared her, it really did feel like I was trying to give her something by touching her, and not just trying to convince her that I would not hurt her. My hand was about a foot from her shoulder when her lips began twitching all wild. I froze. Her cheeks started jumping around too. My mouth opened but nothing came out. It felt like we were both holding half of what it took to be completely warm. All that I could want was to touch that bare shoulder. Feeling that shoulder was a new beginning to everything and maybe I could just touch it from arm's length until the sun went down. Thea's eyes were still wide open and her face quivering. I inched my hand forward again, but this time she covered her face with both hands, and then turned quickly, and grabbed her bag, and said, "I'll see you next week Barry I promise", and I just stood there with that arm out while she moved up the terrace, and then out of my sight, and then for a little while after that too. Then I sat down in a ball and stared at nothing until it was dark outside.

When I had finally picked myself up and stumbled home from the lake the night before, I was nearing the high-rise where the tradesmen had long finished for the day on the balconies, and it was not three seconds after I stopped to look up there again that the pop singer with a ton of swagger leaned over a rail about six stories up, but also up to about eight stories up because the pop singer was over twenty feet tall whether it was a mistake in coding or not, somebody once told me all revelatory that it was a ludicrous ripoff, well sure, but anyway the singer threw a fist up high amidst all of the thick jewelry and tattoos, and "RolllllllllOUTTTT", and I just keeled over laughing, I mean, I hadn't had a laugh like that in some time, oh man, it really got me good for whatever reason. But it wasn't long before the joke was on me again. Stupid me, some time ago I agreed to meet Ron at martbar at eight this morning, yeah, it sounded so easy at the time, and Ron probably wanted to share some good wisdom while lining up a few jerky sticks. I had set the alarm right away, and was so busy laughing at the pop singer and everything else that I forgot to adjust the alarm so I could get to martbar before #ETT morning play, and now had to walk over while the children chased the nicefoam hashtags around.

The catch, for me at least, the catch was that if I made the walk with the phone on, it would show this destination history as probably like ninety-five percent martbar for that time of day, and the kids, well, for the smart ones they could do other things while also collecting a few nicefoam hashtags, and once they got sight of that martbar destination, it was, well, the children picked up on a lot of lines and once one of them got a photo it would circulate and once some comment like, 'off to martbar lol never got fucked enough when young', once that got going there was nothing to do but walk to martbar and see all of the adults in line for the connec.....tittyvity counter look at their phones and then point and laugh, kind of proud that their kids were so astute, and it wasn't the end of the world or anything but it sure didn't make for a good start to the day. So, I know, you might be thinking like I had to have my phone on to livefeed with Ron, or something, because we just couldn't wait to see each other, but that wasn't it. You see, if I kept my phone off, the children had a hashtag for 'why is your phone off' and they'd catch you with a terrible photo and their ideas of what you were up to were far worse than you going to martbar. Again, it was all leading to the adults in line for the connec....tittyvity counter, getting all sentimental with their last ever ridicule before an upgrade, so I probably wasn't going to lose my job at tanning bed or have to answer the question wizard at the morning play perimeter, but still.

I craned my neck out slow and peeked both ways down the sidewalk, still undecided about the phone. I could hear a bunch of children around the corner, on their way in my direction towards a large cluster of the blue nicefoam hashtags. And I was stooping and all uptight and nervous, and thought, damn, I could have been going to the lake if I hadn't set a date with Ron. So I did it. I turned off the phone and I said, what the hell, I will go under and swim to martbar, yeah, just pretend like I'm underwater the whole way there. The mob was on its way down the block. There had to be thirty or so in sight, ravenous for nicefoam and content. Their short limbs and tiny heads jerked around all awkward and goofy, but I tell ya, if one of them got you in the viewfinder, the child would go still and intense, no wavering, like mom was right there with a hand on the shoulder saying, 'take the shot, junior, you can do it. There are too many of them out on the streets, up to no good if the phone is off, for sure, and you might as well put on the big britches and get your survival skills now. Take the shot junior, you know when it's right.' And you could see the clarity in their eyes, suddenly locked in to a comment for the good of everyone, and you knew you were screwed. It was all terrible.

I stood straight, closed my eyes, kept my arms straight at my sides, and I sank. I went down a good thirty or forty feet before even thinking about breathing. And I was off. We would see what the little buggers could do if unable catch me for an instant as a lonely biped skulking down the grid to martbar. I waved my arms languid above my head and twisted through the trench, witnessing from the deep that moment when they detected my dark sonar and redirected from the cluster of nicefoam hashtags. It really was kind of cool, all of the ways you could move in the water when there were no lanes, no optimums. Their running and yelling up there, it was wavy and muffled and their limbs and necks became elongated and then stubby, and it was nice to think for a moment that they were all swimming too. I made figure-eights through the dashes and breaks of the parked car reef, throwing so many shades of watercolor with the loose flings of my hands. When the phones were raised into position up above, they bent out of shape and into starfish, and octopus tentacles, the phones stretched and reached and smooched into cheek barnacles. I puckered up myself and let a bubble rise every few seconds, just for the hell of it, but still keeping the legs going sideways and asymmetrical, like, no patterns Barry, no patterns. Their pointed fingers grew odd knuckles as the bubbles expanded into peripheral wavering. I spun around three times and made one long jump towards the surface before recoiling and slaking back down to the ideal temperature. Their hair, all of the earthy shades of their hair, it drifted outward in wonderful waves and erratic tangles, turned into so many brushes painting at the water, but instead it was the water painting at them and made the brushes the art, it was swirling wild and all of the hues and textures, coils and knots and weightless dissipation into stranding of sand and clay and almond and shale catching light so pure, and all of the wild hair melding along the waterline was so beautiful and I was pretty happy to be able to appreciate it from such a cool distance. I keeled back and to one side, tumbling sideways over myself, and swam away, like, from then on, it was all cool with us, and if they still wanted to tag me with something, well then go ahead and take the shot, follow that viewfinder every last millimeter, angle it down and nose it around until too much of everything jumps through the frame, and fire the spear through the water, and if a split second later it stopped time as the only way to stake the stupid look on my face, well then, kudos, and thanks, because it would be great to have a quick laugh at myself when I showed up a little early at martbar to meet Ron.

I swam past the adults too, while I was at it. They didn't look all refracted up there, and their phones did not reshape like amoebas. Instead they stiffened and their teeth began to show, and it began to sink down there really slow and deep, the determination, the declaration, "You're not a celebrity! Not a celebrity, no….no, no……" Because they had been waiting for their upgrade and it was celebrity this #ETT and that meant some kind of visit from a livefeed star or something, still to come, obviously, to go along with a new and improved charger module. "Not a celebrity!!" Their teeth grew and faces stretched into neon taffy as they stood in a line and became more convinced that I was the one pulling a prank. I blew a few bubbles like slow ellipses, hopefully each one reiterating my total pointlessness, save for disappointing them with my unrecognizable form.

Once inside, I surfaced with an overdue gasp. "CONNECT….TITTYVITY!" The collection of the salespeople heads turned and I could not tell if it was with their bodies too because their shirts matched the back wall so well. I turned in the other direction quickly, looking for the magician, hoping he would engage me. He was busy with a guest, really churning up a good whirlwind through his own suit, and I noticed that he always wore the same necktie on #ETT. I moved along before he did the finger tap, three times in quick succession, the finger tap on the glass which the guest could take as part of the show but I was pretty sure it was a cue to me that he had noticed me watching and my time was up. I hit the three stairs down into martbar and thought maybe soon I'd try to swim all the way past the connec.....tittyvity counter.

Ron and Karim had reached this weird and comfortable understanding of some sort where neither one said a word to the other, or nodded, or anything, while Karim gave Ron his usual. It was a bit strange to be around, I mean, I got used to it over time but it was still a bit uncomfortable to be sitting next to Ron when Karim set down the glass with the ice and then poured the bonus juice from the tumbler, and then laid out the three jerky sticks, one, two, three, and neither one ever said anything, and even though I knew for sure that there were times when they said quite a bit to each other, still, I kind of sat there goofy and wanted to break it with something dumb, like, 'hey, how about that weather', because I was the one feeling awkward.

"I'm going to do the usual here. It is time to ask even though I know the answer. You haven't seen Gehri in the past few days have you?"
"Ron I see him about once every few months, you know that. Oh, but I know what I was gonna run by you. Andrés...."
"Andrés?"
"Yeah, the cool busser who holds together both businesses. Andrés was throwing me a bone about the

big meeting after we carried the big chair back to tanning bed, and I couldn't figure out what he was trying to describe on a cheeseburger. Hmmm, come to think of it, I'm still not sure...."

"Let's slow this down Barry. Take a sip of your bonus juice and tell me, yes or no, if you've seen Gehri in the past few days."

"That's what I was getting around to, with the meeting at Asian Pita......."

"Yes or no, Barry. Have you encountered Gehri with your own two eyes since we last saw each other in here?"

"It's been like, a full #ETT, since I saw you in here."

"It's been five days."

"No way Ron. Karim, Karim......." I could tell Karim was a bit irritated because he knew I had a useless question for him, but he stepped over after a stubborn pause. "Can you make a rough guess of how long it's been since you've seen Ron and I in here together?"

"One second......"

"Well, no, not counting right now."

Karim shook his head and kind of half chuckled with one side of his mouth. Then he turned his back and touched his tablet for a moment. "It was during the last waxing gibbous."

"Was that before megapixel upgrade?"

"It was five days ago." Ron did not go for any kind of documentation. He never did.

"The moon was three of your reserve collection healings from full Barry. Ron you were six jerky sticks from full moon."

Ron rolled his eyes. "You're in here eighteen hours a day Karim. The moon....." Karim brushed off any urge to argue.

"I've met with Thea at least three times."

"Who's Thea?"

"Come on Ron, Thea's my speech therapist. You know that."

"Have you had sex?"

"No."

"Have you seen this Thea three times in the past five days?"

I checked out and thought about Thea for a minute, and sunk a little bit in my stool, and Ron took this as an admission that I was wrong, when it might have been, sure, I might have been wrong about a whole lot with Thea and everyone and everything else, but not this, no way.

"Yes or no, Barry."

"No, Ron…..no I haven't. I meet Thea four times in a moon cycle and if you divide that by pi or something and then multiply back in how many shifts I do at tanning bed per #ETT, I would still not have any answers about all of that."

"Karim, how much of your…..*reserve collection…* have you been serving Barry here?"

"I lose count each moon cycle."

Karim and I chuckled.

"That's wonderful guys. But let me tell you something. If either of you plans on being with a woman, and, believe me, at times I have my doubts, but you will not be doing moon cycles and EMTs, you will living within context of days. There will be things to do on Wednesday, and plans on Friday, an engagement at the end of the month, and you had better take care of this and that by the beginning of next week."

"Your wife is like that Ron, but you can't make that into all women."

"Well, fine, Barry, but if you're going to pick your fights, then I will say for sure that disputing time with a girlfriend is not a winner. You just don't argue about the time with someone who has a few very true clocks in her belly."

Karim turned away, maybe because he had someone else to serve.

"I guess……but Thea, she's late out to the meadow most of the time."

"No, she's right on time, every time."

"You're gonna say that now Ron? After all of that you're gonna tell me that three-thirty is right on time when we meet at three?"

"Sure. You want to have sex with her."

"But…….yeah, that'd be cool, really cool…….I like her…..but, it's still a meeting……."

"Nope."

"Whattaya mean, nope?"

"You know how the caterpillar morphs into a butterfly. Now, you can either stand over the damn caterpillar and swear it's almost time to see it change, and I guarantee that even if the caterpillar has no idea that you're even there, you'll swear it's fucking with you to no end by making you wait. Or you can go about your life, and when the butterfly lands on your shoulder you can just accept the miracle of it all."

Oh man, stuff like that from Ron was usually preceded by his jerky routine. "That sounds like, pay no attention to Thea until she gives me some action."

"No, I'm saying you're lucky that a woman you like is showing up half an hour late, right on time."

He was really in a mood that day, Ron. I wanted him to keep going. "Well, yeah…..sure, I know that……what in the hell even got us started on all of this?"

"You were wrong about how long it's been since we've talked in here."

"No way, no way. It's been more than five days Ron."

"You've been heavy into Karim's powders. Your days and nights might be going on forever. I have tinkered with some bulbs, met several people. I am running on days Barry. Sober, responsible, days. So keep on doing what you're doing, it might even be the best thing for ya, but I do need you to accept that it has been exactly five days since we met in here."

"No Ron it's been longer. Even Karim......."

"Karim is not running on days Barry. He is here nonstop. Women keep the time, and they are nowhere to be seen in this place. Karim does not want anyone else in here running on days either. Which is fine and good. All I need you to do is admit to me that it's been exactly five days."

"It's been longer Ron. A full #ETT."

"Barry you're on a delicate slope here. I am not asking you to change what you're doing or who you're doing it with or where you're going. I just need you to trust me on this. That's it. Nothing else. Trust me Barry it has been five days."

"Ron you know I hate to pull out the devices on this kind of stuff but maybe we gotta touch it to see if there's something about when we set the calendars for today, or something else, we need to check."

Ron rolled his eyes and threw up his arms in shock.

"You've got to be kidding me. Barry come on. Fuck. You know that's no option. Just trust me. I wake up at the same time every day and brush my teeth and take the anti-inflammatory pill out of the first one of seven that is not already empty. You know what the phone does."

"What, disputes what you're saying? Is that what it does?"

"Barry I've known you for a few years now, and you finally seem like you're on the verge of good things. Remember what got you here. You know what that involves, what the phone will do, if you check this."

"No, I don't Ron, and maybe I should. Maybe I should know. I don't know much of anything, period, so I might as well quit knowing for sure that I'm not going to check this stupid little phone for when we set this date. I mean, damn, what was it, the first thing I remember my parents ever telling me, seriously. The first damn thing ever, handing me that phone and showing me that big icon and both of them in unison, very plainly, don't ever touch this. Period. Never touch it. And I listened. I never did. One by one, my friends, classmates, neighbors, everyone, one by one, they all did it. They all did it, didn't look like a big deal, they're all fine, they're getting along, I mean, what the fuck, they all got lives, they all went and did whatever and gave me a chance to touch it, you know, fuck, that's probably what it was all about, one person after another, through and through, some who had already touched it and made hints that I should, or some who wanted to touch it for the first time along with me, but I never touched it Ron, and they're all long gone, I can't even talk to any of them anymore, there's just nothing to say. Nothing to say. It's always like, damn Barry, we gave you a chance and you never touched it, and now what do you have for me Barry? And I have nothing. I meet a speech therapist once a week, and spend pretty much every other waking minute trying to make that ninety damn minutes as good as possible. Sure Ron, you can sit here and know you're not touching that button and go home to Gloria. I don't have that. I have one little meeting a week......"

"Barry you know how much more drastic it is after going all of these years. You were around kids, touching it, college students, hell, even someone in their early twenties can probably get away with it, if that's what you want to call it, getting away with it. I understand that it hurts to think about. But you have to suck it up Barry. Get bent on the powder if you have to, whatever, just promise me you won't touch that icon. Please. No matter what this woman says."

"Thea?"

"Is that her name? Your therapist."

"Thea never touched it."

"Wait..........*what?*"

"Thea. She's never touched it."

"You have a therapist who's never touched it. And you'd like to have sex with her."

"Yes, I like her. Damn Ron, we've been over this."

"No. I would remember that."

"You see? DAMMIT! I'm supposed to trust you on all of this, and one of these days you're not even going to remember my name Ron. You'll call me Brad or something and then lay out some shit in stone about how long it's been and this and that and keep on going until I agree with you, for fuck's sake."

"Easy now. I'm very busy and see a lot of people every day Barry. You know I'm looking out for you."

"Do I?"

"Well, you know what, Barry, why are you even worried about me telling you not to touch it when you're spending time with a woman who never did."

"But she's had boyfriends, like, two-year boyfriends, who did. She can get along with people who've touched it; she's not like me in that regard."

Ron went for a jerky stick. He chose the one on the middle, after a moment. It meant something but who knows what. He ran it under his nose. I was jittery and tapping my hands on my thighs. "Do you know if any of these boyfriends touched it after they had already met?"

"No. They had, two of them I know about, they both had touched it before."

"Okay, okay, that's good."

"Good for what?"

"Good for you, for keeping those stupid fucking ideas about touching it out of your head."

"Ron, I never gave a second of thought to touching it until now, when you were going on and on about how I had to tell you that it had been five days since we met. And you know what I didn't even care about that too much, all I really need to know is every seven days I go out and meet Thea by the lake, but you can't remember that I've ever mentioned her name and yet I'm supposed to go along with whatever you want to hatch up for the day? You know, I'm just having trouble at times seeing what the hell the purpose is of staying away from touching the precious icon, other than coming by here and having you force me to admit that you know everything about everything."

"You know it Barry. I know you do. You know it's too late to touch it just the same as I do. I wouldn't be here if we didn't both know that. And I don't know what it's like, the pressure you can feel, without a family, to give it a rip. But it's too late. I'm sorry. I'm not bringing up the five-day admission over and over just so I can be right about it all. It was my best spur of the moment idea to have a little check on you with the powder, without being a hypocrite. I'm not going to bore you with old stories about me and that stuff. Karim can tell you. I always appreciate the people who made me answer them over the simple things, back when I was going on that powder. That's it."

"Ron?"

"Yeah."

"Have you ever seen someone around my age, around my, whatever else…..have you ever known someone like that and seen them, before and after?"

"I hope you're asking out of more than a twisted curiosity."

"I don't know, I mean, sometimes I need to hear about it to remember why I can't do it."

"This is intense Barry."

"I figured as much. I can take it."

"That's part of what makes me worry over you. You always think you can take anything."

"Just tell me."

"I've known two. There was Ian, he'd been an architect for most of his adult life, an architect, and something went askew at his firm and everything slipped away fast. I mean, he seemed like he did alright with people for the most part, I'm sure there were some who preferred he left them alone, but we all have that. We played in a poker game together once a month. I was hosting when he showed the first time with something clearly out of whack. The location must have been set for him to even wander in. He couldn't look at a hand for ten lousy seconds, it's a poker game, you stare at your hand, you bet, check, and call, and maybe a little chatter, but he couldn't even look at his hand. He had a dozen things going on that phone at once, and he was sticking it in his mouth, rubbing it all over like it was a bar of soap, it was a mess. The chips, we couldn't even slow him down enough to try and see if he could remember how to buy in for some chips, let alone him piecing together a hand. There were eight of us at the table, and for about a half an hour, every last one of us sat there, no cards, we all sat there dead silent, looking down most of the time, like it was an open and empty casket and there was one man trying to crawl into it with hopes that it would put him to sleep forever. Ian showed not a single basic sign of familiarity with any one of us. Fifty different trails of gibberish a minute were coming out of his mouth, and not one indication that he even knew we were there, let alone that we'd all been playing together for a few years. Within a few weeks his family had him back in his hometown, and I heard some corporation pays him a nominal wage to stand in a public space for a few hours a day, you know, one of those people out there as a warning sign, the warning of course being that you can't wait too long to touch it."

"And.......the other?"

"The other........." Ron cleared his throat. "She and Gloria had met each other at a pet rescue event, I think, Gloria can make friends while picking out apples. Riley. We had Riley by for dinner a few times, Gloria was always trying to fix her up, they went out now and again, no rare story, the marriage had fallen apart. I'd never seen Gloria so out of sorts as when she got that message from Riley. That's it Barry. Three days later......."

"She.......died?"

"No. No she didn't die Barry."

"Well then what happened?"

"Gloria knew her better, I only saw her once, briefly, after she touched it. Riley has plenty of company. It's.......I don't know, Gloria has tried to pull her out of it. Karim.....he says someday I am going to spot a woman outside, that I will see it in her eyes that she was born with nothing and has lived honorably with that struggle every day since, her conviction will show, and I should offer this woman a good deal of money to go to Riley and clasp her hands over Riley's cheeks and meet her eyes for a minute or two. It's a better idea than anything I have left."

"Yeah."

Ron crossed his arms. I sat quietly and stared down at nothing. I supposed that I was fairly well ashamed that I had even brought up the idea of touching it.

"Gloria still has her days. It's probably been three or four years now. Gloria still has her days when she is overridden with guilt over her perceived shortcomings as a friend."

I nodded.

"You simply can't even think about it Barry. Don't even joke about something so grave. You have your idiosyncrasies, you have your thoughts, you just can't go back. I can't understand fully the temptation of it, what makes grown adults do it. You're in a decent place Barry, don't ever get impatient and panic and think that's the answer. We're animals Barry. We're......you and I at least, we're not savages, but we are animals. Our past, our history, it has to live in here..." Ron thumped his chest. "....And up here...." He tapped two fingers on his temple. "Sure, sure, we're just little ants leaving a carbon footprint and so on......but all of our efforts, struggles, mistakes, good times, they have to live inside, it's that simple."

"I know Ron, I know."

Ron stared at me for a minute. After a bit I wanted to look away, but I didn't. I kept on staring back at him, knowing I owed him that. "You clever bastard. You clever bastard. That was one hell of a bluff Barry, I didn't know you had it in ya. "

"Well it's the only way to get anything out of you sometimes, you brush everything off until there's danger in the air."

Ron nodded like it hurt just a bit to agree with me. "Did you hear what you needed to hear?"

"I think so. But Ron…."

"Uh-huh."

"Is everyone you, you and Gloria…..are you friends with all misfits and outcasts, people who don't really have a strong social core of their own?"

"Probably, if you'd prefer to put it that way. It's nice to look out for people when it has nothing to do with business. That money is in play and nobody will ever admit to needing anything besides the money."

"Well, thank you, really….."

"Okay, okay, I know we got a bit heavy there but let's not take it all into that now….."

"Alright."

"It's probably past time for me to get on with the day. I'll see you in here soon."

"Yep."

Ron stood, rolled the other two jerky sticks up in the napkin, and pulled his keys from the bar.

"Oh, Ron…..hey, it has been five days."

"What's that?"

"Five days, since we last met in here."

"If you say so Barry." Ron chuckled for a second, then waved as his back was already turned on his way out.

The trees, it was kind of cool how the branches and leaves, well, when the wind came out of the north, that was when all of the finger branches were kind of naturally bent back as result of so many bad winter storms from that direction, so when there was a warm summer breeze from the north the trees were all sitting real comfortable in the rocking chairs with slow and round drifts, back and forth, so many green muppets with strange hair yukking it up and laughing and maybe even getting a little surprise misting here and there, and they could talk all about the weather to their heart's content.

I knew when I admired those trees for a little while that my day, as I had imagined it at least, was not to be. I had these visions of slipping into another day of total placidity with all of my confused thoughts, and feeling those stones against my hands and feet while being otherwise unconscious until I found myself planked all strange and settled into this moment and position where I was in this complete harmony with the water, and everything could go quiet, and it didn't matter one bit if the lake or myself did more work to reach that....agreement, I suppose it was an agreement. These visions were not happening. The water was crashing into the wall with tremendously deep thumps and shooting upwards one organ pipe at a time, in quick succession, blowing skyward into these rolling bar charts unburdened by data and able to open up and splay into umbrellas of a million translucent silver medallions that chimed like firework rain onto the boardwalk. I ran to the edge and pulled up a few feet short and then just walked slow and carefree with my back to the nearest incoming swells, and heard the big and low whoosh as final warning that I was about to be swimming again, even if it was while I walked along the shore. It felt great to be laughing out loud and cackling and cheering as the huge weighty beads drummed over my head and shoulders. All of my thoughts were washed off, they fell onto the cement and melded into the long thin sheet skimming back out into the tantrum to do it all over again.

My phone was in my backpack and I had the urge to catch a good photo or two. When I first grabbed it the thoughts of touching the icon were fresh in my head, and it wasn't like it was a real threat for me to do it, but those thoughts, well, it was pretty damn difficult to not ever think about this little icon, always by your side and ready to instantly change everything, I heard that you touched it and then it said, 'Really?', and then if you selected yes, it gave you one more, 'Really?', and then that was it for the consents, that was it for your life as you knew it, as you remembered it. And it was strange to listen to the elderly folks tell their stories about the simpler times when they were young, you know, an old lady going on about how she put out this cute little photo of her boobies one night after class, and that changed everything, and most people probably shrugged and went, oh, sweet old lady talking about showing off boobies like it was so crazy and wild, that's ridiculous. Boobies. Because it hadn't been about boobies, or an original custom shave job, or the vulva, or dick, or labia, balls, scrotum, or clit for some time. No. The moment that upgrade dropped and the icon showed, it was about the past, for everyone, it was about how each individual remembered their own past, and as a result the history of everything else too.

But anyway. I only wanted to activate the camera. Maybe my thoughts were getting all riled up like the lake. So I turned on the camera and stood there and waited for a wave to shoot vertical in its running stagger of notes and spread into a broken rotunda of stained glass, and bounce into retiring crowns, then I ran forward and pulled up and stooped and waited for the water to again crack the flat mirror of the sky into a million reflections of light, and I snapped away, and then scampered back before all of it crashed atop me, because it was this fun little dance, and I could run back and forth, so simple, so simple, and in the bright sun I could not see how any of the shots turned out, all I could do was step back and admire the long view of the wall's entire mile blowing up into dozens of circular saws rolling up from underneath and buzzing against the land and then falling right back down, in constant rotation, saws of water ebbing and flowing, like they were all connected to a much larger wheel, a half-sunken ferris wheel where each tiny cabin spun however many times faster, and then I could run back right up underneath a single one of them as its passengers let out a big collective grunt and then shot into the sky and the water fell from each of them a little differently and hung still above me for only an instant as I hit the button, laughing, and then ran like hell for twenty feet, yes, twenty feet was all it took to once again see the strange carnival in its entirety.

A bit later, I found a tree that hugged against my back and around my sides with its trunk, and sat back to let the stencils of its bark type into the flesh of my back so carefully, and I think that tree liked having me there as well, kind of difficult to say, you know, nature could only talk back very slowly over time, it could only scream that it was delicate as well after too many people had treated it otherwise, but at the same time, I could not be for sure that if I said good morning to this tree every day, and gave it a gentle pat, maybe it began doing cool stuff with its bark, or learning new tricks with all of its leaves, or maybe it didn't have to change a thing for me to grow and return and notice more about it.

Also, the tree provided nice shade to page through the photographs. One after one, though, they were muddled with no defining shapes making faces in the composite and the light was flat, the water directionless. They were not what I saw. They were not alive. Fifty, sixty shots, I was scrolling faster, writing it off, until the color scheme, with one swipe, took a mad leap to the other end of the spectrum, as I had suddenly come upon this magnificently shaded close-up, not a single flat pixel to be seen as the flesh rolled through the light and into the shadow line between the back of two upper legs and ass cheeks, and I really did think I would have had a memory of holding the camera under a foot away from a butt crack, but maybe not. I had already sent it to Gehri with suggestions for tanning bed art or advertisement or both and envisioned my promotion to, well, I don't know, not having to carry the big chair back from Asian Pita, maybe, for the superb vision and idea, I had already sent it along before I knew for sure that I shot one with two of my fingers accidentally covering the lens. But anyway I thought Gehri would really appreciate the shot, and I was beginning to think he maybe did not hire me for my good degree, and wanted to take a few small efforts to see if I could get a guess why.

It was the last one. Maybe I had an inkling when I took the shot that if I didn't get it there then I was not going to get it at all, and that made it the last one, but no more than an inkling, no way. Compared to every other shot of the water, it was almost as out of place as the mistake with my fingers. It felt as if someone else slipped it into the gallery to do something nice for my confidence. The water was blue and silver trees rocketing upward and just beginning its instantaneous growth of all the branches and leaves and medallions up high. Even the snippet of pavement at the bottom glowed all black and blue and reflective. I sat, very content, staring at my little conquest over the old limits of what I could see. Then I sent it along to Thea and waited for her to send back a link to the nice picture frame which she had just purchased.

Gehri never replied to the butt photo. Thea replied to the one I sent her with, 'Barry you take dick pics to another level! See you Tuesday!' Which, damn, made me think that maybe if I had reached out for her arm when the water was all riled up instead of when it was totally calm, then maybe, well, you know. Yeah.

Brianne had been ramping up the visits to tanning bed in the heat of summer. I had been lucky so far with this. Every time Brianne had shown, unannounced, the Vortex was available. But on this afternoon, it was ten minutes after a young dude came in looking like he had money for shoes even if he wore these orange foam hooves all scummy with dirt, and by the way he walked and made snapping sounds it sure seemed he wanted me to notice them. I steered the fellow into the Everglades, telling him hey, you're all set up first door on the right, and he clomped on off, on, off, and then Dana popped in with the very old and yellowed incoming pile of expired oil change offers and dry cleaner coupons, and I handed Dana yesterday's very old and yellowed pile of expired oil change offers and dry cleaner coupons while Dana asked if Stevie had been around, wow, that Dana, never starved for attention, being chased down the sidewalks while walking around in a uniform which really did show off the pension big time. But, oh yeah, the dude in the scummy orange foam hooves had gone left, of course he had, into Vortex, and by the time I noticed he was already settled in, so I let him be, but of course not five minutes later Brianne opened the door with the arms flying upward instead of forward, and we had a situation at tanning bed.

"Brianne I told him to go into the Everglades, I promise, but then Dana came in and next thing I knew......."

"Oooooh, did Dana ask about me?"

"No......Stevie"

"WHAT?"

"Dana's not giving Stevie that pension, no way."

"MMMM I'd make that Dana walk *all the mail* into the wrong addresses."

"There are no wrong addresses; it just has to be moved around."

"Barry sweetie just let Brianne be a poet, mmkay? Who's this in Vortex?"

"I don't know. Kind of strange that he's here because I know football barn is open and showing handoffs." Brianne sat in the wide leather chair. No one ever sat in the panting bulldog tongue chair. "Oh. I'm in no big hurry. But I could go in and shoo him into the Everglades, ohh, Barry how about it?"

"Noo……..no, I can't, even with those hooves….no."

"Hooves? He took those into my little temple, into my sacred place? No no no, Barry, how could you let that happen…..the beds, Andrés can clean the beds but those hooves, those let evil spirits into the room! Barry you called them hooves I assumed you knew!"

"Like, goat hooves, right?"

"NOOO. Barry those are the hooves of the devil, in my temple! One of the four primary carriers of misogynistic energy! There's monogrammed initials, tobacco pipe, those hooves…..you're sure they weren't sandals?"

"Like, women's open-toed shoes?"

"Leather, or canvas, with a pedicure…..never mind, I already know the answer……."

"What was the fourth carrier?"

"Barbed wire ink…..I'm gonna get Andrés, we need to get him out of there! Oh my, oh my, I already owe Juniper a favor and now she's going to have to exorcise the room, I need to move before this gets worse!"

"I didn't know about this….."

"Barry it's from, like, forever ago, one of the most liked photos ever, of the four carriers…..I'm going to get Andrés….." Brianne jumped back through the door, again the arms flying up and out, but then quickly back down for a double smack on the cheeks before disappearing from my sightline. I tried to settle myself to a place where I could reasonably decide if this could take place.

They burst in together, Andrés being dutiful and walking with just a tiny dash of salt. "Did you see barbed wire ink Barry do you think he has barbed wire ink too?"

"I don't think so, that's usually around the bicep right? No……he had a tank top on, I would've seen that."

"He had a TANK TOP on?"

"What is that, another carrier?"

"No but it doesn't help……okay…..Andrés……"

"Hey Brianne, maybe I should call Gehri first."

"Yeah maybe calling Gehri, calling, asking."

"You guys, no. We can't wait. Come on now……"
Brianne swayed the hips extra big while leading us down the hall, and then stood really close to the door, nose almost touching it, and snapped the wrist a few times up above the shoulder. "…….hellLLLOOOO."

"The musica, he no hearing, too loud la musica."

"I can hardly *bear* to *listen*……the music, it's being ruined!"

"When will the smoke begin seeping under the door? Is the floor going to cave in?"

"Barry I *cannot* with the sarcasm right now……"
Brianne, still pressed against the door, snapped the wrist a few more times. "…….helllLLLLOOO! Andrés, honey, can you pick the lock?"

"Me no picking, no picking! The other guy, waiting the tables, he picking the lock!"

"Ooohhh please go and get him for me baby please?"

"Andrés, dammit….."

"Barry I no picking the locks!"

"Brianne we can't get a server over here, no way."

"Why not?"

"Because he's a server. They wait on customers, that's it. They're very adamant about all of the things they don't need to do. You want a server over here you're gonna have to go try yourself, and you better have twenty-six percent of…….well, something, you better have twenty-six percent of something ready."

The music refrained and Brianne changed course to try another knock. "HellllLLLLOOOO." A moment later, we were in luck, I suppose. The knob shook and the door opened slowly. I took a step back and pulled Andrés with me. He stepped out in his tank top and mesh shorts, not really looking upset, or anything else, just, there.

"Oh my, oh my, please pull those awful hooves out of my temple!"

"HUH?"

"Your, ahem, footwear, could you grab your *footwear*?"

"HUH?"

Andrés shook his head real quick and then walked in and grabbed the hooves, then walked them to the front. Brianne shut the door behind the guy urgently. "Are you here to soil my temple with evil spirits? You can't soil my temple!"

"From the farm maam, but still find a toilet when ineed one."

"MAAM? Oh *my oh* my!"

"Y'all savin' me from a burnin' or sommin'? This place is weird. Music's creepy innere."

Brianne did a full head snap.

"Where are you from man? You visiting?"

"HUH?"

He was certainly almost deaf. "HOME. WHERE IS HOME?"

"OH. Southwest of the wind farms. Yep. Couple thousand acres. Soybeans. Made a video choppin' wood 'n diggin' a hole, 'n this girl 'round here sawit 'n said come one up 'n fuckit boy. What the hell it aint harvest yet."

"I working you need help I working outside too."

"Andrés is the best, but don't steal him full time."

"Ugggh, you guys! The hooves! Have you *forgotten*? Misss.....terrr, what in the *world* made you come in here today?"

"HUH?"

"WHY ARE YOU HERE?"

"Oh. The girl and I, we fucked. 'N then, she's sittin' 'round watching stuff, 'n eatin' a buncha super chips, 'n she said 'here's my card go down the way to tan 'n then come on back 'n we'll fuck again."

Andrés turned away and put his head down into his hands. I grabbed his shoulders and shook them a bit, like, there was so much to laugh over that I couldn't even do it.

"Sorry I don't wanna fuck anyofya, 'preciateit though."

Brianne was not finished. "Well, misss.....terrr, let me be the one to tell you that up here in the city those hooves of yours will bring nothing but trouble for you and everyone else around. You seem okay.....but they're eeee....vil."

"Shit I yousta put on proper shirt 'n shoes 'n then every time I had to hear it from this girl or that back home, just tryinta go shoot pool 'n it's all this 'you tryin' tafuck another girl, whatcha up ta boy, tryinta fuck another girl or what?' 'til I just got tiiiired ofit 'n they don't say nothin' when I put those on. Worked better 'n anything I could say, just put those old clompers on ta show I din wanna fuck 'nother girl."

I composed myself. Back to work, Barry. "Listen, if you'd like to lay down in this one, Everglades, take as much time as you'd like, no extra charge. As you can see, the hooves are a touchy subject, so we just need to keep those up front."

"Hell, thanks, but I've hadnough. Kept ma word, did it for a bit. Girl's probly bout finished with those super chips 'n itchin' to get back to it."

"You needing help I working outside too."

"I'm sure ya can pal. Machines gotit covered though. Hell I just do the diggin' 'n choppin' for the videos, ya know."

The guy tipped a cap he didn't have and walked heavy footed to his hooves near the door. It was strange; he wasn't one of those guys with the sex and violence making this ring of fire around his everything, he was just, well, simple, and at that moment I think simple was better than any of the three of us were doing.

Brianne still let out a horrified gasp as they again snapped against his heels, back through the door.

"I know, I know, they're the worst. Does it need more than a cleaning?"

"I should be able to tell after lying down for a few minutes. It's probably just a little bit missionary for the day."

Andrés was already off to grab the supplies. I had never heard Brianne's voice so flat, deflated, and it sure didn't seem like regret over the fuss.

"He was very quick about paying and stuff when he came in, those things were about all I even noticed."

"Barry, sweetie……" There were lines I hadn't seen before around Brianne's cheeks and forehead.

"You okay?"

"I'm okay. It's a weird life Barry."

"Brianne I can't imagine the half of it. But I'm listening, for sure….."

"Not even that. No. More of…..I meet so many good people, and a few awful ones, and I think to myself, wow, I have such a full existence, and sometimes we all…….congratulate each other on our open minds…..to where…..do we all become too conscious of that? How does a guy who seems like that come in here and blow everything wide open again?"

"He was a rare one, no doubt."

"But…..he looked, everything……so *ordinary*."

"Well, maybe around here, I mean at first he looked like a lot of guys who live around here, like, he was cool but then there are guys around who try to be like him and they're the worst. He had no attitude at all. Then there's so many guys with this attitude that has to be fed constantly, but maybe if more people stood alone out in the middle of nowhere for a little bit, they could at least know how hungry they are."

"Barry, that was…..." I gave Brianne a hug. I didn't know who needed it more. After a moment, we stayed embraced, more of our sides still touching, opened a bit.

"What….have you *been doing* lately?"

"Coming out of a long funk, I guess. Maybe I learned more than I thought I was while I was in it."

"I know those baby. Sometimes I know I'm doing better when I have this *moment* where I feel sadder than ever, and the funny thing is, that *makes me happy.* Ohhhhhh….."

"Yeah. I know."

Andrés emerged from Vortex, having probably given it a little extra attention, just because he was that way.

"Andrés honey, come on in, it's *group hug time!*" He was a bit stubborn about it at first, so I met his eye, like, yeah, I've been there too, it's better this way. So we made a nice quiet triangle for a moment.

"I making a video. Chopping, chopping, maybe wrench too, maybe wrench and changing tire."

"Ha ha, yes! Okay, Brianne, yeah? We'll all make sure it's done right."

"This. *Yes.* Amazing."

"Wrench and changing tire. No chopping, me no chopping."

Thea kept her sunglasses on. I mean, it made total sense; it was just that she always had them off before. We stood a ways apart, and I kicked at the grass a few times as we did this back-and-forth about how we were going to get started. I still wanted her to teach me new things, but was a tad afraid she was only waiting for me to jump in the lake again. I wondered if Thea had made up her mind about quite a bit. In the past I found myself trying to make this or that happen when a woman had already made up her mind over what would, and, well, there probably could have been a few more good friendships in my life, if it weren't for all that. So I had to be cool. Just be cool and do some stretches and one-legged poses.

"Did you go in the lake on that day you sent me the photo?"
"ARE YOU KIDDING? What kind of lunatic do you think I am?"
"I didn't think you did Barry. I only wanted to make sure."
Thea scrunched her lips a few times. I pulled one arm up and back with the other hand on the elbow, not so much eager to get started as much as something to do besides opening my mouth.
"Barry….."
"Uh huh."
"Do you think you're…..healed?"
"I don't know……I haven't……in a while. You could, well, you could probably still catch me by surprise……."
"No, not that, your back…….do you know how long ago that was when you hurt your back out here?"
"Here we go again. I meet up with everyone so they can ask me if I know how long it's been, why does everyone want to make so damn sure that I know what time it is? What's the difference?" I immediately shook my head as flash apology for getting kind of snappy.
"I'm not even bothering you over that Barry! Man! I barely even recognize you week by week! I shouldn't say that, sorry, because that's not, you're the same person, we're on a steady ground. I don't ask myself 'who in the world just said or did that' when we're out here, but your……presence, the way you carry yourself, Barry I deal with adolescents all week, outgrowing shoes and pants every six months, and then you come here

and look changed more than any of them.

Just…….different. And your back goes out, and the next week I'm driving over thinking of some exercises to do to ease into it, and you're jumping in the lake like it's a bathtub!"

"That's exactly what it was! A bathtub! I'm not a kid but when a lake that goes on to infinity, and, seriously, it might as well actually go on to infinity, none of us ever see the other side, the other shores, but yeah, when this lake that's always moving and sloshing and crashing and hiding everything beneath the surface suddenly stops dead and shows everything, but I shouldn't even use that word dead because it was so aLIVE, yeah, it was a bathtub, it was the best damn bath I'd ever taken and I know I can't just turn a faucet whenever I want to do it again….."

"How do you know it was all about the lake being alive, and not you being alive?"

"I am alive! All of the sudden I'm rarely bored and people are talking to me and listening to me and most of the time it's not really about much at all, but we're both there for a minute at least, and it all started when we began meeting out here, everything gets better and better and you're helping so much and I'm so glad to know you and, and……."

"Go ahead…." Thea did a cool thing with her eyebrows.

"And…….I……"

Thea had a very kind look on her face. Hopeful too.

"You can do it." She nodded a touch.

"I……..WANT ALL THE CHOCOLATE! I WANT THE CHOCOLATE!!" And I sunk. I felt all of me sink.

Thea stepped in a tight circle like she did a year of, well, something, in like two seconds. "Are you okay?" Her voice was soft.

"Well, there's your answer. About healing."

"Don't be so hard on yourself. None of us are ever completely healed Barry, I'm glad you didn't tell me that you were."

"But.....we weren't.....I wasn't even.....balancing or anything......"

"I think you know that's not what it's all about."

"Well, yeah......but, my back......"

"Do you even remember when we first met? What do you remember about that?"

"You had on a tan sweater and the zipper was halfway up. You had caramel ice cream and the guy sitting next to me said something about your body, and I was, like, well, sure, but look, she has good taste in ice cream. And I remembered trying to get him to notice that your flavor of ice cream, like, look, caramel is the best, and that was when it seemed you overheard me and gave me a glare."

Thea had her hands over her mouth. I didn't know what she was right then, but I knew that she wasn't terrified or anything, so. Her fingers slowly crept down, one by one it seemed, over her lips, until her mouth was exposed. "You're wrong, but it's the nicest wrong, it's the best wrong....."

"Well I know they sell it in like five different languages, like they're still making them up to be more luxurious, oh, you thought Italian was fancy but they don't have anything on the Danish when it comes to this, but the color of the lid was that tan, so it was definitely caramel, right?"

"That's so cute Barry....so, touching......."

"Unless there were cookies or pretzels or something in there too, I know that sometimes that stuff is in there too, but I can't quite keep up with the fine print all of the time."

"And my sweater was tan?"

"For sure, yeah, the lid blended right in with your sweater, like for a second I thought the lid was off and you already had a few spoonfuls."

"Wow. That's……..wow."

"The lid was on, right? I can't picture you wolfing it down with the little paddle in front of the freezer."

"The lid was on. The lid was on. And my sweater, it's, it's green. It's a green sweater." Thea smiled and laughed a bit.

"Nooooooo……"

"Like I said, it's the best wrong."

I shrugged and we stood there smiling all weird, and I didn't really worry for a second over how I saw her sweater to be tan, and that was nice, but also, unbelievable, I know, also, I didn't just do the obvious and say well, let's go and get that caramel ice cream, but instead stood there smiling for a while until the moment, well, like we went over the top of the hill and then began walking another trail back down into town. The lake, it was a little bit ripply, not rough, but definitely cloaking the magic down there. I think I looked off at it for a while after some kind of runaround in my brain routed me right around the obvious.

"Are you looking to swim?"

"Do you want to?"

"Let's not go through that again."

I turned to the water once more. In it I saw promises that it would be perfect the following morning. "Ron and I had a long talk at martbar about touching it."

"Pardon me?"

"The icon."

"Oh. That. That's never an easy subject."

"He peeved me just enough to start acting as if it was time for me to touch it, and it got heavy quick. He told me some stories about people he knew that touched it when it was too late."

"Oh, don't look at it that way...."

"What?"

"Being too late. Don't look at it like that, please?"

"Noooo, I was just saying, for them...."

"Oh. Okay."

"I told him how you'd had boyfriends who had touched it."

"I used to have an inflated sense of what I could do for people."

"Well, that's.....you really got that.....to the point."

"It was tough to deal with until I was able to accept that. You've never had a lasting relationship with someone who touched it, right?"

"Oh no. No those women don't want to be anywhere near me."

"You're sure that's still the case?"

"I don't know why it wouldn't be. It's not like I can do something more for them now. I'm just the fool who didn't touch it, to them at least."

"If you go in thinking that way, then yes, you'll be right about that."

"Oh come on Thea......I love your support but that's a little overboard."

"I'm just saying....." She shrugged and cocked her head to the side.

Hey, big surprise here, I know, but I was confused again. "A minute ago you may well have sworn that you'd never again go within ten feet of a guy who touched it."

"I'm past it all. But I wouldn't be able to do this with you if I hadn't gone there."

"Oh. Of course." There was some kind of question stirring within me. I took a step or two to help it out. "Do you think it looks obvious that I've never been with someone who touched it?"

"A little bit. It's certainly not a bad thing though........ do you feel like doing a few poses? I could go for some poses."

"That'd be nice."

"Let's try something new. You're ready for it."

"Okay yeah. Will it be new for you too?"

"Always. Always."

"Fair enough."

Thea went for her bag and pulled out the blanket, and my memory for color wasn't much to be trusted it seemed, but the blanket, I think it was maroon. She felt out the ground for some consistency and then somehow unfolded the blanket like it was a flag, or something, and in the ritual of it all I became nervous. "The grass, it itches my legs more than I'd care for."

"Of course."

"I hardly ever use this blanket."

I nodded and shrugged and looked around wondering how long it had been since anyone else had been in sight. Thea tried to kick her sandals off, a few feet in the air, into her tote bag. One of them hit near the top and folded over the canvas, then rested on the slant it had created. "I can't believe I've never asked you about the image on that bag." It was a photo of a woman's face, with her glasses kind of crooked, and she clearly was not having the best of nights.

"I found it in a vintage shop, and I loved it the moment I saw it. It seemed......honest......about the struggles of our parents' generation."

"I can see that."

"Other women ask me all of the time where I bought it. It usually makes for a decent conversation. And it's nice to tell them exactly where it's from while knowing that they can go to that store but are going to have to find something else for themselves."

"Yeah."

Thea had slipped into the split where both of her legs went outward, not the front and back kind. I threw my hands onto my sides and awaited instruction. I didn't even want to guess. Any guess would have been way off, even if it had been close when Thea first saw that I was guessing. She was looking at me in a way where I was pretty certain she wanted me to get that look where I thought I knew everything, and was, like, sure, of course it was time for me to settle my toes right up front and center, and, yeah, pretty close, and then lower myself into a toe touch or I supposed my hands could land somewhere else too. I threw my arms out and laughed, like, WHAT? I'm just waiting for you to tell me! And Thea laughed too, and repositioned her hands, setting them back down further out, behind her knees. We kept laughing. My bumbling about and cackling finally faded into standing straight again, to see Thea was finished laughing too, and suddenly it was very obvious that she was not about to tell me what to do. And just like that I had a million thoughts about it all, the visual catalog going on forever and all of these voices too, not saying anything really, the voices just all a ton of people who were so damn sure of what I should have been doing, and it was this huge jumble of the voices and the images, like one particular voice matched one particular image, and it would be like, 'we have matched codes and attained target lock. Set course.' And I tell you, I knew I had lost it for a moment, lost

Thea, but she was so calm and patient and understanding, and when I shook off what my mind was trying to do, she was just as before, welcoming me back to the moment. It was such a gift. Thea being like that was the only reason that allowed the small miracle to happen, the small miracle of me motioning to do exactly what I had imagined her telling me to do, and it was ours together, that vision, I knew that we both took our own way to this comfortable place as I took tiny barefoot steps and Thea peeked up tenderly, and our eyes met as I settled my toes really close. I began to lower myself, little by little, and heard her breathing. My toes wiggled and became warmer as I spread my hands out to eventually set them down just inside of Thea's. I brought my head up and we were face to face, and her eyes were big but calm, and telling me to keep on going. I sank further into this nice bouquet, rousing from all of these places into this one beautiful cloud that turned itself inside out as the tangled braids of pressure opened and released new color. I set my hands down. Thea kept hers planted while bringing her shoulders back, which I could tell by the slow and slight wave the movement sent down through her torso. My forehead touched her chest first, and then her next breath, I heard it just before it grazed my chin. I turned my head while lowering a bit more, until my cheek was against her and I could feel it roll very slowly and easily, again, like losing track if a wave was going in or out and it didn't matter one bit. And I stayed right there for quite some time, really awake and really asleep, my toes basking in the warmth and my long fingers inching out just enough to graze against the tops of Thea's hands.

It was not #ETT, instead, you know, just one of those inconsequential days in between, no strange phenomenon of people showing up in a line because they could be around others waiting for the same thing, but still, I went under and swam just before arriving at the connec....tittyvity counter and had some thoughts about some sweet moves underneath the magician, because he was probably worn out on me looking and peeking around for a show every time I came by, so I'd play hard-to-get for once, but it might have all been result of me, oh here we go, a few hours prior I had called Thea and asked her to the martbar for ice cream, yeah, all that after I had thought it over about martbar versus syrah cottage and maybe I'd wait another week to call, so my thoughts churned and then I dialed, and it rang, and I had practiced for both Thea answering or voicemail, you know, just a quick tone check, but anyway the call went to voicemail and I started out all big-voiced and assertive like nothing could be better than ice cream at martbar, but then began tailing off and repeating myself and, yeah, by the time I terminated the call I was just lambasting myself real good and turning seconds into weeks waiting for a response which I soon guessed would not come until long after I was already here, swimming beneath the magician as he stood stoic up above the water and maybe it was simply the conditions but he wasn't all distorted and I could even make out the pattern on his half-serious necktie as I passed.

Karim greeted me from an odd distance and probably he knew I was about to exhale, took a good guess as to how long I'd been under and decided from that the volume he would tolerate. He was looking at me like he could reel off the last quarter of a moon cycle of what I'd been doing just by the way I slid the stool out a few inches, to get situated. It was a good thing, even if I peered down a little longer than I had to, to let him know that however I felt about whatever that was going on, I wasn't going to ask Karim to go all lifecoach, or, even worse, go all lifecoach on him. So he set down my bonus juice and, well, it wasn't ice cream with Thea, but still, martbar, man, martbar.

Not two sips later, five of the big round buggies with the total roll protection came all banging wheelies down the three steps and all of them had such grand gazebos, or pergolas, or facades or something built up over the top of the cabin that I could barely make out that it was three mothers and two fathers, definitely not just caretakers, you could somehow tell, navigating the rear knobby tires over the stairs, but we had some kind of ritualistic chariot race on our hands around the martbar as they split to both sides, and I think they were all calling out their own infants' names but more certain they had entry numbers for some kind of organized runaround where they paid in to have a runabout sanctioned by, well, I don't know, but they tore around the coolers in the back of martbar, really bouncing good with every stride, the showoffs, and we all knew there would likely be many waves of this happening over the next hour or so, and the uproar was instant. Karim loved it all because everyone was suddenly riled up, professor lifted himself out of his chair and caught a few of them at the cooler and knowing professor he probably said something like 'you know one of you could just come in and get this round, and then so on at the next place' but that logic was beside the point of it all, and a few of us threw our arms up in exasperation as the name chants persisted while the group came around and scanned out for the peppy squares, and the whole place was just bonkers in protest until we saw the silver fox motion to Karim to ring the tiny bell, and that meant a round of schmootzies for everyone seated, and also that the silver fox was probably going to use the toast to draft a plan of action, and we all knew that he had two grown boys of his own so we didn't feel ridiculous for being irked over the infant parade.

This was when Karim showed off his quickness back there. Most of the time he let everyone know that his calm was better than their impatience, but when there were fifteen or so schmootzies to get out he wasn't going to let the moment pass. Really, his footwork and changes of direction were superb. He had the bottles and glasses set beneath in a few separate places and poured them out in clusters of four, each in front of a senior patron but so a few others had to stand and come to it, and just like that, we were all huddled and raising the schmootzies, and awaiting the silver fox's best idea for when the next wave of chariot racers arrived, surely all too soon.

The coliseum trough master was very loose on both reserve collection and awareness of his unique technical knowledge, and the bill of his cap was tilted at captain strum; big easy and mad man were unmoved in different ways. Eagle eye was being dry to the opera

singer, always warming up his voice. I slipped in by happy Kenny as he pulled a cookie from his pocket. I felt included with several nods, not having to small talk. The silver fox raised his schmootzie and we all did the same. "My good men! The future of the martbar has been challenged, quite brashly, I do say. This....retail excursion....at the hands of fleeting passerby, has made us all too aware that our great tradition is at risk. Despite Karim's PROUDLY done service and rather fine selection of offerings, we cannot allow everything we have built here to be swept into consumer oblivion by such a.....blatant *affront* to our genuine sociability."
"None of this *tiki taka* bullshit!"
"People should not be doing that. I swear....." Old Steve shook his head. "It's not right."
"Compadre. I think maybe the belly dancing on the screen might be good, yes?"
"I believe a song is in order my good men. It will be a PROUD song and we will sing with the panache of gentlemen and the gusto of our love for the martbar. SCHMOOTZIE!"
"SCHMOOTZIE!"

silver fox brainstormed one up quick, and it, well, to come up with that on the spot and then run us all through it for five minutes, that was pretty damn impressive. We gathered near the bottom of the stairs with designs on lining up along both rails as soon as any chariots were spotted up the hallway. The door swung open at the other side of the connec.....tittyvity counter, beyond the smattering of browsers up there.
"HEY! LIS....TEN! HEY! LIS....TEN!"

Many of us shook our heads and chuckled. Karim had tried several times to stop Jimmy from calling that out through the hallway, but it was of no use.

"Jimmy get your ass down here! None of this *tiki taka* bullshit!"

"HEY LIS…TEN get everybody a refill HEY LIS….TEN!"

"Jimmy you're gonna have to shut it, there are chariots blowing through here and we have a song."

"HEY LIS….TEN what's this about?"

The big easy pulled Jimmy in to explain further.

"AAAAA…..ve…..maaaaaRRRIIIIaaa!"

"Not you now Raymond!"

"I have quite a bit of range to warm up. HAHaHaha."

"My good men! Here they are……."

It was a good nine or a dozen this time. They poked through the door looking like robot crabs and retractable Swedish furniture. We jumped to the sides of the stairs, and, as directed, extended our low-side palms outward, like we should have all had top hats. silver fox addressed us quickly with his eyes, letting us know he'd lead it off. The parents were probably doing something similar behind the chariots, even if it kind of looked as if there were unmanned, rogue dune buggies coming at us. silver fox drew a big breath into his considerable pipes.

"WELLLcome to MARTbar, much more than tasty treats"

"It once was a genERIC pit STOP til Karim put in the seats"

"HEY LIS…TEN!"

The buggies had come to a halt a few feet from the top of the stairs. Some of the infants began crying.

"We showed up here LONG AGO in search for bonus juice"

"Now it's mountain drone, a second home, somewhere to be loose"

"HEY LIS…TEN!"

"Karim maintains a GREAT SELECTion but WATCH your BABY with that resERVE collection"

"FORgive our LECture for their proTECtion"

"We made our own SENIOR SECTION"

"HEY LIS….TEN!"

"I'm an OLD MAN I can't deal with the running….it's not right!"

"Pull up a CHAIR it's only FAIR but do not TALK about your BABY'S hair"

"TAKE YOUR PICK of a jerky stick YES WE KNOW it's shaped likeadick"

"THE ONNNNNNNLLLLLY RUUUUUUUUULLLLE………….IS DONNNNNNNNNNT BEEEEEEE A PRRRRIIIIIICCCCCKKKK HEY LIS….TEN HEY LIS….TEN that's not right, no AAVVVEEE….MARRRIIIIIIIA none of this *tiki taka* bullshit HEY LIS…TEN nope, nope, can't be that DONNNNNNNNT BEEEEEE A PRRRRRIIIIIIICCCCCCKKKKK!"

"HEY LIS….TEN!"

Everything went silent besides a few cries. Some of the chariots turned around immediately. The others stayed still. We all gradually relaxed from our officious postures, and one of the fathers stepped around from the rear of his chariot and asked politely if he could step in for some ibuprofen, and of course, was welcomed down. The rest made way back up the hallway, and we began laughing and hitting each other on the shoulders and such.

"Yeah, yeah, that was good and creepy!"

"Scratch this one off of the trail map!"

"HA HA you nailed it silver fox! Brilliant!"

"HEY LIS....TEN!"

"Jimmy shut up the song is over!"

"HEY LIS....TEN!"

I looked to Karim, behind the bar. He was laughing and it looked like he had filmed it all.

"I think it's best from this angle, come give this a look Brianne."

It looked like Andrés had his fill of Brianne taking the lint roller to his black tee shirt, thus my suggestion. Brianne slid the platform heels over to the front passenger side of Andrés' friend's old royal blue pickup.

"It's perrrrfect. Only, Andrés baby, I can still see some lint don't you go running away from me, I'll be right back with this brush. And with something for those cheeks, gorgeous."

"I no needing the makeup Brianne, no needing for changing the tire."

"Don't worry baby you won't be all glam like Brianne here. Just a touch for the camera."

"You gotta get just a little pretty buddy. Believe me you've got plenty of manliness going when you're changing a tire."

"I do it two times very fast, me changing very fast."

"Remember your audience Andrés, unless you wanna send this out for pit crews."

Brianne went back over with the brush and took a makeup kit from the handbag to set it on the curb.

"No knowing the pit crew."

"For the RRRRrrrrrrr RRRRRrrr vum vum vum." I spun my index finger in circles.

"Oh HA HA, no, me no working there. Too much hot suit. Nah."

Brianne moved in with blush, or rouge, or something, and I think we were all in understanding that I would cut it off if it started getting a little thick and bright. Passerby on the sidewalk didn't really flinch over our production. I looked up and down the block and could see another group filming.

"Hold still baby Brianne's not gonna bite."

"We do need to hurry on getting this set, unless one of you wants to pay for the second hour." It was still a few decades until the parking meter deal expired and there were already whispers of mass celebrations and citywide holiday and no parking regulations of any kind within city limits on that date.

"Andrés! You *made* me *smudge* you beautiful man!"

"I think you got it perfect Brianne."

"Barry, there's perfect, and *perrrrrrrrrfect*. Two minutes *honey*, two minutes."

Andrés shined up his black boots good at home, that much was for sure. Half of the damn sun was jumping off of each toe. And if I said something about his polish job he would shake it off all nonchalant, like he always had them so prime, no, not that they were usually beat to hell or anything, but he did them up right for today. So I thought about how I'd have to work those in with a quick pan. Yeah, we'd run the shot down the side panel for a few seconds, then give him a once over, before he took to the tire........

"Brianne, what do you think about doing the jack while I shoot? I think we should come in with Andrés with his hand in the wheel basin, make it look like he's lifting the truck himself, you know, start off with a laugh."

"Ohhhh, I don't know Barry….."

"It's as easy as can be, a nice handle to push on a few times."

"It's not that….." Brianne looked up and down the block.

"Oh, yeah……..is it that much of a worry this time of day?"

"It iiiiiiissss early, buuuutttt……"

"It's like fifteen seconds and you……I can shield you off for the most part and hold the camera right over your shoulder, I mean, someone would have to be walking right here……."

"I don't know…."

"We need to get Andrés off to the right start with this….with some humor……Andrés, you like the women with a sense of humor best, yeah?"

"Me like a funny, yes."

"Okkaayyyyy, for you baby."

"Yes! Thank you thank you, it'll be quick and painless I promise."

We got the jack and everything else set, after the belated discussion of Andrés just reaffixing the original tire because we didn't want the video to finish with that flimsy spare in the picture. In my nearly professional opinion, we were ready.

"Barry honey you have me at your convenience for the one-time spectacular of Brianne stooping over this………thing."

"And Andrés' video."

"*Helllllooo!*" Brianne did a slow head roll towards Andrés. "*Obvious.*"

"¡Vamanos! Barry! Time for making." He was. I could tell by his body language too.

I got a quick shot of the side panel and then Brianne lowered to the jack as I made a crushing artsy pan of the streetscape and Andrés got his one hand up under the wheel basin, and I had to stoop right over the back of Brianne's shoulders and head, and it seemed as if the exercises were helping me to contort and keep the camera steady as I got the shiny boots real quick and then made it up to Andrés' best cool face, pretty good really, and then back down to his hand as Brianne began pumping with the hips and legs on those very inconvenient shoes, getting all theatrical with this full body gyration that ended with barely a push on the jack, like Brianne thought it could be pumped with absolutely everything except for the arms, and I was trying not to break and laugh but had a big and dumb smile pushing its boundaries while zeroed in near Andrés' midsection and he would probably keep his distance from me for a few days for this one, even when I knew that Brianne was fucking with me somewhat while we were not exactly capturing a rocket-launch-style liftoff. But anyway, very soon Brianne raised up, and I hit another crushing artsy pan of the streetscape and it was time for Andrés to get busy with that wrench, even though it really wasn't time because the chassis was not lifted, and Andrés had the socket wrench while I tried to keep the camera steady in my left hand as Brianne began tapping both hands on my shoulders from behind, and I could tell Brianne was making all kinds of exaggerated gestures behind me, and again I was close to totally cracking up as I hit that jack with my right hand and started pumping away like a madman as Andrés made a ton of great faces every second. It was all falling apart and it was so much better than I could have imagined. I think I got the chassis up enough while pumping and trying not to crack, and then, and then, Andrés spun the socket wrench back and it made those little clicks, and it was like he suddenly heard a song in his head through those clicks and began dancing just a bit each time it ratcheted back and he made it all very rhythmic as Brianne shouted out compliments and encouragement, and Andrés kept making beautiful sounds with the wrench as if he had given the tool, and everything else, to song over practicality for the occasion.

So, here we were, again. The last time we met Thea was doing the splits and I bent down and rested my head on her chest for awhile, and then I followed that up with a call to see if she'd like some ice cream at martbar, and since Thea probably tried to tell me something by never responding, I supposed the only thing to do was tell her what a blast it was to sing that song and shoo away all of the chariot racers with our brilliance and unity and what not.

"So you guys are chasing off parents of newborns in there now?"

"Well, yeah, but it wasn't necessarily that as much as how they came in all running around and chanting. They started it."

"They sure did Barry. They're parents."

"Thea I think you had to be there, the first group was really shoving it in our faces, and a good number of those guys have kids, grandkids even. I mean, they PAID some organizer who had nothing to do with martbar or probably anywhere else and then every damn place takes their stupid money and annoys the hell out of their real customers and those chariot racers or whatever they're doing won't even come back until they can pay another organizer for a dumb tee shirt to run around and make everywhere dumb. Except for martbar."

"Do you have any idea how badly new parents need to blow off a little steam, and get out?"

"Well the infants might actually be able to observe something for real if they weren't being run around constantly. That's probably their lasting impression of it all is just move as fast as possible from place to place for a couple of years, until they're like three and get a phone."

"Oh, are you an expert in child psychology now?"

"I don't think I have to be an expert in anything to see all of the space out here, and look, no babies being set down in the grass to fumble and pick around and fall on their butts a few times. Not a one, anywhere."

"Are you trying to claim you guys were sticking up for the good of the babies now?"

"No way! We wanted the parade gone."

"Parents, Barry."

"I'm not trying to say no having kids, I'm saying we shouldn't give them free pass to interrupt whatever they please."

"Are you saying we shouldn't give a damn Barry?"

"Of course we should give a damn! About challenging them to go do something real with their kids instead of these victory parades, like they're taking revenge because no one liked them around before. Come on Thea! These are some of the same children at school who dismiss what you're trying to do for them, the same ones who do their best to terrorize me if I have to walk through their morning play."

"Walking on your way to........."

"martbar!"

"I rest my case."

"AHHHHHHH! Are you upset with me for asking you over there for ice cream?"

"Not at all. That was a nice invite. I was simply busy."

"If I had asked you over to syrah cottage nothing would be different?"

"Barry don't be silly. I just think you spend too much time there, for your own good. Besides, syrah cottage is my place to ask you to, when I need to get something off my chest."

"Well I just hope it's not my head you need to get off your chest."

"Oh, Barry, that was wonderful sweetie."

"Yeah. It was." The word 'sweet' had suddenly become irritating, like it had finally grabbed me by the arm and yanked me into a pottery class. I had a brief thought of stomping into football barn, smashing a stool through one of the fantasy pods and yelling PREEEESEEEESSSSEEEEAAAASONNN. I locked my hands behind my head and turned towards the water, which was quite calm and looked like a laid out sheet of twice-used tin foil beneath the heavy overcast.

"Are you going to go swimming?"

"Yes. No. Not right now. Unless you'd like to go. Do you want to go?" Every time lately, I had been waiting for Thea to show up with the colorful little straps sneaking out of the neckline of her shirt and making a little bow tie on the back of her neck. It was wishful thinking, and it seemed like yesterday when I had an endless budget for wishful thinking.

"Barry I'm not going to swim in that lake with you. I'm sorry."

I could tell by Thea's everything that she was not only talking about today. "Don't be sorry. Please don't be sorry."

"I'm……..I don't know…….it's so complicated……..I really think you're great………"

"The lake……it's not complicated, it's simple……..in a way, at least, it's simple, maybe, um……more things could be simple if we could swim sometimes…..more things could be simple……" And I knew all of the sudden that I had thrown the last coins into the fountain in the square.

"Barry, don't………"

"I'm sorry."

"I don't want you to be sorry either Barry."

"I know…………..I know."

We both kind of took some kind of long step into our own spaces. Mine was blank. It was like a shutdown or an overload or something, where everything had to go blank, so there was nothing there to move towards or away from too quickly. I took a very long and deep breath. When I finally exhaled I didn't mean to make any sound of it, but this noise snuck out, it was a very weird and fractured noise, like something from both a lone, wild animal, and one of those with its nose stuck into the butt of another, in a pen, conscious of little more than its ultimate fate. Thea covered her face and dropped her head. We were in the empty acres of grass and trees but every moment we stood there was like a fence being built in a spiral about us, a huge constrictor snake somehow being kind enough to tell us what it was about to do.

"Thea?"

"Uhhuhhh……"

"I'm gonna go…..in the water, and I would really like………I would really like it, if you………if you would do some exercises on the shore for a bit……and I won't bug ya, I won't bug ya about the lake or anything like that……."

"You're too nice. Why aren't you at least a little upset right now?"

"I don't know. It's not like you're screwing me over or anything. I'd like it if you stayed and did some exercises."

"Barry why won't you just call me something AWFUL and tell me to GET LOST? TELL ME TO GET LOST!"

"NO no no no no way you're too great to me and probably everyone else too, you're the last person ever that I'd tell to get lost, just do some exercises on the shore for a little while please…….PLEASE."

"I'll try. I'll try."

"Okay, good. I'm gonna walk down there now and give you some space."

"Barry, are you sure you're okay out there? It doesn't look like you can see the rocks underneath."

"I don't need to see them anymore. They're just there, I can feel them I know where they're at, somehow, a big pile of underwater rocks….the one thing on earth I know exactly what's going on, a big pile of fucking rocks……." Already half-turned, I threw an arm up in the air, loose and resigned, as I walked very slowly towards the water.

I stood and looked at it for a few minutes. It was an eerie silver and black, like a mirror with so much ink on it that it wasn't trying to sell you on anything, only trying to keep you from looking at yourself. I descended the ladder facing the wrong way. When I pushed off and sunk into the liquid Braille stretching forever, there was the one simple rule of keeping the feet high and hands low, one simple rule to navigate the same old terrain beneath new water. It only took a few immersive touches against the tough little crags and bumps and my feet were on, it was back to radgames as I hurdled gorges and bounded sideways off of sloped faces, sometimes catching the next boulder with my hand first and going horizontal to do gymnastics atop the sunken croutons of the blown upon soup, garcon there's a fly in here, yes sir but it's faster in the broth and doesn't like dog shit, well okay I won't send it back but could you take it off the bill? I flew and drifted and twisted and dropped until my toes curled around the top edge of a stone, only a calf-length or so beneath the water, and I rose carefully, slowly, until I was standing and looking down again at the blank slate of liquid metal, and maybe I made something out of a cloud reflection and into what was below, or maybe I had no idea except for some bodily sense that I wasn't going too radgames for my well-being, but I sprung forward off of that perch and had my legs tucked in and arms out wide and there was something fantastic about that slow reentry into the unseen, and it was forever in a second before my feet did another moon landing. I turned back to the land for the first time. I supposed I wanted Thea to have seen that one, but anyway it was extremely nice to look past that slimy and rusty wall and up the four huge cement steps, which for the first time looked like gigantic martbar stairs built long ago when somebody probably thought people of the future would be outside in their free time instead of near the connec.....tittyvity counter, but anyway up atop the terrace Thea was doing something like slow motion martial arts, taking turns with each leg sweeping outward in different directions, it was really cool and fluid, and I went back to swimming after a moment, thinking of her as much as I could and glad to see she was moving and not feeling all terrible about things.

Thea and I traded a quick wave from afar as she packed up. I think we both understood that more words would have gone awry quickly. I drifted to the ladder not too long after, and on the last rock, felt some sort of smooth and round pipe with my foot. I pulled it up between my feet. It was the left handle of the ladder, maybe eighteen inches long, which had somehow been broken off from the top of the rungs. I set it down on the pavement, muddy water dripped from its open end, and went for my shoes. When I turned back, there was a crawdad or crayfish or something of the sort, peeking all slow and alien out of the pipe. It crawled onto the pavement and all I could think was, what the fuck, I moved a stupid pipe ten feet and now this poor thing is lost on the worst planet it's ever seen. It was facing the terraces, and, given the speed it moved, could have spent half a lifetime before it ran its tentacles into the wall and did an about face. So I made my shoe a wall instead and the critter turned all slow back towards the water. I stood and watched and smiled and cheered as the little bugger made a five-foot odyssey back to the edge. And it did not stop for a moment when it got there, didn't turn to look for a better angle within the serration or anything, it just went over, real radgames, like man that is one badass little sucker taking a cliff dive fifty times taller than it was long. I didn't know if it was the right thing to do, but after mulling it over for a minute, I dropped the pipe back into the water as close as I could to where I picked it up.

"What in the world is in here?" Ron had just slapped a bag onto my legs, which were tucked under the overhang of the bar.

"A pickle. And some cash. Slide it under the Asian Pita office door after, you know when. After the managers are gone for the evening."

I noticed Karim looking over, observing, out of the corner of my eye. "Ron I only go over there when that big chair needs to be retrieved after the meetings."

"Big chair? Just get this under the office door so Gehri can grab it in the morning."

"Pretty big pickle to slide under a door here, Ron."

"You can slice it if you need to. That's not an issue."

"Good to know. Yeah. You hand me this bag with cash and a pickle and no questions asked I carry it around "and then slide it under the door but as long as I can slice the pickle, well we're all set here."

"You got it. Easy as can be."

"Do I get to sit in on the next meeting when the big shots come in to Asian Pita?"

"I don't know a thing about meetings. This needs to get to Gehri."

"The meetings, Andrés told me about a pickle at the meeting, you know the guy who sits in the big chair, at the meetings……"

"Barry I don't know anything about these meetings. I am sending cash and a pickle to Gehri. With you."

"I don't like going into Asian Pita. Why can't you meet Gehri?"

"You really should get a General Tso tzaziki."

"What are you talking about? A motorcycle?"

"I don't have a motorcycle."

"General Sahzeeki.....isn't that a motorcycle?"

"General Tso tzaziki, at Asian Pita. You should try it. It's fantastic."

"On a pita?"

"Yep. The proportions, the spices, it's all spot on. Exquisite, Barry."

"So you love a dish over there and can't stop in and have it and take this to Gehri?"

"I just had it no more than four or five days ago Barry. It's great but I'm not going to eat it three times a week. Don't be crazy."

"No Ron. Crazy was what I pretended to be last time so I could get a straight answer from you about touching it. Now you're calling me crazy for asking why you can't meet with Gehri."

"Yes. That was an impressive bluff Barry. Now I'm asking you as a businessperson to not be crazy, and simply deliver the bag."

"How much cash is in there?"

"Twenty-five thousand."

"*Twenty-five thousand dollars.*"

"Yes. Pull it out at home, count it, hell, roll around in it for an hour or two if you want, just make sure it all gets back in the bag, and to Gehri."

"I wasn't questioning the count Ron."

"Well good. Okay."

"This…….it'll be all over the scanners."

"Just keep the bag zipped up when you're outside."

"Of course. All of the tracking is helpless against this special blue bag."

"No no. The pickle gives off a strong odor."

"This is unbelievable."

"It's quite a pickle. Help yourself to some of it, we're fine with that. Even if only a quarter of it gets to Gehri that's no problem at all."

"That's my payment I suppose. Carry cash around under all the scanners for some of a pickle."

"Settle down now Barry. We'll take care of you. I thought we were working on a solid base of trust here."

"Well sure Ron, but this is changing things quite a lot. I'm supposed to walk all of this around under the scanners?"

"If you want to stay off the scanners you can stay parked at the tanning bed desk, safe as can be. Forever. Just because some eye-in-the-sky picks up on this stack doesn't mean anything more than it being logged into some massive cloud of data. Twenty-five grand is not really much of a red flag."

"This is a lot of money Ron."

"Just pretend it's a year's rent and you're walking it to your landlord. It's nothing."

"Damn Ron now you have me nervous and depressed all at once."

"I've told you before when I have a studio available."

"I know but your places are too far from everything."

"You're paying too much over here."

"No, everybody else is paying too much and I'm paying to be close to the water."

"It's a big city Barry."

"Yeah, for the mayor and the sports teams."

"Have it your way. But back to what's at hand. Those scanners are no big deal. And what, you have two or three blocks home from here, and then about the same to tanning bed?"

"Yeah."

"So how about it Barry?"

I felt Karim peeking over again, from beyond the reserve collection cases. I was going to say yes. I knew it, Ron likely knew it, Karim, hell the pickle and the scanners and Andrés and the Asian Pita line cooks probably knew it. I supposed I was only trying to show Ron that I wasn't going to be a total sucker. It was tough for me to see opportunity when I could not see it from the top. But of course when I thought about it Ron might have been carrying things back and forth in the dark too, as much as it seemed that he never really answered to anybody. We looked at each other. He was quite calm. I supposed the short end of a deal with Ron was still better than the long end with most others.

"Okay, okay. I'll get it into that office at the end of my night tomorrow."

"Thereyougo. We'll get you up to speed soon."

"What does that mean?"

"It means welcome."

"Yeah, I was worried that's what it meant."

It got kind of weird the night before, with that blue bag sitting around, I tried to go about my evening with it sealed up over in the corner, but had troubles with doing much editing of Andrés' video or customizing my own special original seven-ingredient trail mix while that bag was in the room. So, yeah, it wasn't long before I had cut into the pickle and had one of those wraps of cash in between the first two toes of my extended leg, shaking it to make an odd flopping sound and trying to toss it up and back to land on my head and then eating more of the pickle after a handful of unsuccessful tries, until it would certainly fit under the office door, no problem, yes, that's what I could say in the morning about it all, I was wolfing on slice after slice of that fantastic and transcendent pickle, I mean, wow, it sure was good to know that the bag would fit under the door.

So, here we went again. The blue bag was zipped into the compartment-inside-the-compartment in my backpack, just in the event some cowboy intercepted the government scanner and then stole a patrol horse real stealth and cool out from the back side of a mass protest, and began clomping away towards this little dot which was my backpack, and, quite frankly probably making that horse as happy as it had ever been, but anyway, cowboy was on me without a worry over being chased himself because the cops who got to be a presence at the protests were all on overtime pay and busy talking over what their actual work week entailed while the crowd stated its case, so if cowboy was gonna burn down the avenue until he zeroed in on my dot and then hit me with some kind of dismount tackle, well, he'd have to get through two zippers, and me, of course, so I was feeling alright about my journey. But I might have had to go back inside. I was not for sure that I had turned off my iron. I was never quite sure that I had turned off my iron.

I had turned off my iron. Okay.

The heat, it was so balmy and thick, I sweat past the used drone store window, and my back had grown very tight, and I really needed a soda, which was rare but very clearly at that moment I needed a soda and pushed myself through the door and into the three-booth burrito joint at what must have been the peak of afternoon meat prepping, wow, and it had probably been a few years but the counterman and I definitely recognized each other and made it known with our greeting, and after a quick moment of us both kind of standing and trying to show each other that our physical energy was good, he almost certainly doing that better than me, I asked for a soda and then tailed off with some nonsense explanation, and he insisted on making me a burrito, on the house, and I tried to politely say no but was overwhelmed by his hospitality to where I felt rude declining, and after pouring myself a soda sat at the closest booth to the counter, facing the window but also kind of opened up sideways to conversation the next time he turned forward and gave me a rest from thinking about how everything that was so right about this place at three in the morning was so wrong at three in the afternoon.

"Amigo! You know Karim right?"

I think I might have looked back and forth between he and the window three times in an instant, like I could move all hummingbird now that the pack was set beside me on the wall side. "Karim, yeah…..sure…….um, you go into martbar?"

"I seen you in there once or twice. You were dancing all goofy up to the front."

"Ha ha, yeah, I treated myself to the reserve collection a few times of late."

"It's good. It's good." He nodded all warm with memories and probably at the feeling of forgetting too. I sucked the second half of my soda through the straw and stood to refill it.

"Oh, let me at least pay you for the drink, can I do that at least?"

"Sure my friend. Six dollars."

"That includes the refill?" Not bad. I pulled out my phone.

"Refill and tax included. No cash amigo?"

"NO no no cash sorry usually have some to walk around at least……" I think I probably peeked at my backpack, as if someone from that sedan with the tinted windows was going to sprint into the empty place and make a grab, any second. I turned back and the phone beeped through the transaction.

"All set my friend. Burrito al pastor for you one moment."

"Too kind, too kind…..thank you." I stood for a moment and let the idea of introducing myself pass, as it was his place to decide if he wanted to give his name and remember mine. Finally, I tore into the burrito with thoughts about how easy the bag was to get home the night before when I was stomping off all salty at Ron and probably just looked like a guy all jacked for preseason at football barn. I made the soda gurgle once more. I should not have done that. Only a few blocks to tanning bed and I was not going to make it. It was the heat, the grease, the soda; my gut was not used to the strain. Something was on a very aggressive slide and I was not easing a thing with my worries of how strange it would look to carry the backpack into the restroom. But I stumbled, sweating, into the little corridor and twisted the loose knob and burst into the single-toilet cabin which, like so many others, had given up on trying to stop people from writing on walls and instead provided a few markers attached to chains, and so there was already shit everywhere, just absolute shit layered over more shit, some of it appropriate and unapologetic for the forum and then some of it, much worse, all smudged with a lone thought as if people really got the smarts out in there with some kind of four word revelation for everyone at all times, and there was so much shit of all kinds already in there that I was getting more uptight about adding to it, it took energy to not read, to avoid ingesting all of the terrible little streaks of goo that would stick in the brain and intestines and heart and soul, it just stuck everywhere until it became the duct tape smudges that held everything else together, and a hideous fly hatched within and flew around to fiddle its legs together on all of the shit which took so much work to expunge. I had to close my eyes and take a few deep breaths. My hands and feet eventually made contact with the rocks, the money already delivered, water moving gently about me, until the matter at hand was settled.

tanning bed. tanning bed. Oh, what a beautiful place to see. I fell into the big chair.

After unlocking the front door I felt like returning to the big chair and waving whomever past into surprise free day at tanning bed, especially since my back was very tight and stretching felt stupid right then.

There was always someone passing by outside, filming video, no big thing, but I saw those two and it was something about the way they were moving, the woman with the camera and the guy, he was wearing traditional Hindu clothing, maybe it was called a sarong, I could not be for sure, but more certain he was celebrating that his heritage was from India, and I knew they were on their way in. And just like that, all of his easy and free gestures became all stiff and he turned himself into one big shove of the door, the woman right behind, filming.
"YO this place IS RACIST! Everything about tanning bed IS RACIST!"
My back tightened some more. I suppressed the initial thought of simply telling him to get lost. He wanted a response, was frantic.
"You hear me tanning boy IT'S ALL RACIST! Tell me how you SLEEP at night!"
It was kind of sad. This, that, a lot of it was kind of sad. History and all of its ugliness, the worst individuals past and present, and then all of those things ingrained into the cultures and institutions, I did not know the half of another's suffering and never could even if I spent several lifetimes trying to. So of course I had said things

here and there which were lacking for compassion and displaying the limited worldview of my privileges, and when someone pulled an aside and said, Barry that was a little racist, I was glad to listen and consider, and wished I was better at stopping others the same way. But then, well, there was this kind of thing. I knew there was real progress happening, and maybe some of it was funded by those who had found a way to be popular amongst their peers that was probably easier than being good to them. I sure hoped so. Because, well, the comedy was powerful stuff, and could either be food for progress, or some kind of....irony, maybe? I still did not know exactly what irony actually was.

"YO…….." He was stunned, his mouth agape. And then I noticed that the woman had the camera on me, and that I had unconsciously rolled up onto my right toes and my left leg was up and out to the side with my toes pointed, and I kind of shocked myself with how high it was, and my arms were stretched out with my hands parallel to the floor, and we stared at each other, not all football barn like two guys wearing the opposable jerseys or anything, just staring, both of us quite stunned, but I supposed he was going to see how long I was going to hold the pose, or maybe I just supposed that so I could show off how much work I had put in to just be better about everything and with everyone, and I tell ya, whatever the reason, I really did keep it going for a pretty impressive amount of time, all things considered. Finally, I brought my left leg down, but stayed on both tip toes and just leaned my shoulders back with my hips forward and hands behind me. He turned, calmly and slowly, and made two steps back to the door, past the woman, and I was kind of glad because I could tell he was suddenly content to reconsider for a little while. I rolled onto my heels and brought my shoulders forward, and, well, the woman, she had been a good cameraperson and made herself invisible like a pro, but now she had the equipment down and such a big and true and full of character smile, one of those that got wider without the corners of the mouth stretching, her upper lip rolling up and back too special for her to give it on the cheap, and I was transfixed, that was really all I could see for some time, and then she bit one side of her lower lip for a quick second, then turned and rushed out, we didn't say a single word and immediately my world turned into hoping against the odds that she would come back by or I could run into her again, somehow, somewhere.

Thea showed up at the meadow. She really did, bless her heart.

"I don't deserve this help Thea."

"Oh, shut it Barry. Give yourself some credit."

"You see, that's exactly what I was talking about......."

"Okay. Let's call that the last talking we're going to do for awhile."

I nodded and zipped it up fast, and my cheeks ballooned out because the words that were all cruising, windows open, around the bend of sweet country air had suddenly pulled up to a train crossing. Thea gave a soft grin as thanks, for the obedience I supposed. Her outfit was eggshell and sleek and minimal, almost like it wouldn't have been all that surprising if there was a sword holstered along her hip. I had a quick wonder if she was gonna start running me in place and demanding push-ups and making me into one of the poor souls I shook my head at from afar.

There were actually some people about out there. It seemed as if this happened when summer grew short and it was almost time for football barn. Thea was not walking as if she was on her way to football barn, though. She kind of paced out a semi-circle, looking downward, and I didn't know if she was gonna blast me in the chest with some kind of kick-punch.

Suddenly a recent dream resurfaced, something twisting or pulling upon that hidden little splinter and blowing open this projection of being out on the terraces at night with Karim, sitting under bright stadium lighting, the water placid until all of the sudden a lone wave froze just before breaking and Kid Tippy was on a board and shot along the curl, and it actually made the sound of skateboard wheels bumping quickly, fronts then backs, over the uniform separations of sidewalk cement, and then he jumped off, and the tsunami never broke but just disappeared. All of the others with boards were then in the water but it was not going as well for them. Everything was chaos and some were trying to pull others back out of the spooky night water lit not quite enough by searchlights. Another perfectly formed and gigantic wave appeared, as far as I could see identical to the last, and Kid Tippy again shot across the tube like it was a hidden urban gem of some rogue genius working the cement mixer. Again, the clacking sound, it was as profound as if I'd heard it while awake the day before.

The dream fizzled into a bunch of whitewater and foam. I came to, of course unaware of time, thinking Thea would be marking out that intense semi-circle. I spun around quickly until I spotted her maybe a few hundred feet off, running towards where the trees became tall and dense. I called out her name but she did not break stride. I began running after her as fast as I could, thinking that if I could close the distance enough maybe she would pull up. I sustained my pace for thirty seconds, tops, and stopped and gasped and grabbed for my shorts while calling her name to the sight of her still going strong and disappearing into the woods. I gathered myself and pressed on down a small swale and into the canopy, kind of jogging while knowing I only had a chance if it was hide-and-seek instead of cross-country pursuit. Abstractions of her appeared in tree curvatures and wildflowers spotting from overgrowth a few times. A squirrel made a ruffle on the periphery and the erratic scratch against the trees' gentle soundtrack made me hopeful for an instant. I was sucking for air and dropped my ear onto a cluster of soil, root, and twigs, wondering beyond reason if I could hear her strides. Then I looked upwards, for some of the trees had low branches and I couldn't put it past Thea to have climbed up into a v-shaped perch. There were only a few acres of magnificent forest out there, I mean, it wasn't a national park or anything, and in time I moved slower and wiser, to the odds of where I'd have to see her. That is, until the thought came that she simply wanted to run for a few minutes and I should have stayed put in the meadow. Thea could have easily lapped back around on the parking lot side of the woods and been back there. Stupid, Barry, stupid. I jogged back towards our spot, chiding myself for turning it all into some action chase when our entire thing all along had been stillness together.

She was gone for the day.

It was a big unknown whether I'd see Thea the following week, and if I did, would probably never know if she had returned to our spot or just kept running. I lumbered down to go for a swim with hopes that maybe someone would walk up and sit on the wall and talk for a bit, because one person in the water and the other on land seemed to be a relatively easy arrangement between two strangers, yeah, at least at first with someone else it was a relatively easy arrangement.

I had tried to be all nonchalant with Karim about getting my hands on another one of those pickles, pretty sure that he knew about my errand for Ron and that it was not in any direct competition with his reserve collection, but it seemed that Karim could tell I was really after that pickle. Andrés and I carried the big chair back over from Asian Pita and I didn't ask him about anything specific; it was only a few days after we got his video out there and he was showing signs of frustration that he was not neck-high with offers. He was carrying himself kind of rigid. I sensed he felt the video came off a bit too goofy and was curt when I tried to reassure him that the right woman would see it in time.

I only knew that I could not call Ron, no way. And there you go. I wanted some pickle from anyone except the guy who had slapped one into my hand, and hoped that if someone else gave it to me that they wouldn't let word of it reach Ron because I wanted him to trust me with another errand even if I did not really want the bother of it, especially when I didn't know if I'd ever be paid, but of course Gehri probably told Ron that I had eaten most of that first pickle, and for all I knew there were people everywhere who ran one errand for Ron and then we ate most of the pickle and then scurried around tight-lipped like we were doing business when, really, we were the business, and there was maybe one person who ran an errand without eating any pickle and now they were down in some tropical location at open-air martbar while the rest of us weren't even sure why we needed more pickle other than to relax after being tight-lipped around others also looking for pickle, and I did not know what to call the whole situation, but it sure was a tricky one.

So I was even happier than usual when Brianne came into tanning bed because Brianne never checked the tongue, unless a nerve was struck as to what kept the account flush, in which case, well, let's just say I knew not to ask Brianne what kept the account flush. I inquired straight up about the pickle, and Brianne motioned me to follow into Vortex, reassuring me that I could leave the front door unattended for a moment.

Brianne's shoulders dropped with a deep sigh upon entering Vortex. I took in the panorama of Sedona and the outer shell of the bed which matched the sky, a bit uneasy about what was about to happen. Brianne spun around once, quite deliberately, with arms extended, almost as if ensuring that there was still at least a foot or so to spare on all sides. I nodded, grinned, and noticed, for the first time I noticed the rectangular patch of sky, with a singular bird, painted into the ceiling, to resemble looking up and reaching up through a car's sunroof. Brianne set both hands atop the closed bed, a heat check. I used the top of the doorway to stretch a bit.

"Barry honey, how about letting Brianne settle in? I need a perrrsonal *moment* and then we can *chat*."

"Oh, yeah, of course." I pulled the door from against the side of the bed and closed it. My mind raced through a whole lot of thoughts, including Brianne hanging clothes upon the little wooden hooks. Brianne and I were pretty well in tune with one another's comfort zone; probably how to gently challenge each other's comfort zone too. However, that was all outside. I did not know how much the boundaries changed in there.

I heard a voice from inside and knew only from context that it was Brianne's. Inching the door back forward, I was unsure if I had any chance of keeping the conversation to the pickle. The bed was on and whistling a soft and consistent exhale. It reminded me of the one morning I stood outside with coffee before sunrise, the wind pushing very low cloud smudges over the rocks with tea kettle sounds rising until the jagged thumbnail of an opposing peak lit afire, and the whole world went quiet and still.

"I first came upon a pickle when I was, ohhh*hhhhhhh*, not quite adjusted......." Brianne's voice, it was, well, I didn't know if the bulbs somehow loosened up the pipes or what, but we all had one place where we thought our voice sounded best and if there was an audience it probably noticed.   "I was, well honey, you get so many different types of attention for so many different things throughout life. To feel fresh, and excited, and not at all afraid to show it, people are drawn to that no matter what it is, and it's pretty easy to lose what's good for yourself. Sometimes what's good for yourself changes so quickly that you can only hold onto a few nice memories. And that pickle, it's, Barry it's like that caboodle you always want to notice you but doesn't until you're with someone else, if that makes sense baby. It's that mint resting on the pillow…….some people can enjoy the mint and rest easy, and then others, you know honey, they start running the floor of the hotel until they can grab two handfuls from a housekeeping cart. The pickle, it hasn't shown itself to me for awhile, and that's fine, I'm comfortable with that, but who *knows*, maybe it will be back? I sure don't………"

"Brianne?"

"I'm *right here* honey."

"Have you somehow heard about my speech problem? What I scream if I get too uncomfortable and my back gets all tight?"

"Noooooo…….tell me about it."

"No, it's just, well, you what you said about the mint on the pillow, it kind of sounded like what I used to, well I want to say 'used to', but I can never really say it's done, but I yell about wanting all of the chocolate….."

"Baby it's *choc*-o-*late*. It's hard to trust someone, ooooohhh there's no explanation when someone says they don't care for chocolate. Barry you run *like the wind* baby if any woman tells you that she *never* eats chocolate."

"Ha ha, thanks. The thing is…….ahh, sorry, didn't mean to get you off the pickle thing……."

"Brianne's here for you baby. Anyhoooo, I went through some wild times where the pickle was always around, and Gehri, more than anyone else, Gehri, this was before tanning bed, before Asian Pita. Sometimes, ohhhh my, sometimes it's tough to know if nobody wants to see you before midnight, or if it was you all along, you never wanted to be seen before midnight. And Gehri, now he had his interests at hand too but if there are fifty people holding out a glass of champagne, well sweetie sometimes there's one angel who walks over to grab you a glass of water. He had me over to his place for lunch a few times a week. Barry, he'd cook for me, and I was so happy to have some true company during the day and Gehri, well honey, I don't know too many people who keep inviting you back even if you barely touch their food on some days. Oh, *dear*, I was so *ashamed* the first time, this wonderful meal, I took two pecks and died on a couch. He stayed at it, the less of an appetite I had the more he invited me over, not out of some crazy insecurity over his cooking, no, he just knew I needed that steady ground. Over time, my appetite came around, who knows where *ole Brianne* might have ended up without this kind man tailoring meals for me. And.......and......." I could tell Brianne was welling up in there, in a good way. "......Barry, there's those people who you always think of and say to yourself, I'll find a way to return the generosity in time.......and now, here I am, lying in this bed, sitting in that restaurant, he's still giving me steady ground, I can make things all about me with the best of them Barry, but make no mistake, I was his kind of his first audience of for all of this. He narrowed it down to what I'd like.........and........and he put his heart into it........*how*......how do I thank him Barry?"

"You probably are, somehow, most every day."

"Ohhhhh I don't *know*......."

"Don't ever forget how much Gehri probably likes knowing how much you enjoy being here, that he built something which is a real part of your life."

"Ohhhhhh......"

"Seriously. Everybody needs a number one fan of something that they do. It's like, if I can make one person crack up over something, I just keep on trying to make them crack up, you know, not like, hey, when's this someone gonna make me crack up in return......"

I could tell that Brianne was kind of tearing up in there, and figured it was the best time to give some space. I stepped forward and tapped my palm atop the bed a few times. "I'll let ya settle into the bed now."

"This is gonna be a nice one today Barry, oh yeah, a nice one today....."

Here came Dana, right on time, always right on time to swap out the old and yellowed oil change offers and dry cleaner coupons, and usually we didn't talk much because, well for one Dana had to keep on schedule, that was the rub of it all, the schedule with all of the oil change offers and dry cleaner coupons had to be kept, and people were following Dana around everywhere trying to get at that pension but all begging for it right then and there, and hopefully someone every so often could talk with Dana about giving that pension and then they could arrange a get together for that evening or something, but for the most part everyone out there needed that pension right away, they couldn't wait another second, and if Dana cut out for even, well, who knows for sure, but it was probably fifteen minutes or so leeway at most, and if it was longer than that, well, there went the pension and they might go all hysterical that it was gone, but that usually seemed to be the case when out and about, people coming up and needing that pension immediately and going all bonkers to be the one who Dana blew the whole thing on right then and there, I could only guess some of them promising they had a pension of their own, even if they didn't have the uniform to prove it and show it off proper, but they'd say they had their own so Dana could break the schedule and go nuts and blow the pension right then and there, and so had to be pretty damn strong about it all, at least until the evening when the pension wasn't at risk of being stripped, even if that took just a bit of the excitement out of the matter.

But the neighborhood was being resized for me of late with this pickle stuff, so I wanted his ear for a second to see if I could get another measurement.
"Hey Dana."
"Hey blondie." At least a bag did not need to be lugged around too. Just had to carry the tiny stack from the last stop.
"Dana, real quick, do you know Ron?"
That question prompted a look. "I'm sure I know a handful of Rons."
"Oh yeah, but this Ron has a mustache."
"Mustache.......no.......that's one I've never had going for the pension." Dana took a step back towards the door, like a ten-second warning.
"Okay, of course, I just thought I'd ask, he's been around the neighborhood forever but his home surely isn't on your route."

"Can't help ya blondie."
"Oh, no, that's cool, thanks, I just wanted to ask."
"Alright, wish me luck out there."
"Have a good one."

Dana hit the street again. Still, I was kind of frantic for answers. Suddenly it was this brilliant idea to check the addresses from the expired coupons and offers. Also, man, I was so used to Dana swapping the same old boring mail and walking the gauntlet that I never even considered that every other mail carrier was looping something similar around a different neighborhood, maybe for different types of shuttered businesses, but I wouldn't have been surprised if all of the neighborhoods were marked out by the last nearby dry cleaner and oil change pit to stick offers on paper, that certainly could have been the case. To start, though, I was going to stroll by the address for the dry cleaner after I closed up tanning bed.

My guess was it would be a speedy spoil. The speedy spoil was across the street though. The old dry cleaner had not been redeveloped or leased again or anything of the sort. The brick was tan with this feint greenish tint to it, certainly more the shade of decomposition than rebirth. Both lamps hanging from the street post, which was mere feet from the door, they were both out, the only lights in sight that were burnt. I looked around for cameras, but that was dumb. It had been a long time since those could be spotted by the naked eye. Any signage that might have once existed was gone, and the only window was a porthole turned opaque within the splinter and grime of the door. There were scattered people out walking--on the other side of the street. I felt guilty of something, just lurking about in a dark patch of sidewalk, guilty of cultivating suspicion; if I had any reason for walking around to the alley that was probably it.

Well, Friday night, here I came, ready or not. Barry had some momentum going now, just no stopping it.

Sometimes I wished that every year there was a different color of asphalt patching used, so that the streets and alleys that never got a full repave job would have like fifteen or maybe even thirty different colors of patches here and there, and they all at least looked kind of cool, and a stupid alley such as this one had this tiny chance of being some kind of accidental masterpiece. I turned my phone to infrared viewer. Before I stepped up to the dumpster, no doorman that night, the dumpster free and clear, I stooped and looked through infrared beneath the dumpster, a rat check. All safe, as expected, just had to make sure. Ooooh, the eyes of a rat through the infrared, to see that once is enough, forever.

I stepped up to the dumpster, which looked like property of the small Moroccan restaurant next door. I was not committed to jumping in or turning things over to see it all. Then again I had not opened the lid yet. I flung it up and back into the wall, and held up the infrared after a first glance did not reveal anything beyond typical restaurant waste. Boxes and bags, it was all just boxes and bags. I went to pull the lid back down, disappointed, maybe, about what, I had no idea. Just as

I did so the back door to the restaurant flung open, and it was a bit jarring for me, and the cook too.

"Get lost, eh guy……"

"Oh, I'm not a digger or a beggar I just……"

"I didn't call you a digger or beggar I only said get lost."

"Yeah, okay."

I tailed off as the large bag he had carried on his hip thudded into the dumpster. I must say, I did respect sound logic when being asked to leave somewhere or someone. Still, I had my head down as I loafed back behind the old cleaners, and this is why I spotted an oddly placed iron cap, like a manhole cover, between the wall and a patch of knee high weeds. And, I don't know, it could have been a number of things I suppose, but most of all it had that look of the one thing on the property still attended, or used.

"Hey, come on now….."

"Okay, okay, I'm not even on your lot now."

So I walked. And thought. I walked and thought and hardly ever knew which fueled the other. But there was something to that cap, and maybe even to how protective the cook had been by not going back in until I was around the corner.

I was able to swim again on my way to martbar. It was not even a morning play #ETT where I had to do go underwater, just a wade beneath the officious stream of corporate workday dusk, the current knifing to both sides of hurried retirement, all of the heads up above steaming from temperature change of music and data. I had not seen Ron again and did not expect to on this day. It was getting to be reserve collection time, because I was bored and lonely, and in the seasonal wane of daylight was impatient to be stirred before layers of clothing began accumulating between our warmest wills.

I stayed under while the connec….tittyvity counter salespeople's heads wagged independent while torsos blended into the wall. The magician, I swear his back was turned as I snuck a peek, but suddenly there was a gigantic ace of spades, waterlogged yet floating, rolling with the water, taking over the entire surface and hindering the light from above, so I kicked myself upwards because that card was kind of like being under a tipped canoe which needed to be pushed over. And that was that. I nudged the card over while surfacing, never saw the other side of it, and was face to face with the master. I was really interacting with the magician for the first time.

His eye contact was brief, as if he saw into my soul and if it had persisted an instant longer I would have seen into his. I reached for my phone instinctively and held it out in that space where his eyes had settled on my chest. I was a bit nervous that he would simply try to sell me jewelry. Not to disappoint him by saying no, but rather that it might mean I had already disappointed him in some other manner.

He mumbled something. The top of his mouth must have been like a slanted tin roof, funneling sound to only the adult side of a picnic table. His hands, palms angled downward, were hovering a few inches over and to the outsides of the phone, his fingers in a relaxed state. Each of his fingers had a unique, independent bend to them. It would be foolish to think that they started that way. I admired them for a moment, but then focused on his necktie so that I would not begin wondering how he did the tricks. I certainly did not want to be thinking at all of how he did the tricks.

The magician's necktie was a deep and burnt red, one I had seen before from too far to see the repeating diagonal trio in the pattern. There was a turtle shell, a mushroom, and a stocky mustachioed man in overalls. Okay then. My wondering over that ceased when I realized that my phone was no longer in my grasp. The magician's hands were positioned exactly as before, the phone out of sight. I snickered, peeking up quickly to no reciprocal facial reaction. "herrrgh we're gonnahavetafindyourphonenow herrgh."

He clapped his hands together and then showed his palms over a two-foot square of green cloth strewn out atop the glass encasement. "let's seeheeeeeere……" He turned one shoulder, and then the other, forward, the wool of the black suit having collected feint scents of travel in its fibers. Then he lowered a palm onto my shoulder and simultaneously there was a thud of a phone dropping onto the cloth. It was antique. Somehow it was always easy to tell when one was over two years old. The magician, eyes fixed upon my chest and one straight patch of hair gradually veering away from the rest and down his forehead, he snapped a finger and a woman in a red dress appeared on the screen. "isthisyours?" I shook my head. The way he spoke made me wonder if his tongue was occupied elsewhere within. He chuckled and flipped the back of his hand against my chest like an old buddy, only it was not the feel of his hand, and there was another strange phone on the cloth, his knock on the glass prompting a photo of my own face. It was spooky.

"howaboutthisone?"

"Well, not my phone……"

"okayokay" He knocked again and the image flipped to a full and tasty looking glass of bonus juice. Then he folded the cloth over the two phones, touched the top of it, and lifted a suddenly empty cloth with a pinch of his fingers while I stood in amazement that the two phones were now under the glass, on the encased shelf and still showing both the woman and the bonus juice. I felt the urge to simply have one of the phones in hand, for the show to be over and I could have a phone in my hand. But he did not break pace, and laid the cloth back over the glass top. "saaay I almost forgot here herrgh." He pulled up the cloth, and there was my phone atop the glass, with a consistent image of wind-rippled lake water. The desire to simply have one of them in my grip was growing. The magician knocked on the glass twice, and the images shown on the three phones all rotated from one to the other. Then he tossed the cloth over my phone, knocked again, pulled up the cloth, and mine was beneath the glass with the others.

It was safe to say I had very much given up on figuring his methods. A good part of it all was that he had minimized his presence until I could not feel his, or my own. The only physical force to be found was the movement of the phones. His identity and mine, whatever the dynamic at the onset, it had dissipated, we were the ones in the glass encasement. We were two mannequins frozen in a store window as the phones went about their day.

The magician told me to knock on the glass. I did so. That's when it really began. All three phones down on the shelf suddenly flashed to it. The big icon. I was afraid that I had accidentally touched it, or would soon enough.

He laid the cloth back over the encasement. Then he told me to knock on it. I hesitated, and met his eyes for a moment. The contact was brief but reassuring. He told me with a fleeting glance that my worry was either outside of his powers, or ethical code, or both.

I knocked on the cloth. He pulled it off again, and now my phone was gone, the other two still showing their big icons while resting on the enclosed shelving. Then he told me to lay my palms flat on the glass, absconding the two below, but still, it's just, craziness, he knocked again and, yeah, the cloth was still there but I could already feel the phones in each palm, and, yeah, I may be getting a detail or two wrong about the phones moving around, because there was a lot going on up in the noggin.

So anyway, now I was holding the two strange phones, both with the icon up, and the routine so far had made me feel mystified and vulnerable, but also as if I had agreed several lifetimes ago to lay my defenses down for this very instant. The magician played with the cloth for a moment to show it was empty, then crumpled it, knocked, and unfolded it again, to, of course, my phone. It was either off or showing no image.

"saaaayyyyy I never caughtyername."
"Huh?"
"yername."
"Oh……uh……wait…..huh?"
"okayokay….it'sokay."

He covered it and knocked and made it go under the
encasement, further away, another degree of separation.
He nodded once, confident I knew what that meant. I
curled both of my thumbs over the top of the two
foreign phones, and I pressed down. They both ran me
through a few double-checks, but those did not slow me
down at all. I knew. I just did.

The magician, he went away just before everything else
took hold, no big trick to it, he just walked away because
there was not going to be much point to standing near.

The first thing I remember is sitting on a couch in the
middle of nowhere. There were not walls or really even
a floor, although it was not like I was floating, but rather
simply sitting on a brown couch, with endless grey all
around. No sound either. It was not like I was afraid to
get up from the couch, but there was no urge to do so,
not an adventure or even curiosity anywhere in sight. I
sat still. I was quiet on the inside.

I was eased under in a growing distortion of last waking
thoughts. My head bobbed several times as I lifted
heavy eyes with unfulfilled expectation of seeing

something besides the grey. Then I was out. Like a surgery, I was out.

The reawakening, after time indeterminable, the reawakening was prolonged, and profound. And also it was kind of stupid. People began showing up on the grey horizon, and the first to step forward was this was, well, by popular standards at least, good looking doctor with a glorious voice and extremely calm manner, as if she had been picking daisies the entire time I was out, not rushing off to a dozen other rooms while nurses and technicians all lunged for her frantically in the hallway. Doc said I came out fine and complimented the dimple on my chin and said it seemed I had a strong grasp on happiness. Others began to step forward just behind the doctor. This was as international as could be; not a blemish to be found on the globe. Men, women, children, pressed pants and bright blouses, wonderful headdresses and hats, traditional gestures, oh, I was the star of an airline commercial and the entire world had been excused through the security checkpoints to meet me at the gate. There was a chef without a single stain on his coat, a mechanic with shiny and attended hair holding a golden wrench, a programmer really laughing it up and enjoying rapport with a Pacific islander propping up a surfboard. Three children, likely all hailing from different continents, rode tricycles in perfect circles. There was a jazz duo off to the side, both wearing tuxedos. Nobody really said anything. They all smiled huge at me, not even a tinge of yellow to a single set of teeth. Not a one out of the dozens even had a phone in his or her hand, let alone their face buried into it. A country looking baseball pro without any dirt on his uniform, yeah, he was speaking Japanese, well, that's my guess at least, that it was Japanese, but he was speaking in this language to a mountain sherpa maybe? with hair dyed platinum blonde. When they noticed me observing them, the ball player tipped his bat forward off his shoulder and winked at me. A group of college students all wore the fantastic cardigans. The doctor, still standing in front of everyone else, held out a phone. I took a few steps in and she handed it to me.

"You're doing great here. Welcome. We're all very proud of how far you've come."
I looked at the phone. There was a cursor flashing.
"Go ahead. Write out a message, please."
She was nodding kindly. I looked into the crowd. They all had big eyes, expectant. Even the kids had stopped cycling. I felt like a three-year old about to blow out the birthday candles.
"You can do it. You've made it."
It was tough to say if I had the ability to think out a post or not at that moment. I did not attempt to do so. Instead, I belted out, 'I WANT ALL OF THE CHOCOLATE! GIVE ME ALL OF THE CHOCOLATE, YOU FOOLS!'

Everyone pulled out their phone for the first time, and, a moment later, let out a loud cheer. The doctor smiled and touched me on the shoulder. I shook my head at everyone in disbelief. When I looked back at the phone, the 'like' counter was spinning digits. I gazed at them and made a fist to shake it loosely and slowly. The 'likes' kept piling up, far beyond the number of 'people' I could see.

"You're free to stay right here until it reaches a number that makes you happy."

"How do you know it won't stop?"

"Pardon me?"

"The like counter. How do you know that it will keep on climbing? How do you know that in another instant it might just get its last like of all-time? It should have never received a single like in the first place. That's what I was trying for, not a single like. So, tell me, how do you know it will keep climbing?"

"Please excuse me for a moment."

She turned with clipboard in hand, walked into the crowd, and vanished just artificially enough to be noticeable. That's when it dawned upon me, that I had asked what certainly was the simplest logical inquiry possible, and it had broken the algorithm. Unbelievable. It had not even dawned upon the programmers that the question, or likely even a hint in that direction, could be asked.

I checked the phone again, the counter had accelerated. Everyone in the crowd had been standing all proper with their hands cupped together in front ever since the doctor left. An urge to be devious overcame me. "Anyone up for giving me a foot massage?" Well, not much logic in that question, but still not a one was able to react. "I WANT ALL OF THE CHOCOLATE! GIVE ME ALL OF THE CHOCOLATE, YOU FOOLS!" Still, nothing. They could not bridge the same words through two separate contexts. I pointed my finger at the crowd, not really at anything in particular. "You guys are lame!" Okay. They were awake. Each of them scolded me in their own 'personal fashion' for that one.

The doctor reappeared out of the mass. Who knew how many people and machines were involved for what was coming. She approached, and I scrambled to think of another simple question that might confound everything.

"Are you a terrorist?"

Well, it looked like she beat me to the punch. "How could you possibly ask that?"

"It is proven terrorist behavior to state a desire for no likes for your post. And also to desire that the likes cease."

"I asked you how you knew that they would keep accumulating."

"It is progress of humanity."

"You had to go talk to the boss to give me that? That's it?"

"I had to use the restroom."

"If that's what you'd like to call a rewiring......"

"Are you a terrorist?"

"No."

"Would you prefer the likes to continue?"

"I am indifferent."

"Pardon me?"

Oh boy, here we went again. "I am indifferent to likes of my post and to likes in general. I am indifferent to likes."

"It is *progress* of humanity."

"I disagree."

"It is progress of *humanity*."

"Once again, I disagree."

"It is progress of humanity."

The doctor's look had morphed during that interchange. The lines of the face were losing curves, becoming angular and robotic.

"It all seems to me like another sketchy currency exchange."

I thought this one would make the doctor 'go back to the restroom'. But it did not. "It is progress of love." The voice too. It seemed to have expended the last of its inflection, if it was not in my imagination in the first place.

"It is a thrift store selling a cheap knockoff of the real thing. Which would be fine if it was not turning the real thing into something to be judged as if the knockoff was made with more care."

It nodded. It was silent, and shifted its hips as if choreographed. It made these skeletal imitations of seductive lip movements. Maybe if I was so immersed in digital impulses I would have seen it to be sexual. I have to say, it was pretty impressive programming, even if I wanted to flip the bird at someone behind it all.

"How can a human being possibly be concerned with a large number of people before they even learn to be concerned with just a few?"

It grazed fleshless hands upwards over what had become a conical chest.

"That is not attractive."

It stiffened and the expression became hard. "Are you a terrorist?"

"No. Can I go now?"

"Have you ever wished physical harm upon another?" Oh my. I was immediately wary of this one, legally. "I asked your friends back there if any of them would like to give me a foot massage, while you were 'in the restroom'."

"That is threatening."

"No, it was an invitation."

It made this weird roll of the shoulders and chest, and its tongue inched along its upper lip, real cat style. "Would you like me to fellate you?"

"No, I don't trust you."

"I cannot let you leave until you trust me."

Uh oh. "I'm happy to hand you my phone."

"I do not want your phone in my hand."

"Okay."

"At the same time, I do want your phone."

Uh oh.

"Do you know where I would like your phone?"

"A guess can do no good for me."

Its eyes turned bright red. I snickered over its frustration with my ease of declaring not to know. It was sheer metal and bolts by then. "You have many choices for where to put your phone."

"I do not care. I want to leave."

It began moving about, apparently an effort to make me gesture towards a certain part. I crossed my arms and did a fake yawn. Finally, it stood still, and, I suppose, presented its response to all of my indifference. This considerable protrusion crept out of the pelvic area and towards me, it was actually fleshy and I stepped one of my feet back so I was not squared to it as it neared. The eyes were flashing all different colors and there were all kinds of images coming and going, bright enough to show through the clothing. This….thing, it was human looking I supposed, as in a fifty-foot tall man kind of deal. There was something of a female part along the top of it as it stretched horizontal a bit closer than I preferred.

"This could have been much more straightforward for you."

"Yeah yeah."

I kept my fingers along the far edge of the phone to try and push it into the limb without touching anything. But it was not going to be that easy.

"You have to grab the underside to open it up."

I narrowly headed off an expletive or three and remained silent. Then took a deep breath. I reached under and tried to tell myself that it was only a bulk roll of tin foil, even with all of the numbers streaming through the veins of it. The facial features of the doctor began returning. Not ideal. I pushed the phone and flesh returned to other parts of its body. I told myself again and again, those were droid noises, they were not human moans. Finally, the phone released from the tips of my fingers. I stepped aside quick, fearing....yeah. Instead though, the protrusion retracted and all kind of images and numbers and words lit up. I could only help to guess that it was mildly disappointed by my phone's relatively low amount of content.

My balance was so shaky. I had my head down and my arms clutched around my torso. It was approaching my cheek to kiss it. I winced and grimaced and tightened myself even more for those facial appendages to make contact. They did, and then it stepped back. I hoped that punishment for my impudence was served but very afraid that it was not.

I heard the phones knock into the glass as they fell from my hands, and I tumbled to the floor. Instinctively, I got to my feet as quickly as possible, but immediately spun around all wobbly and top-heavy, and fell again. I have no recollection of whether there were others nearby or not. I regained my feet and kind of staggered into the counters on both sides of the hallway. I did not even glance at martbar. It was straight, well, except for all of the jagged stumbling, it was straight to the door, towards as many anonymous people, towards as many people who found me anonymous, as possible.

It was indeterminable nighttime. I felt as if underwater but not swimming as much as being whipped through rapids, narrowly avoiding people in the river. I found enough coordination to avoid bumping into them and then was rushed into the next group, between the hot white glare of retail and menacing wind blast of a city bus. I swooped into an oncoming group of three, clearly engaged with one another, and by the time I was twisted back away from their energy pocket, all sexual snapshots were clipped into pieces and rearranged, imagined parts rubbing into my upper arm, my kneecap getting into the action, all of these crazy pings shooting in and out of the least sensitive spots, and then the whitewater overwhelming it all, churning up its deep laughter at such fragile visions. It jettisoned me towards a lone man who opened his mouth and it kept on growing wider and breaking shape, and I was blasted feet first into the striped orange and golden ribbing of the smoothly contoured cave, shooting towards the escalating pitch of the teardrop hanging from the ceiling like a sound fixture, flying through the octaves until I passed on my back beneath its reverberation like it was a hospital scan, and it blew the clog right out of my ears, and then I vacuumed through a constriction and out into the video images blooming as if the most bountiful rain of the spring had left the ground abuzz, and suddenly I could hear all the footsteps of different treads and heels and strides kicking out a beautiful drumbeat over the heavy and low undulations of the blitzing water. I listened to that song for a good long while as the wane of traffic slowed the current and I caught a few magnificent breaths of air sweet with kisses of both neon and mist.

Before I knew it the water had funneled me into the stillness of wide plaza banks, overgrown and absconding any tributary fingers. Scattered parishioners were waist deep and in uniform. I lowered my feet slowly, and discovered they were bare as my arches cusped on smoothed and rounded wood. I inched my left foot along the easy taper, inching it back as well until my toes were wrapped about the tight curve, and then my pinkie was stung by a jagged shard, and I slid it back up to rest both feet on the barrel head. I stood. Up ahead and near the top of all the grey beams crisscrossed into a huge tic-tac-toe board of all x's, perched up high was the ancient red clock that had been struck by lightning and frozen at one minute before midnight, forever ago. The parishioners were in clusters spread about the plaza and tuned to a frequency which I was not. Vendor shouts came across the calm flooded plain as if a quarter-mile was twenty feet. Trying to move would make the conundrum of distance just the opposite. Some of the parishioners pumped their fists or did high-fives, and then a moment later a huge collective roar from the coliseum engulfed the plaza and ruffled the placid water, so who knew if there was a frequency ahead of real time or not. Huge lightbulbs beneath the clock began flashing, 'THIS AMERICA'S FOR YOU! THIS AMERICA'S FOR YOU!' and the same message came across in various forms of the eras, on all sides of the plaza. The water began to rise as masses of people descended the ramps and began the displacement. My feet began to lose contact with the broken bat, and I felt my big toes press into engraved lettering before lifting away, and I was floating again, quickly losing any space to spread my arms in the suddenly thick crowd of uniforms. No one said much. There were loudspeakers barking out the repetition of 'Thank you for sharing a tiny bit of your joy with our concession vendors'. But you could only hear it if not plugged into something else. I supposed we were all in very slow transit towards celebration but everyone, including myself, was turned inward, into themselves, many either reviewing statistics or watching replays, and it was frustrating and slow. My thoughts died even as the water lifted us upward. I tried a few times to make eye contact or small talk but all efforts were rebuffed. Soon enough I was depraved and mad for food and beverage, food and beverage alone. We were coming upon a narrowed pass out of the plaza; I could see the parishioners ahead slipping into the funnel and down the chute. This was about to get interesting.

The water began bumping our shoulders together as we neared buildings which rose three or four stories above the canal. Aggressive faces behind big round goggles poked out of all the windows up high, loaded and ready. We gained speed and our torsos fell back. The slide became a crazy mess. 'Take this motherfuckers!' and the like was screamed from above as the torrid onslaught of barley grenades came down upon us from all sides. The gunners had to throw enough barley grenades into the river so that there was enough for all parishioners and there would be no fights over limited quantities. I must have exploded my first grenade in two gulps, the second not too far behind in this mad twisted rush beneath the sky, metallic with torrential downpour. There was a fork in the stream in sight with huge flashing arrow warning us to stay right. The water pulled in knots, we twisted about one another, the emptied grenades clacking between, and in the chaos a horn buzzed in unison with the flash of the arrow as the gunners continued to spike the river from two and three stories up. We all needed to get our third grenade down in order to bond and avoid being swept left. The gunners were doing their part with attitude to spare. I drained my third grenade, clutched the shoulder of the nearest parishioner, and in the barley backfire yelled out, 'hey, what a service, yeah!', even though I had no idea, but it spread until we could all have a hand on another's shoulder and scream about what a great service it was, and it was enough to not lose anyone off to the left where there appeared to be precarious netting to catch the empty grenades along with any lone and sober parishioners.

We floated easy, with exuberant nothings, under a massive fielder's glove which was missing its webbing. That folk tune from the sister and brother, or husband and wife, nobody knew for sure but it was this great folk tune from ancient Detroit, blasting, dah…….DAHdah*dah*dah…….dah, dah…….DAHdah*dah*dah…..dah, and we were able to put our feet down in another wide pool shored by fortified bunkers, with a ten-foot high wood carving and a lone skylight from which a bearded man with a weird leather bag glared through. I took a few bullets with two firemen and a man with a museum of historical torture devices shirt. Soon enough I was splashing around like an infant and trying to sing a song with a wedge of citrus between my lips. I thought it bad news when the word 'bellhorn' appeared before me, but the woman ushered me kindly to this huge bank of tin foiled masonry, and I unwrapped one after another, the gooey cheese stuck to the inside of the foil and bun sponging up blood, I ate a hole in the wall while not knowing if I was being yelled at in Polish or not, and then this nondescript door came ajar and the water sucked me through the tin foil and then the doorway, and I tried to remember the rule for how long to wait after eating to swim as the rapids twisted me into a tight cement bunker with minor league caps and ammunition of all types stacked high and a few gunners hiding in between the piles. The gigantic ice machine opened its lid and the pile inside alternated between tints of red and green each time the motor grumbled between sheets. I pulled in my arms in preparation for shivers as I was tossed past all of the gas cylinders and into the ice. Immediately I was frozen inside of a cube and could only wiggle slightly and hear the slightest indication that it might, one day, crack open. Another sheet would fall with thundering weight, allowing me momentary sense of what was up and what was down. The shifting tint of red and green; that was all I could see filtering into the frosted cube.

I had many thoughts about those cheeseburgers and hibernation, about the minimalism of winter. There was a prevailing image of streetlights coming on at three in the afternoon and the profound memories of heartache attached to it. I laid there and saw that heavy rollback day of many years.

After some time, I began tumbling end over end, sliding, stopping, tumbling again. The light prism had changed. I was lifted out of the bin, I could tell that much, and then, everything around was blurry colors, and then I was moved, steadily, and could feel hints of warmth at both head and toe. The cube was engulfed by flesh. I wiggled my arms and legs as much as possible to the supposition that I was noticed. I was rolled over a few more times as the melt continued and one of my toes caught a whisper of the outside. The fleshy shade released into other colors; I was on the move, somewhere, in a hurry. Heavy contact jarred me. The sound of the ice cracking was a prolonged tectonic quake. My eyes were freed to look up and a gigantic barrel-chested guy with a goatee shaping rhymes, waddling away with a green pickle bucket. I broke from the top of the cube as water rushed about me and drew closer as it whittled the ice away. I was eased into the current and in a flash all that I could see was many identical round holes in the rust, and knew only that struggling against the water could do nothing but change which opening I would slide through.

Darkness. And stench. The smell was unbearable. I was gagging. A huge flock of bats or something shot past all crazy and flopping and some of them hit my arms and chest. Every second brought a different touch with another preferred unknown in the water. I had a terrifying concept of forever down there. More bats. It was a slow descent. The reek grew in complexity, collected awful hints that other pipes were leaking in their discarded signature recipe. I was paralyzed with the fear of encountering a rat ten or twenty or a thousand times my size. I could not say for sure that I would not drown myself first if one of those monsters even came near.

Darkness. And stench. An eternal sludge drift of darkness and stench.

A voice came down there. It was impossible to tell how many corners it had turned, how long ago it had first echoed into the piping.

The voice was incoherent for awhile. Then, interrupted by a familiar, and escalating, sound. Now, don't get me wrong, I never had some dream of the day when another man's piss was coming down my way from above, but at that juncture, it was quite alright and maybe even better than that. The voice returned, and I recognized it. I recognized the voice! There was no mistaking that weird and slow drawl. It was that funny fucker the coliseum trough master, probably all bent and singing into the damn drain. Ha ha! And here was the thing, too, he was singing a song to his own piss, well, because he was a crazy bastard, of course, but also, because he could. He was singing out distances and diameters and turns and bends, leading his piss on its journey, probably to somewhere he was gonna go soon enough, maybe even martbar. martbar, yes! And, damn, he for sure had a few bonus juices the way it was coming out of both places. It finally tapped out some staccato, then ceased, and then, much clearer than those measurements and stuff, I could hear him go, 'ya put your RIGHT HAND IN, ya put your RIGHT HAND OUT, you put your right hand in, and ya *shake it* all *about*, you do the *hokey pokey* and you turn yourself around, that's whaaat it's allllllllll aBOUT'. Oh man. And, I don't know, it wasn't like I could follow his directions or anything, but damn hearing that just saved my ass. I was on an adventure, what the hell, the pipes were going somewhere, anywhere, and if another man could sing to his work I sure as hell could enjoy the unflattering miracle while there.

Now, again, don't get me wrong, I was still terrified of running into one of those giant rats.

I drifted along to memories of his goofy ass song. It repeated over and over in my mind, kept it occupied with a simplicity which did not beg for dissection. It was all about the hokey pokey for awhile, and that was just fine.

In time, the water became pocked with dollops of blue. They splotched onto the dark rippled meringue as if there was a single dribble of blue up above and a dozen unique rolls of water contorting and angling to reflect it, for an instant. My sense of time returned to those brushes of color. There was something inside of me which simply knew their rhythm, for how long they appeared. Soon, the soft fluid lines of the shapes morphed to include strokes of grey and puffy white too, while the rest of the water, waiting its turn to catch a slice of the sky, had eased into a deep green. I have absolutely no idea what was up above, the thought never crossed my mind to even look. However the water kept intensifying, bubbling into many shades with every elastic tendon. I had never been as sure of one single thing in my life: the sun was to peek over the horizon within the next few minutes. My eyes went so still that they were blurry, and all of the beautiful squiggles and puffs and rolls went through my temples and massaged my brain into total bliss. The rounded and doughy knuckles dusted grains of orange into the charcoal and slate. One sideways candle flame snaked and burned inside of a stringy fumble of blue and grey marmalade. Time was assured, but what was internal and external, well, that seemed very uncertain. Also, I did not care. The jelly kept returning, clouds smoking and churning within, the flame eating further from the curvy fringes and blowing its tint into the texture of the vapors, as the jelly continued to appear in one splotch and then stretch apart like two huge wads of bubble gum in each hand. Over and over, it was such a magically therapeutic envelopment. Then the wads, still doing their elastic ebb and flow, they became the negative space to the huge splatters of orange, and my brain was total jelly and my body followed suit and shook and trembled in the hot light and in the impossibly sedate intensity, and I did not know if I was inside of the sunrise or if it was inside of me, but my body's first sign of return was a response of incredible trust that it was definitely in the right place.

My hands felt as if they had been cupped very tightly around the top of that submerged rock for some time. The sun was five or ten minutes above the horizon and a few more below the cloud range hanging all of its blushed cheeks and smoking secrets. I was horizontal, and released my hands from the stone. I waded towards the sun and set my feet on another, then stood and realized I had no shorts on to check later for evidence of what may have happened just before I gained my bearings.

I stared at the yellow ladder while clutching it, searched for tiny spouts in the rusty wall, ran my fingers along it, beneath the surface, to no avail.

My keys were resting on the cement, and, oh boy, nothing else though. I waited for a jogger to pass before climbing fully out, then quickly stepped down again to think it all over. The major concern was sneaking to my apartment without being logged into a very bad list for life, any defense very, very shaky. Even trying to speak my piece to the authorities, yeah, you know me, I would try to tell them the whole story honest rather than just pass it off and admit to a morning pervert run, and if my first words were to the authorities, well, you know how it goes. Suddenly you were being passed from one authority to the next and the harder you tried to just tell the truth, the deeper they checked you into the maze of authorities, and it would be three lifetimes of talking to authorities until your family could show and pay with their blood for them to release you. So, yeah.

I sunk back in and stood, submerged to my chest, on a rock. I waved and hollered at a few joggers, and there was no way they did not notice me, but those headphones sure made them good at pretending so. I wanted a phone, but as I waved ten feet from shore, unsuccessfully, time and time again, the realization crept in that I did not know a single phone number nor any of my passwords to get remotely into one of several other platforms to reach people. I looked up and down the cement terraces. There was often unexplained clothing out there, but not that day.

Another jogger did not break stride. I was asking people to speak for a brief moment from fifty yards away while I was in the damn water, and, you know, never mind, it was too fucking aggravating to even consider why they couldn't at least turn and say no.

I swam up and down the shoreline for a while, widening my search for a mystery pair of denim shorts.

I yelled and I waved. I racked my brain for passwords in the dying hopes that someone would stop, let alone hand over their phone for a moment. I thought about how much I loved that lake and yet how it would never be quite enough as the only love in my life.

A couple was strolling together, hand in hand, a few hundred yards away, approaching. Their strides were reassuring, and this helped thoughts of my best option of what to do with a phone. Their arms swung back and forth together. Andrés' video, I could get to his tire change video and reach him in comments. However the username would not match and so I could not introduce myself straight, he wouldn't believe it was me if the username did not match.

This couple, the way they moved, I liked them. They rounded into more definitive form as my plan did the same. It was going to ask quite a bit of them and if they declined then I was just going to make a run for it and hope I got very lucky.

Beyond the waves and hollers, I had not spoken a word to another person, for, well, yeah, some time. I was nervous over the words pouring out so fast and so many that they had no choice but to run. Plus, even though I had tried to keep moving to stay warm, I was freezing and shivering. So I kind of blurred my eyes to their hands swaying together, a gentle lean of a shoulder, a head rolling in and up or down for a moment, and that relaxed me until it was time.

"H….h…h….hey there guys……" I forced a smile and shook my head, which was about all I had above water. My teeth clattered. "……I, uh, hu…hu…had a b..b…bit of a strange night which luh….luh….left me here in a……I don't know……."
They nodded, real ones too, they were actually taking me in.
"L…..l…..long story short, if if if if…..one of you could spare your phone so I can try to get a friend out here…….I huh…huh…hope you can't tell, but I nuh…nuh….need a friend to bring me pants."
I believe the woman stopped short of offering to go themselves and bring me something back. They did that thing couples did sometimes, where they each kind of shrugged and nodded first and then began turning to one another, for a consensus.
"You guys are the best for stopping……." I was about to tell them there was a bit more too it all. The guy though, I could tell by his expression, he already knew there was a bit more to it all.
"Did you get all messed up and pranked by some friends?"
"Um…m….m….m…maybe? I'm not quite sure just yet…..I've b….b….b….been out here since……..before

sunrise, and now, it's……." I motioned upwards to the sun, a few hours up in the sky.

The woman leaned into him and placed her hand on his arm. My rough guess was that they touched it, together, in their late teens. "I can dial for you and set it down on the edge here……"

"I wish……um, you guys are so nice…….the thing is, I d…d…d….don't know any numbers, can't remember any of my passwords to get in for a message. The only wuh wuh wuh way I can think of r..r..r..reaching a friend is through the comments of a…..video we made of him, ya ya know, tuh tuh try and find him a woman, and it's……"

"I'll open up the video platform for you."

"Okay, but……there's……" I shivered; was nervous about them turning on me. "……he w..w..w..won't trust it's me with a different username, and…..I hope this isn't asking too much……"

"Go ahead."

"If you guys cuh…cuh….could shoot a photo first, you know, so he he thinks he's r..r..running out here for some company……."

They began doing that couple thing again, only this time it was not all nods and shrugs. I looked down and away, not really knowing if that made the ordeal more or less creepy. "He's not some……d…d…deviant, it just needs to be a nice smiling photo and then I can write something to go along with it, guh guh get him out here……" I tried to nod at them both.

He turned himself away from me and stepped out of the decision. I looked away, and then at the woman.

"We would need to delete it later today."

"Oh yeah, oh yeah, I mean, an hour at the v..v..very most, he'll be out……again, I don't know how to not sound weird about this, but he'll see it and be on his way in fifteen minutes, for sure."

"Okay. Sure." The woman turned to her guy and brought him around with a few seconds of body language. "Sure."

"We need to read what you write before posting it."

"Of course. Nothing obscene at all. You guys, I can't……..thank you……you can….." I thought of offering free sessions at tanning bed or bonus juice at martbar, but both sounded dumb. "Thank you! I'll give you a minute to take a shot."

I waded and did my best to move and keep warm, but what really kept me warm was peeking back to see that they were having fun taking some photos, maybe they'd never done it before or it had been awhile, they were really into it and I felt so much better about everything and waded out a bit further to hopefully allow them to forget why it was happening in the first place.

They huddled together and smiled over the photos. A minute or two later they chose one and then the guy walked the phone over to the ladder. He was smiling. I nodded and grinned at the photo and declined to say that it was real and true and would have Andrés on the move immediately. I punched in, 'Hey you strong and funny man I need you for good company and times right now at the lake right in front of first birdhouse north of harbor, you must wear sexy jeans from video but bring swimsuit too I MUST swim with you! XOXO'.

The guy nodded, still smiling, then showed the phone to the woman, and they posted. "You want us to wait around to see if he responds?"

"Nahh, he'll be out here pronto, not a worry."

"We'll stick around for a few minutes, no hurry."
"You guys are the b...b...b....b.....best, really."
They returned to taking photos, for themselves I was sure, and I felt better and better every second. It was not too long before they told me Andrés had responded with a quick, 'on my way!' And soon after the beautiful strangers were off.

My heart nearly sank me under when he appeared up above the terraces. He was so excited, his stride was a bounce and his chest all pushed out. He turned each way a few times, with hurried exuberance, then rushed towards the birdhouse I had mentioned. I was afraid to yell out and break it to him, and also afraid to wait longer. His first steps on the top level of cement revealed the shine of his boots. He was no fool, far from that, and from my distance it was easy to notice in his body language that very first moment of considering realities. It was the least worst time.
"Huh...huh....hey buddy it's B...b....barry can you c....c...come down here puhpuhplease?"
Andrés stood still for a very long moment. It was tough to watch.
"I'm suhsuhsuhsorry I swear I d...d...didn't know what else to duhdo."
He rubbed a hand over his face, and did his thing where he looked down and shook his head really fast for a second.
"Andrés p...p...please I've been stststranded for hours."
He didn't have a bag, or a suit in his hands. I think he considered, for a hot instant, leaving my ass in the lake.

He did the head shake once more, then began lowering himself down the terrace. I waited, silent.

"You make me leaving, first time me thinking pretty lady liking the video, Barry you make me leaving home man this not joking, no funny, not joking."

"No no no buh buh buddy it's no j...j...j...joke, I have no pants I can't g.g.get out of the water with n..n..no pants."

He froze and let another wave of shock wash through.

"I huh..huh..have no pants, no phone, I couldn't get out I'd be arruhruhrested."

Andrés started falling out with laughter. His laugh was great. It went on for awhile.

"You d...d...didn't bring a s....s....swimsuit?!?"

He looked at me like that was a crazy question. "Me bringing, me have it, I wearing underneath."

"Ohhhh no.....you've gone Euro too?"

"Shit, no man, me no Euro!"

"N...n...never mind, c...c...can you sneak up behind a t...tree and take them off so I can g..g...get out?"

An unfamiliar expression came over him. Both his face and body, I didn't know what was up during that pause before he left for the trees.

His gait was more recognizable when he reappeared. It made me recall a few instances at tanning bed where he left a fart behind for me to discover in the hallway. Andrés maneuvered down the terrace. The slight hunch in his back, it somehow was transparent to a prank or something. I still could not see any evidence of a damn swimsuit.

When he got to the edge, he pulled them from his back pocket and pulled them straight and taut to show me, like a parent-to-be might do with infant clothing opened at a baby shower.

"Mexican flag wrestling tights?!?!?"

"Now you making video, me making video of you in these, I make!"

We laughed together, at different things.

"Boy you sure were bringing it all down here for that woman Andrés."

"Me making video of you!" His laugh ran up several steps into a giggle.

"Okay, okay. Ooooh, boy, you were aiming for a bold move, stripping to these. Toss them on down."

He giggled.

"I'm in for the video, just toss them on down so I can get out of here."

I slipped them on, unable to keep from wondering just how in the world this was making me decent. The red and green wrapped around opposing sides, it was a double-image with the band of white and coat of arms running through the middle in both front and back. They did not fit at all. My crack was pulling it in from the cheeks, over and over, there was no stopping it. I pulled it out a few times with my thumbs and also cupped at my vacated front side in a futile effort to bring something back out of my gut. I had to just remind myself that they were keeping me safe from arrest and get on with it.

Andrés kept giggling. I smiled. "Alright, I'm coming out, get that camera going, I'm not gonna stop and give you tips for crushing artsy pans of the landscape or anything." I hit the ladder and got my feet on the pavement. Andrés got his phone ready. Now, I really wanted to own the walk, strut it out proud and all, but I was shivering and exhausted, my nuts were probably on the other side of the world for ten days, and my bare feet could only take the lightest of contact with the pavement. So it was my toes and bent knees pointed outward, which did not help the pace at which my crack wanted that fabric, and my arms and shoulders shaking, one trembling and tenuous step after another as Andrés made circles around me, giggling like all hell. I smiled and laughed and told myself just to keep my mouth shut otherwise. I shook my keys in my hand to some kind of song I could listen to as I kept thumbing out the fabric with the other and Andrés zoomed in for a second on my vacated front, narrating in Spanish here and there as the only recess to his laughter. He continued to catch me from all angles and distances and I thought he might get enough before we hit all the traffic of people and good coupes. But when we did get to all of that, he was still filming and giggling, and I was really glad he was still there and enjoying the hell out of it, so I could simply know that he was having a blast and not give a damn about what all the people honking and hollering and whistling thought.

We made it to my building. My longest walk was through. "I'll wash these up and bring them back in, on, ah hell, I don't know, do I still work at tanning bed or have I missed a week and been fired?"
"You keeping the pants! For you Barry, you keeping!"
"Okay, I'll hang them up proud somewhere. We're good here?"
He was still laughing.
"Okay, I think we're good here. I'll see ya soon buddy I need a hot bath."

The magician was nowhere to be seen behind the counter. It seemed very possible that I would simply never see him again. The salespeople behind the connec....tittyvity counter, however, after so many years of me being invisible, they were jumping out of their shoes, all three of them with eyes wild at my fragrance of eager commission. I passed indifferent as their assured pitches wilted into virginal failure of their instincts.

Karim was standing in front of Ron, in his stool. Both were silent. I made a quick, unacknowledged wave from the bottom of the stairs, then slid in to the left of Ron and opened my mouth to say hello. He turned away from me before anything came out. I deflated, and waited for a moment just in case it was an odd tic. It was not. Slumped over my forearms on the wood, I finally raised my heavy chin to look at Karim, and got more than I bargained for. I had never been stared at like that before. His brown eyes looked like they were each suspended within a tear, welled behind a statement of what was a byproduct of what. I met them for a good time, aching, until I was sure that it was no contest unless I wished to make it a losing one. I shifted my glare about and kept returning it briefly to Karim's eyes, still and calm and trickling deeper into me. Ron remained turned away. The weight of even thinking that these two might ask me to disappear, it overcame me. After looking back and forth for another long moment, I summoned myself for another meeting with Karim's spirit. One side of his mouth curled up and pinched his cheek. He leaned over just enough so that Ron could see his nod through peripheral vision, then stepped away to more conventional definitions of work.

"Barry dammit I thought we had an understanding."
"You…..Ron, you said I could help myself to the pickle each time don't sit here and pretend you didn't make that very clear. And what was this all about when I sat down?!?"
"Pickle? *Pickle?* We had to do our best to check and see if we'd lost you after whatever the hell you did the other night."
Karim set down a bonus juice for me and moved along. "Some way to check, yeah, why didn't you just ask me about it instead of acting like I wasn't even here?"
"Here we go again. Like you know. We were seeing how you handled the rejection, if you would simply look to anyone you could, on your phone, for answers convenient to you. So I don't know what you pulled, but you're lucky. Very lucky. Dipshit."
"The magician sent me off on a wild ride, but I knew I wasn't really touching it before I committed."
"And how do you know that he's not an agent for where the technology is going, rather than where it is now? Think about it. All you knew was that it was different than the way it happened for others in the past. Huh? Tell me how you know."
"Eye contact. The same as Karim and I a minute ago." Ron did a strange wiggle of his lips, his eyes still burning from under the shelf of his brow. "That's it. That's how you knew for sure."

"Do you have a better case for why he is some kind of agent, Ron?"

"I don't have to."

"Of course you don't."

"I don't have time for another back and forth here, as much as I'd love that Barry." He pulled a blue bag from his far side and slid it onto my lap. "Same deal as before. There are three pickles in there this time, try not to eat them all at once. But what do I know."

"Are you only handing me this because of what I did the other night?"

"I already needed to give you this. I just switched what's yours to take and what needs to be delivered."

"Yeah, right."

Ron shrugged. Sometimes the most believable thing of all was when someone honestly didn't care if you believed them or not. He stood, rapped me on the shoulder, and walked out.

Karim stepped back in front of me a few minutes later, squaring himself calmly. I didn't know what to say.

"Ron was greatly concerned over you. As was I."

"I know. I know. He's.......you know, never mind, it's fine."

"He is aware the time is nearing when you won't require his guidance or advice. Possibly, it already has. He can be this way when he feels he's needed no longer. Do not neglect the significance of healthy confrontation Barry. Ron will challenge you until you are not here to be challenged."

"But I'm not going anywhere. I'm not taking off."

"I am not going to say it is best for you to be leaving. However, you are going somewhere. If you do not have this place in your mind, then I kindly suggest finding one. If you do not, then the unfortunate places shall find you."

I nodded to show Karim I would process that further very soon. "Hey, I have no idea, and didn't ask Ron, how did he even know I went into……whatever it was?"

"I told Ron. I stood in this very spot and observed yourself and the magician."

"What did it look like?"

"It was most curious in that, recognizing you, I was confident it was not a jewelry pitch."

"How long was I standing there, or was I lying down, or running around down here?"

"Professor showed me an old book, I tinkered with the glassware cleaner to remove a noisy straw, and silver fox asked of an ideal powder for an abdominal pain. I looked up into the hallway once more, and you were leaving with an unnatural and foreign gait."

"Wow. That's it?"

Karim glanced around the bar and gave subtle hint that his time was short, without undermining the weight of our talk. "Ron, he is unable to see the spirit animal within the magician. Hence his mistrust. I see it, as do you. However, Barry, a spirit animal can only watch over those seeking understanding, not gratification. For this reason, you cannot repeat, or even experience some variation, of your recent actions."

I nodded, again showing my desire to digest his words further. "I have this feeling right now that I understand less than before the other night."

"This is likely true. However, the bridge which you have tried to walk in your mind is now beneath your feet."

With that, Karim excused himself.

I brought one of the pickles with me into tanning bed, unsure that I could tolerate the boredom of the shift without a bite or two at least. But it was too slow and scarce for me to park myself at the counter and intensify any senses while gazing out at the passing sidewalk activity. Andrés was not even around, which was odd. He was one of those people who you didn't know whether to be glad they took a night off, or worried that something was wrong. I stood, bored. No visit from Brianne or Kid Tippy sighting either. I was unable to concentrate on anything that could keep me occupied. So I stood beneath the lighting, which rose in temperature as the night asked for more of everything outside.

The instant I noticed her passing I jumped into a wave. But she moved along without noticing. I pushed through the door and jumped to a stop on the sidewalk to see her down the block, her pace very much slower, and she was holding her phone up above her shoulder, not directly in front of her face, and I supposed she might have been using the viewfinder as a mirror. I stood for a moment without waving, not wanting to embarrass her if she was in fact looking back. She continued on after a brief and slight hitch in her stride. I returned inside, hopeful, happy.

It was many segmented jogs of nice thought later when she appeared again. I waved once more. She turned and I was too happy to witness her smile to wonder if it was with mock surprise. I stepped from behind the counter and held the door open.

"I'm glad to see you again."

"Yeah, me too. I was in the neighborhood for….." She waved her hand towards her walk in a manner of those who did not want to bore others with details. "……your video is something else. Pretty gutsy stuff."

"My video? Like, what you caught me doing when you guys were in here?"

"NO! The boy never even put that up, he felt so silly about how it turned out. Your video…of the walk…."

It took a moment to remember. "Ohhhh, yeah, oh boy. You've seen that?"

"*EVERY*body's seen it. How are you handling all of the crazy comments and name calling?"

"What is this now?"

"Oh my…….." Her mouth went agape. "…..you're serious, aren't you?"

"I've had a lot going on of late." I fluttered a hand upward as gesture that much of it was upstairs, would be lost in explanation. "Do you want to sit down?"

"Sure." She took the weird chair. She took the weird chair. Now, there was good chance she was being kind and knowing to let me have the big one, she was of petite physical stature, but still, she took the weird chair. I sat a moment later.

A concerned look overcame her. "I've been worried that, well, we came in here trying for that video bit about this place being racist, and you were great, and I'm so sorry about it, that boy paid me to film before I really knew what he was going to do. I've been worried that your video was kind of provoked by what we did….."

"Ohhh, oh no, no, ha ha, let's see, I was stranded in the lake without any pants and had to borrow a couple's phone and I didn't have any numbers or passwords to reach my friends so I had to trick Andrés into coming out there with a swimsuit with a comment on his video page where he was trying to meet women so he came out there thinking he was going for a swim with a beautiful lady, but then it was me, and he was a bit pissed and let down so he had some fun shooting me in his Mexican flag wrestling tights, which I thought were a bit risky to unveil on a first meeting with the woman who, of course, wasn't there anyway. Yeah."

Her mouth went agape. She stared at me. My happiness began to show as I realized that she was stunned at the truth and not at perceived audacity of a lie.

"Oh man, I'm gonna have to call Andrés, he's not here today……how many views are we talking about here? Actually, forget it, I'll find it later."

She raised her brows and I took it as a cue that we were over a million.

"Okay then, well, my name is Barry….."

"Hey Barry……Carly."

We shook hands, smiling awkwardly for a moment.

"So do you pay the bills with the video stuff?"

"Ha, no, I have a stupid job downtown. Here and there a guy pays me for something of the like. Usually it seems they're afraid to just ask me out." Carly bit one side of her lip and I remembered that from before.

"How long have you been here?"

"Probably too long and also not long enough, every day I come in."

We talked and laughed and shifted around in our respective chairs. It was not all mind-blowing with commonalities, not like, 'you were there that night?' and 'I put that on pizza too and everyone said I'm nuts!' But it was very pleasant. I had this warm feeling that I somehow relaxed Carly, was an escape from some worn social norm. I was not exactly accustomed to being a relaxing presence for women to whom I was attracted. Maybe the video, and knowing what she'd seen, had something to do with me being calm. I was quite happy to hear it from Carly first, and felt as if the rest of the world could say whatever they pleased and it would not bother me at all. That was a powerful tonic to sip.

Time passed quickly. Her brows were always on the move, and sometimes dove into a 'v' which was outright intimidating. But that hard expressiveness spoke to me on plain terms, an easy language of likes and dislikes. Somewhat more complicated was Carly's tendency to bring her arms into her torso and then flare them back out over the sides of the chair. She ran her fingers over the ear of her tightly cropped hair as she paused for the right words, and caught me staring all goofy until that reprieved her from needing them.

It was closing hour, just like that. I checked myself before, and believe me, the thought was there, I stopped myself before asking if she'd like to go to martbar or syrah cottage after I locked up. But I had, dumb, I know, I had already mentioned it was closing time because I couldn't quite entirely forget about being on the clock. So there was a heavy pause going, and the thought had never even crossed my mind before, but suddenly came rushing up in this bundle of anxiety and excitement and surprise as my hand moved out slowly into the space between the chairs and as if I was asking for an extra slice of cheese on a sandwich I said, "Would you like to lay down in one of the beds for awhile?"

"That'd be nice."

"I think so too."

We touched hands and shared all kinds of looks for a little while. Eventually I stood and made that door latch real sweet and talked over how there were three beds, the Vortex, Bronzeville, and Everglades, and two of them were kind of special to people and I didn't feel right about those so Everglades it would have to be, and I think Carly knew that I was talking in part to not fully break contact while taking care of the minimal closing necessities.

She walked just in front of me down the darkened hallway, tossing her shoulder back into my ribs once or twice. The lights and sounds were waiting for us inside. I remained stoic on the outside but freaked out for a moment. I mean, a nearly total stranger was suddenly after hours at another's workplace and taking in the panorama of trees rising from the swamp while frogs burped and birds chirped and crocodile tails swooshed at the water, and any second I knew I'd be telling it to her back that I wasn't a murderer as she ran for the door. "WHOAH! This is *coooool!*" Carly turned and probably could see my big smile in the deep green canopy. I was too happy with her reaction to think much of it at the moment, but I soon recalled with glee the adventure and wonder in her voice, and her wise sense of character that allowed it to speak in the first place.

"I would be in here all of the time!" She slapped a palm atop the bed.

"Yeah, it's not bad." I neglected to say that I felt as if I was seeing it for the first time, too. "I'm glad you like it. There is some love that went into this place. This is the least used room of the three, by far."

"It's perfect."

We milled about in the oncoming gravity of what was to come. It was strange and new for me, well, everything was right then, but the sense that she would be comfortable lying in the bed with me but not me going in for a kiss first, while standing, somehow the levels of intimacy had rearranged and I was simply glad to be there and realizing so clearly what made her happy.

"Should I get into the bed first and let you take a moment before coming in?"

"That'd be nice."

I peeled off my shirt and lost my shoes and dropped my jeans, like, what the hell, everyone's already seen that and more. "Please note the traditional boxer cut here...."

Carly laughed. Her voice was far bigger than her stature. A lot was; I knew it already. I smiled at her and then hit the sensor for the bed, climbed in, and shut the top.

Carly opened the lid, topless, and then cupped her hands under her chin, trying to seclude herself as much as possible with her arms. I reached a hand out towards her hip, glowing green in the light. She quickly accepted that as invitation to cuddle in, face to face, where there could be no bodily staring. Her face was an impossible wonder in the shadows and color. It went on forever. We would brush noses and with each pass over the ridge there was something new and beautiful on the other side. Her lashes and lids went up and down with the pronunciation of all her thoughts and then freedom from them.

"I feel like we're drifting along on a great raft through the swamp."

"I like the frogs."

I suppose that not kissing was somewhat more on me by that point; I was a little self-conscious over my mouth, whether it be from opening it too much against all reason, or cheating on the commandment of four dentist visits per year. My hands had been lightly about her hip and forearm. I brought them up to grip her tighter.

"Get ready baby, big Barry's gonna rub your shoulders real good."

"You weirdo!"

"I know! EVERGLADES!"

We stared at one another some more. Her upper lip rolled up and seemed to collect the weight of her smile. I crept my mouth towards it and it felt like a dozen invitations for every inch. My lower lip made a silky fabric snag of contact with her upper. I tried to lift it off by bunching it together; instead she pulled at it lightly until we tore a tiny imperfection into the gown that no one else would ever see. My hands left the knitting of her shoulders and I spread my fingers in wait for the next breath of her ribcage to melt with them. I motioned for her lip once more but she pulled another blemish in the fabric already new. One of my index fingers snuck away from the pack and crept slow and firm to the lipid bubbling of her sensitivity. It made just enough contact with the cornice of her bounty to feel it elevate into the weather of her easing concerns. I was free with a total loss of any gulf between her happiness and mine. With next to no idea what I was doing, I slinked my other hand down and stiffened my palm against her hipbone, and she kneaded it into purpose with rhythmic wiggles against it. After another near miss at a lop of hot breath and visual journey through the sleek new history of her face, I brought my nose down to the taut muscle of her neck and let the cartilage run hard passes up and down the extended ridge of her natural fragrance. Everything became a rich green fog of sweet musk curling through with the breeze of our motion together. I was there and waiting for her. I continued with my hands and after breathing against the grain of her hair, my nose gave way to my lips upon her neck. I bent a leg to run my toes over the top of her foot. I was so lost in the building ensemble of our song that the crazy sensation seemed the only hint that she had even altered her movements to take me into the warmth of her otherworldly responsiveness. We were no longer at all separate. And we flowed together as if we had never been in the first place.

We went on through various stages, gradually losing notions of beginnings and ends, until our excitement reprised into easy caress and heavy eyelids.

The first startled motion in the bed woke me immediately. "Ahh! I'm going to be fried how long have we been asleep I'm going to be so burnt!" Carly rubbed at her arms, searching for pain.
"You're fine! I set the bulbs to warm only, no ultraviolet. That's how we got away with no goggles."
"Oh. Huh. Do people pay for that?"
"Yeah. They don't get it as good as we did for free, but yeah."

"That was…..um…..I was in a trance." She sat up on the edge of the bed.

"It was very very nice."

I moved to turn off the bed lights, and my back peeled away from the puddle of sweat on the glass. Then I lied again and grazed at her back, keeping at it for a moment to not let on that it was soaked and cold. We both got the chills very soon. Carly stood and redressed without self-consciousness while I looked on with a big dumb smile.

"Hey, um, Barry……" I raised my chin as she buttoned her jeans. "……I don't know if we can……do this again….it really was great, don't get me wrong….."

"Oh yeah well it's not a worry you can always come by just to hang out if you like, I have plenty of time up there and that weird chair you sat in, well it's never taken."

She reacted with her hip alone. She seemed taken aback and I supposed maybe she heard some other reply enough times for it to become typical. "I might do that."

"Please. I'd love your company."

"How old are you?"

I was a bit stunned now. "Younger than I was in college."

She laughed. "But really…."

I went for my jeans on the floor to pull out the identification. I didn't like to say it. There was just no way to say this number and get everything I felt about it into my voice, and even if I could it would probably just sound as if I was trying to sell something by it, especially when finding myself naked in front of a woman most likely in her mid-twenties.

"Wow…..not far from my guess, but still, good for you."

"You know…..eat bananas, avoid responsibility……"

"And crazy women?"

I supposed she was halfway calling herself just that. "I try to stay weird enough so that only smart women can see me."

She smiled wistfully. We were out of things to say.

I walked Carly to the front door, telling her I'd have to get Andrés back with a better prank than leaving a bed all dirty. We hugged and turned ourselves awkwardly a few times.

"Seriously, come on back even just to say hi."

She nodded and grinned. Maybe it was my unusually contented state but I felt good about the chances she would.

The message, it definitely came through while Carly and I were in that bed, and I was a tad spooked over the timing of it being even more specific. I had been out to the meadow at our time twice to no avail, and nary a peep of any other sort, it was all okay and understandable even if it was like an ingrown nail where several times a day you just are reminded that it's sore, but now out of the blue the silence broken, apparently responding to a message I had sent but did not recall at all, and despite my foray, courtesy of the magician, I could not check back for time or content of that or anything else outgoing on my phone. So I was conflicted. It was always nice to hear from Thea but the timing of her message had my mind all revved up like I had been disloyal on some astrological level, when I was looking forward to some easy stretching and breathing in the cool reminiscent haze of my time with Carly. So, yeah, Thea was already back even if I declined to meet her, and let's face it, that was not going to happen anyway.

I did not get out to the meadow too soon though. Playing it cool now. After all, I had been in the water earlier, for some morning sideways planks and boulder jumping. A strange bipolar sky had arrived since then. Clouds from the planets of northeast and southwest were hanging in a divide and it did not seem either would cede the last hours of the day. The treetops were without pattern as to which embraced the breezes and which ignored them. I was uneasy with thoughts, all of them jumping to the front and raising their hands as if they were the one and only to alleviate lost touch. Even the lake, it was not rolling yet, but either it or myself or the both of us knew of disturbances on their way from the northern woods. It was a strange afternoon to reconcile that I was beneath the same sun which spiked my morning coffee.

Thea appeared in the distance, far off in the long tussles of color as the overgrown grass was wiped over by the practiced mop strokes of the breeze. She was wearing an orange jacket cut well above her hips, no bag, and carrying drinks in each hand. I did not pretend to be looking anywhere else as she neared, attire showing to be unsuited for exercise. I waved long after it was obvious that I had seen her.

"I brought you a hot pumpkin drink."

"Those are out already?" I shook off my initial candor as ungrateful. "Thanks, that's nice of you."

Thea handed it over and I quickly got the feeling it was a beverage of significance.

"I believe they make sure they're available before football begins."

I chuckled and realized how deep the reality of her statement. "I got a swim in this morning already. Usually I know the day by then."

Thea turned herself and I followed. We loped over to the top of the cement, to sit. "Your message was really sweet Barry. I thought there were many more to come, so I waited, and then it turned to worry."

"Did I say I'd write again? What did I say? When did I send it, or, um, when did you get it?"

Thea tried to conceal her smile with a long sip of her hot pumpkin drink.

"Nothing? I don't even get a hint?"

The zipper of her jacket pocket made a sharp zuumpfff. She pinched one end of her phone with her thumb and forefinger and flipped it over into her palm, really quick and coordinated. Thea looked at it with a satisfied grin.

"Come *onnnnnnn*.......pleeeaaase?"

She whisked her thumb a few times to indicate the length. Then smiled some more. I made a half-pretend grab for the phone, forcing her to turn away and cradle it in. I snapped my hand together in the air a number of times, playfully.

"Ohhh Barry, you're something else."

"You gotta give me more than that thumb swipe."

"That's against the rules, you know that. It's *mine* now......" Thea cocked her chin. ".....it's extremely nice. All of it."

"Ooooooookkkkkaaaayyyy......" I dropped my shoulders into a happy slump. ".....so at least tell me this. What's all the autumn stuff, your outfit and the hot pumpkin drinks, what's this about? I mean, you know I'm not disappearing into football barn….."

"I'm trying to get you to slow down before you get caught riding the summer too far."

"Oh. I see."

We both sat, gazing off, in our own spaces. I wasn't really big on thinking too much about it all right then. So I started back up with the play swipes for the phone, Thea tucking it away, and both of us starting to laugh as she was turned from me, until I tried to call a truce by hugging her from behind and squeezing her tightly and settling my chin on her shoulder, where everything was just perfect, the touch and the scent and the closeness, all of it was just perfect until forever wiggled itself back out of the moment.

I continued to hug her, and the elements became more prevalent in our stillness. There was a warm flush on one of my cheeks and a dewy frost upon the other. Nature was careless of our embrace. The two of us could do nothing with our touch, or our hot pumpkin drinks, to generate current alternative to the wild electricity of the fronts. They were shooting too many tickled lashes about the skin for our own sources to be anything more than reverent.

Thea was right there and I was, well, I was hesitant to know of the climate in which she was immersed. We sat together and gave ourselves back to a weather that would destroy us if we gestured to steal what it was trying to give.

"Thea?"

I was still wrapped around her from behind, but it was surely mutual that the hug was finished. We were staying put out of decorum and respect for each other, also bittered with that pesky dash of self-loathing, shading the ice in the complicated drink of life.

"Uh huh."
It had to have been the most involved breath of air I ever drew, truncated by its complexity. "I know I can't.....you know, count on this at all, but maybe.... maybe I could call you when......maybe when dandelions come back.....I don't know......maybe this winter I can make myself full enough to catch up with you in the spring......."
Thea was nodding and her cheek was twitching. It felt like we were agreeing to take a lap around the earth and trying, with any luck and fate and will, to arrive right back in that spot during the same sunrise. It hurt. I think she was pretty sure too that it was the best chance we had.

I promised myself that I would wait to view it for the first time with Andrés, hoping when that moment came he would believe as much. It had not even crossed my mind whether Thea had seen it or not until now, well after we sat heavy in the conference of the seasons, and I guessed not for no other reason than having a spare moment to do so.

When I walked up the hallway to open, I hoped the chair was not there. I just wanted to carry that chair back over from Asian Pita with him. No such luck though. So I went into Bronzeville to configure a projection range along the wall, since it was toned without pattern and would tint the video slightly as the only interference. Then hit the sensor from the counter to notify him that it needed a cleaning. He was probably keen to what was happening, given the time. It was a better way to do it than to go over to Asian Pita all waving and beckoning while whomever else had seen it over there heckled up the invite.

He came in through the back. I heard the door and the proud duty of his steps. I touched play and made my way in.

Andrés did his head shake as I filled in the doorway. I ate half of a cut pickle and held out the other for him.
"No, man, me working, working."
"This won't change that. Plus you can tell the guy in the big chair what you think of it."
My dumb ass stepped out of the lake.
"Okay, okay." Andrés shrugged, then bit into it and for a second it looked like his entire face was going to suck in through his nostrils.
I chuckled. "Well that will make sure it's only on special occasions."
"No good Barry, too much sour."
I turned and looked at myself fumbling all goofy and pulling fabric out of my ass. I was not winning any of the radgames, clearly not, but still felt like I had won something, being able to smile at this. Andrés was looking at me and trying to determine if I'd seen it

already or not. His giggle on the video escalated, and I began laughing. It was all so ridiculous. The camera zoomed on the tights and then made a lap around my gingerly waddle, Andrés laughing on screen but still tense in Bronzeville. There was such a heavy dichotomy in the room. It was so simultaneously easy to see why this video was the best--for the two of us--and absurd to see how anyone without any back story or context whatsoever could dive in as judge of meaningful content, and then be reaffirmed by the seven-digit grizzly parked in the river and playing a game of virtual salmon snatch. Possibly that was the very core of the allure; maybe a lot of people yearned for something they could not quite believe was either staged or spontaneous, maybe it freed them to make and balance those choices in their lives.

I became wary of my weighty thoughts and how Andrés could see them as irritation. I refocused on, well, myself, shaking keys and shivering like a misplaced ostrich beneath the sky, tinted by the wall. In the video, Andrés burst out with some slang that made every Spanish lesson on earth toss two question marks into places where camaraderie was the dialect. On screen I shook my head grinning and in person I gave him a playful shove on his shoulder. He was loosening. A moment later we reached the exercise superhighway, and I froze and peered back and forth real slow at the traffic, looking like a gargoyle that had been underwater for a few centuries, and Andrés in the room giggled just an instant before Andrés on the screen made the exact same giggle, and everything, all of it, kicked in at once as it seemed he had thrown his voice, and I just lost it. I was stooped over laughing, then sitting down laughing, then curled on the floor laughing, and then he started up and his laughs and snorts and giggles were coming from two different places, and I couldn't stop myself, not that I was trying. When it had finally waned a little, Andrés stepped in, motioning to speak, but then his mouth opened to another spasm and sent me back into helpless fetal madness. Soon enough he had to collapse against the side wall, and we both looked up to see the tights really wedged up my ass and me doing slow mocking hand gestures at the good coupes, and it set us off again, and we were beyond good with this and everything else.

We got to the door to go our separate ways in the hall, and I put my hand on his shoulder and said something of the like that this was his time, this silly video was his credit for all of his daily art which was often taken for granted. I can't remember how I had to fumble around with words to express that, but in his grin I knew he understood and had ideas for living it up.

When Carly showed about ten minutes prior to closing, even I could take the hint that she was not there to chat. Her attire was extremely similar to before and I sensed she was like me in preferring to keep it out of the equation. I was just plain happy. Carly saw that and tenseness left her. Somewhere along the line I had lost any response that she may have feared upon walking in, vulnerable.

She sat in the weird chair which molded body language but let her face relax into dreamy sensuality.

"I'm really glad you came back."
Her lips, man, they moved so slow and true into a smile. They could laugh at application. "How was your day?"
"All of the sudden the boredom was worth it."
We smiled at each other, her eyes leaving and returning a few times. I moved to lock the door and stubbed my foot on the corner of the counter. "That wasn't there before!"
"I like knowing you're far from smooth."

Carly sat atop me in the stool opposite the bed. I warmed different areas of her body until they called for the clothing to be removed. We moved to the bed at the stool's warning of first wobble.

It was all entirely new. Trust was the only foundation. It eliminated wrong turns as all else became progressive paths through the natural hinting, further movement into the woods of our lost inhibitions. I began occasionally timing out a big suction pinch of Carly's butt to the sound of the frog. It was the best light moment to collect along our strange trail of determined pleasure. We ended up somewhere on the other side of a peculiar contorted tangle of those Florida trees which might have been sharing roots.

We left the bed and lied undressed on the hardwood floor, keeping the top open for the subtle glow of retired heat. I snuck out and grabbed a pickle. Clearly, I would be bothering Ron soon. When I returned and offered Carly half of it, we both became too cool, because she had never seen it before, yet ate it without any more than one wise glance of hesitation.

"What's it all about?"

"It seems like it's the best if you're doing something real; and probably a disaster if not."

"Sometimes this doesn't feel real." Carly pinched some flesh on her forearm, somehow finding it curious.

"I think that's because we're strangers but very familiar in that bed."

"I wish I didn't have to wonder why. Do other.......not that I think you are always with other women.....but have some felt this comfortable right away?"

"Ohhhhh no. No, it's usually felt like, I don't know maybe like I was being sized up as a potential long-term partner and I never liked to make a bunch of promises or anything, but was just being kind and maybe that sent off wrong signals especially when I couldn't simply say I only wanted to take the clothes off and didn't know much else or have some great life plan so, I don't know, looking back it often felt like by the time we were in bed there was this weight of what it meant for everything, and maybe sometimes it was just in my head from other experiences, and a lot of insecurities, but it seemed that we were supposed to redress and immediately get our lives together, of course probably a lot of that stemming from being convinced that sex was the only thing that could make me happy and going without it for too long, until there was just too much going on......" Damn that pickle really could stir up in a hurry.

"Oh. Wow, that's, I'm sorry....."

"Ahh." I shook it off. "How about you?"

"The boys, they don't have any patience. It's like they're trying to pick a lock before an alarm sounds." Carly pulled her chin in, seemingly wondering where that came from. I nodded, like, yeah, pickle. "But the patience…..is it just age?"

"I think I've always had it to some extent…..it was difficult when younger because patience made me the slowest one in that scavenger hunt for a little self-esteem, and I kind of realized it was a losing game but didn't know what else to do other than go with it, occasionally wondering WHEN IS THE PATIENCE GOING TO PAY OFF, but then eventually I suppose the self-esteem comes from patience itself, after hanging on for dear life for so long……."

Carly gave me a brief glare which was kind of terrifying, like at any given moment she could just say that she hated me and walk away. I realized I had been speaking casually of a decided male privilege. Still, I was pretty sure she wanted candor over protection, with the words at least. So I could not bring myself to say sorry; it felt like it would be apology for way too much. And I sure did not want her to say it either. We slipped silently back into comfort with one another after the hiccup.

"What's on your mind?"

"That I probably should have just said how enjoyable it is to be patient with you."

Carly smiled while staring at me inquisitively. It seemed that she let a thought or two pass without speaking. Then, "Are you a warlock?"

I chuckled. "Well if I am, no one's sent me a certified emoji to stick in front of my name."

We laughed together.

We remained on the floor for time unknown. Carly, well, maybe I wasn't asking good questions, my questions could be a total bore for sure, but she was not talkative and seemed to prefer me rambling about. I was fascinated by the rearrangement of everything I was accustomed to a woman protecting and sharing. It made me feel that I had become evolved enough to be let into an exclusive club. Then it made me remember that I was probably let in because of my hands. And we were off, going at her calves and thighs, tracing shapes along her back and sneaking a finger up into the top of her neck, maybe wondering but certainly not worrying if her sighs and gyrations were owing to the technique or the effort. I don't even remember how we ended up in the dark hallway, going after one another as we could see sporadic passerby, oblivious on the sidewalk, we were spurred along by slight chance of someone stopping and cupping their hands to the glass for a peek, inching slowly up the hallway in all our fury, some tiny part of us wanting the entire world to see, every successive foot a mutual agreement that the new odds brought excitement over hesitation, all of it becoming raucous to the power of taboo until we made a dive to the floor just beneath the chairs and collapsed into laughter over our peak of exposure and many other things too.

Ron did not ask over the phone why I wanted to meet him, but by the way he was making these weird 'hmmm' and 'urrrr' sounds like he was air traffic control after a thunderstorm, yeah, he knew, and set me three days out to slow my roll. Now Andrés was hitting me up for pickle, oh boy, he was shooting videos of women and being grandmaster of parades around his neighborhood park, and I was going back and forth with him since he was in on the big chair meetings at Asian Pita with the guy in long white shoes, so it seemed he had his own avenue to the goods. Carly hadn't asked for any on her way out the tanning bed door, not yet at least. It seemed she stopped just short of doing so last time by, so it wouldn't be long. At least I got out to my favorite rock to plank sideways and scissor kick, knowing my time left out there was in question and wondering if Thea had already bought a turkey and named it after me.

And now, even though it was not celebrity #ETT, patrons from the connec….tittyvity counter were at my heels and following me down the hallway, four or five of them not saying anything, just, 'hey, it's you', and my acknowledgment and smile were not enough, I got the feeling they would simply follow me anywhere, no matter how banal, so I turned at the top of the stairs and said, "Oh, I get it, you all want to see me in underwear again!", and by the time I whipped my belt through the loops, they had all sheepishly turned back to the counter, and we wouldn't have anything where silver fox had to buy schmootzies and make up a song again.

"Here's another three for you Barry. They're one-seventy five."
"Wait, what?"
"Volume discount. I usually sell for seventy apiece."
"But Ron I wanted to compliment your bulbs. Seriously, Everglades, that green heat is something else."
"Nice try Barry."
"Alright, alright."
"You spent some time in the bed?"

"Yeahehhehhheh."

Ron looked me over. As much as that mustache could hide it, I saw it. It was almost completely obscured by the big thicket, which I swore could hang there like an otter with its arms crossed even when Ron turned his head the other way. But I saw his lip twitch towards a smile for an instant before Ron summoned all his shrubbery back over the clandestine palace door. I didn't know if he could tell I noticed, so I had to assume he did. "Don't play with that third sensor in Vortex, okay."

I stopped myself before running into a wall of his frustration by asking why not. "Nah. It's just so nice to unwind with my thoughts for a bit in Everglades."

"Karim I take that back, I will go for those jerky sticks." Karim acknowledged while continuing with some powder mixing.

"It's like I can feel those frogs jumping on my shoulders and back, man, you ever do that after some physical labor?"

"No Barry I go home to Gloria. I cannot design light bulbs to make the illusion of frogs and toads throwing a lily pad party."

"Oh. Well I can dream up some crazy stuff in my loneliness but it's really good to chill after a long day." Karim set the jerky sticks, quietly, and I had the feeling he knew most, or all, of what was happening. It seemed that he avoided attempted eye contact from the both of us. Then he made way to the far end of his bar.

Ron did not go for a jerky stick. "I suppose you haven't run into Gehri over there."

"No, of course not."

"That's too bad. That weird cat could probably suggest some kind of game, for those frogs of yours."

"I don't know if he'd be too happy with me, staying around after close."

"Well that's how places work sometimes; people get fired and then become the best customers."

"Oh, I need to keep the job, especially at one-seventy five for three."

"We all have our choices to make."

"Yeah."

I broke off for a moment, kind of thinking the pause might prompt Ron to go for a stick, and throw out some wisdom. But he stared ahead, actually seeming just a bit low. It went on for too long.

"Ron, really though, I don't know how you do it. Those bulbs, they're something else."

"Ahh. A little forced creativity, and research, and we were lucky enough to find decent use……." For a second it seemed he was going to clam up on the matter. "…..decent use for some land, since redeveloping it is on hold for……well, probably on hold forever."

"Wait…..you mean? What?"

"You've probably seen the addresses."

"The old mail…..damn, the old mail! I was right!"

"What? Settle down now."

"I went by the old dry cleaner some time back….."

"Why? Oh kid, you have too much time on your hands."

"Well, yeah, but…….but what is the point with the mail? Why the mail?"

"There is no point to the mail. None at all, save for a few jobs. It's just all that's left in the area. The rest was either for a continuing business, and was grabbed, or if there was mail floating about from another shuttered business, it had to be pulled when the address was redeveloped. So those are all that's left in the neighborhood. Free advertising for nothing, for almost everyone."

"So you keep it hush…..keep the technology secret?"

"Sure, but it's more on the down low to keep the damn city away. The groundwater is all tested, it's totally safe in those bulbs. We could give the city all that documentation and samples, open and closed, they could verify with their own experts, if that's how it worked. But in reality, if they get wind of this, they'll shutter tanning bed temporarily, order the same tests, some asshole will literally sit at a desk and make up new permits, and we'll be a few hundred grand into those thieves, for extracting contaminated water from the ground and setting some of it securely behind glass bulbs……" I could tell he wanted to pound his fist on the wood. "…..all from properties that they initially approved for redevelopment and then reversed course for no clear reason other than they already got us on the hook for the taxes." He really had to take a breath there. It was scary.

"Yeah. Sorry. But, as it is, amazing, really."

"Well, thanks. We're happy with it all, hopefully it can stay that way. I better get moving here."

"Of course."

Ron's story of resourcefulness, and the considerable hit for those pickles, had me inspired. We needed funds, or the good times were going to freeze up and we'd be caught shaking our fists at a November slush, icing our hair for months. I was pretty sure the date was coming up soon, and checked to see that it was a week out. It was too perfect. An #ETT to boot. We had to try and clean up before the wind picked off the leaves and buried the video beneath a new season.

Brianne was at tanning bed too when I tossed Andrés a pickle and began working him in on the realities of the situation. And then the realities of Mexican Independence Day, "El Grito!" he shouted at my first mention, how he probably knew that everyone went out and fell on their face every Cinco de Mayo, even while far too many erroneously thought that was the independence day. So we'd catch that #ETT line outside the connec….tittyvity counter and start the celebration right then and there, hitting them with as many tee shirts and selling them chips and salsa and tamales and guacamole and probably making for the best time any of them would have in a month. Brianne was on the edge of the big chair, hysterical with some crazy image of the scene, blowing up at every word of my pitch. Andrés, however, was reserved, maybe even close to downright opposed. That was, until I told him it was definitely his photo to orchestrate for the tee shirt. Then we were in business.

"You wearing the pants and…..and…..me hitting you with the toalla……no, no, too much hurt, no toalla……..maybe me having a vihuela, playing vihuela……no piñata, no way…...Barry maybe it say El Grito, maybe saying……you wearing the pants and me……me with vihuela….no……El Grito y el gringo…….Dia de los Muertes……no, too much, too much, maybe…….shiiit….."

He slowed from his brainstorming, but still pacing with shoulders up and head down. Brianne had fallen back in the chair, and motioned to speak before reconsidering.

"Me thinking……thinking…….la comida too much pequena……vihuela, no…..no…….MAN."

"Andrés, *baby*, how about you wear *those tights* that Barry had on in the video?"

It was perfect. I kept a straight face for a minute to stay out of it, and Andrés went for it immediately.

"Yeah yeah! Me wearing the tights and you having no pants, me wearing the flag! El Grito! Maybe kicking the futbol at you! You having no pants and me kicking the futbol at you!"

I laughed. Here we went again. "I love it. Okay, we need to get the photo soon so there's time to print the shirts. We'll make some food……they won't know what hit 'em."

I was circling my chin into the small of Carly's back to the brassy musings of the music's full wander. The warm tones of Bronzeville pooled into instrumental glares on her skin and I chased them across time signatures. Her face was an intimate cabaret of unbroken sultry lines and her eyes played the room with understated magnificence of slow motion from another era. It was our first time in there; it seemed our hungry experimentation would be chewing through drywall in search of hot wires in tanning bed, soon enough. We were floating about on intermingled saxophone fluttering when I heard a noise.

"Did you hear that?"

"There's always strange sounds that seem out of place in the jazz."

"No, I heard something, for sure……"

The music crawled into open space a few moments later, and it was unmistakable then. Footsteps.

"Uh oh." Carly whispered into my chest. "Do you think someone broke in?"

"Maybe….I don't know why they would, but maybe."

I jumped out and threw on my pants, trembling. I did not feel very manly about my impending burst into the hallway. All the foreplay was like throwing a boomerang into the distance and if there was interruption before it came back around, well, I had been in better states to face confrontation. I had been dreaming up some menacing poses to make a bluff that I could really unload at any second, so there was that, I supposed. The steps seemed like leather soles, nearing the front. I held out hope that it was Andrés, that he had discovered the secrets of the beds on his own accord.

"What should I do?"

"Besides get dressed and lock the door behind me, I don't know……"

"Be careful Barry….."

"I'll do my best…." But I probably shot her a look like, nice knowing you, I'm about to be badgered by a meth freak too stupid to hit a place with cash. I pushed into the hallway. A voice rolled in from the front and the source of nervousness immediately changed. Gehri. There was nothing to do but come clean. Well, sort of, of course. I moved a few steps into view. He was with a woman in a full length dress and a guy wearing a beige suit and holding a large plate of nicely arranged sushi. "Gehri, I'm sorry, I was gonna lock up as always and then my girlfriend stopped by and we couldn't decide where to go and just wanted to talk for a bit I'm sorry I don't want to take advantage........"

He laughed. A kind one too, not one of those at the satisfaction of his devised torture. "Please, please, Barry. I am....elated....that you have discovered this for yourself. Do not let us interrupt you for another moment. These are my friends Nadine, and Vincent."

"Hi." They nodded. We were all of quick understanding that the small talk was off.

I looked back at Gehri, kind of waiting for him to tell me something more. But he just stood there, his wavy black hair messed in a way so many others tried to arrange, and all the defined, prominent features of his face making it an unlikely one to state nothing, but it really felt that way right then.

"Oh, yeah, okay, well I'll get out of your hair, or way, now, yeah.....be outta here soon."

"We were simply in the neighborhood and I wished to show Nadine and Vincent the place, briefly."

I waved, smiled, and turned. I didn't think that was true for a second.

Carly must have been glued to the door, trying to listen, when I knocked. She pressed into me, looking up with beautiful concern, as I shut the door and restarted the music.

"It's the owner. I'm not completely sure I'm home free, he might have been that way in front of his friends, but I don't think so. I think he was honestly glad to see me doing this."

Carly rubbed her palm on my chest, ready to not wait another second, as if the entire ordeal was simply another unpredictable touch. I chuckled and shook my head. "They……his friends, this perfect tray of sushi he was holding……what the hell."

"Are they staying?"

"Oh yeah, they're up to something good and weird……."

Carly looked surprised that my hands weren't at work again already. "Is everything okay?"

"Yeah…yeah, just that feeling of, you know, being at the boss's house…..it's that curse of the dutiful employee…." I moved to sit on the edge of the bed, able to faintly hear Gehri and friends moving into Vortex. "……probably nothing a little more pickle can't solve….."

She brought herself to my new speed so effortlessly, so seamlessly, and it really was pleasant. "Did it look like they had a dragon roll?"

"*What?*"

"A dragon roll!"

"Is there something I don't know about a dragon roll?"

"No you freak! I've only had sushi three or four times in my life, and I always remember the dragon roll."

"Oh haha….okay cool, yeah, I don't know…….it's just, oh shit, they were all standing there dressed to the nines, the guys likely have just a few years on me but it's like they saw me and it was like they were thinking to themselves, yeah, eighteen, those were the good times…..you know, I get that look sometimes from people and it's so apparent they have never known prolonged loneliness, they've never been unwanted."

"What's wrong with *that?*"

"Oh nothing, just strange.......I guess......I'd been fancying myself as a man of experience and then all of the sudden it feels like I'm supposed to get back to my biology homework......"

"You're a goof. How about we order a dragon roll? My treat!"

"Wait....what?"

"Let's order delivery, there has to be a place open."

"Oh....I don't know if we should."

"*Come* on! You said it yourself how little it seemed they were bothered about us being here......"

"Okay......just leave a message for them to text from the back door when they're here.......now, about that pickle........"

"You're off the rail with those things."

"Our fundraiser will have it covered."

"Hold that thought."

We lied and talked. The room began to feel larger than ever, after really shrinking for a little bit. But still, the feeling that we were breaking some rule had slipped from the situation at tanning bed, and to the situation of us. Almost like we were so happy to frolic in our liberation from respective societal constraints, until that escape itself became the restraint, and a room at tanning bed our only refuge. But it was all too clear that neither of us were itching to jump back into what the world had waiting for us, even when I could tell it was going to call her first. Anyway, yeah, the pickle was at it again, and the sushi text came none too soon. When Carly went to grab it I had a freaky thought that she might knock on the Vortex door and suddenly there'd be a little too much dragon roll and distinguished gentlemen going on. But she came back in with a smile for all of the simple things.

"Did you hear anything across the hall?"

"I don't…….*know*?" Carly made another new face, like all at once it was flush with an intrigue of goats about to mate, and the disquiet of actually seeing it. It was adorable.

"Yeah, I'll learn my own twisted tricks if it comes to having to do it."

"There were noises, maybe some of it was the music……….it reminded me of being alone and bored and seeing a couple through their window across the street, just cooking dinner together or something, but suddenly I become so convinced that they're about to get into it that I'm making up a story in the space between."

"Yeahhh…..of course. Normal……*stuff.*"

"Shut up! Jerk!" Carly swatted me on the chest. "Let's eat this."

"Is it squid in there?"

"I think it's eel."

"Like one of those morays from dolphin drone?"

"There's enough personality in the room without you giving one to our dinner."

After we ate, I could tell Carly wanted to start up, and I did too. Something remained different though. Gehri's presence made me feel on the clock, as if I should have been walking around offering bottled waters and warm towels. Carly must have sensed this. She had me turn the bed back on and then get down to my boxers and lay on my back on the floor, telling me to close my eyes and forget where I was. She stood over me and traced this toe and that across me, and my eyes found themselves little pillows up there as she teased and brushed with her feet, and I was exactly halfway asleep and off in some distant instrumental place, coming to for the occasional instance of another one of her clothing articles hitting the floor, and I laid right there while going further away, her toes communicating to me across some wide divide, like I could feel all of her from planets away just through a brush of her foot, losing all sense of my own proportion and shape to those gentle lines until it all came rushing back in a blurred immersion of her against me, and Bronzeville was aflame with the crazy smooth electricity of her skin and mad implosion of her easy patience.

A lot of the #ETT crowd probably woke up thinking they only got one holiday for the day, until, BAM, Andrés and I would drop the double holiday on them and turn the street upside down with food and dancing and tee shirts. I had seventy-five printed at the rough estimate of selling to one of every three people outside the connec....tittyvity counter. Andrés did the tamales and I had my guacamole and chips all portioned out, Andrés shook off my departure from traditional ingredients, but it had been gringo approved, many times over. We had the combo package all ready for when they fell out at the screen print of me hunched and naked, cupping my junk with both hands while Andrés wore the flag tights and kicked a soccer ball at my ass.

We both pulled our two red wagons down the sidewalk, having minor difficulties with the nicefoam blue hashtags foiling up the wheels. Both of us were loaded with all three products so we could start up at opposite ends of the line and spark up the wick from each direction. It was daybreak for awareness, even if some of that awareness was the kind from abundance of pickle.

The crowd came into view from a distance. It was a good one, and still building for sure. This was gonna be a celebrity #ETT for them to talk about until, well, probably just until megapixel, but still.
"Okay, remember how little time we have for them to be trying on sizes. We put all three items for forty in their mitts and work backwards from there if need be."
"Hecho en Mexico. El Grito!"
"Yep. Let's check our pay transmitters one more time, then go start the wildfire."
"You eating the pickle? Me wanting calm, too much excited."
"Well, it only seems fitting......"
We stood for a moment, nodding and scratching our bellies, composing ourselves with a nice sour chew.
"There's a link to buy the shirt on our video site too, for when we run out of them here."
"My friends they liking the picture, they buying, wearing."

We pulled the wagons closer and began to sense the general cocktail of interest and suspicion which permeated the most basic of street commerce. There was a fair deal of pointing and, I could only guess, discussion of whether we were the official celebrities for this #ETT.

The colors were predominantly navy, black, and grey, the spacing and posture very much dictated by some unspoken more, and it had been awhile since I hadn't swum through this on my way into martbar. If I took one more step without asserting our presence I might have just given up and wheeled the barrels under a tree, to gorge myself on the food. "HEY! IT'S MEXICAN INDEPENDENCE DAY! HAPPY INDEPENDENCE DAY!"

"La revolucion! El Grito! Diez y seis de septiembre.........Michoacan de Ocampo!"

They stirred. I might have become recognized from our video. "We have tee shirts and snacks......it's a flash fiesta! Happy holidays!"

We arrived at the tail end of the line. Andrés and I shared a nod before separating. "I taking back the pants from the gringo, me wearing the flag, kicking......HAhahehehehaha......"

"Damn good tamales folks you won't get this stuff in the corn flakes."

I rolled through the heart of the line, smiling, expecting to be stopped eagerly for product. I unfurled a shirt, nodding, but being met with questions which seemed to want some verification of credential, above all else. I fought off the rising sadness of thinking how many had been to a Mexican beach and impulsively waved off what could have been the best lunch of their life from a family which dragged it from the sea a few hours prior. "Have you seen the video? Here's the sequel to the video......"

I did not have much in the tank for the disregard. I had to remind myself that I had spent three winter months standing on downtown sidewalks for entire days, fundraising. "It's a holiday guys! Let's celebrate!"

"It's #ETT!"

"Where's our real celebrity?"

I sank to the reality that celebrity was not about popularity or notoriety so much as a dose of validation that they were making the best of their free time. I turned back to see Andrés, it appeared he had made a few sales, but there was certainly not a wave of tees and food washing out the block. When I spun back, deflated and hesitant, I was face to face with a woman, definitely of Latin heritage, buttoned up in navy, hair pulled into a tie, looking as if years ago she reached for a morsel of security, then blinked, and suddenly all of the generations of her soul were bound down further within, even special occasions becoming futile to untie the knots. And for an instant, the weight I felt in front of her was unbearable, I wanted to jump in the lake and never come out. I'll never know if that was what sold her. She went for the full package and reached deep for her youth, pulling up an intoxicating bomb of carefree energy, blowing out a million smithereens all thundering some tone of YOU'RE DAMN RIGHT IT'S BEEN TOO LONG SINCE I'VE BEEN OUT. Oooh, was she dancing. It was way too much to be good and way too much to be bad. I was smiling. It was hers from long ago, right now, and it was beyond contagious. We were in business. Others could not help but feel the tap into their depths. I had to hang back for a moment, to let them all settle into their mad jags before offering up more fuel. There was screaming and singing and some really alien looking moves, and I was thrilled to see it. It seemed Andrés had even caught some momentum at the other end. It was madness. Within a minute or so I saw a man shooting the double finger pistols into the sky, someone try a backspin which made it about one-quarter turn, and there were screams of both 'La Bamba!' and 'Cinco de Mayo!'.

I had inched back in and began trading on the wings of the positive energy when I heard a few deep clunking sounds just up the block, on the other side of the street. I had never seen Kid Tippy roll the wheels over the top of a parked good coupe before. Then he did it again, and alarms sounded, and a siren cleared its throat for its first high loop. I hoped I was wrong about what was happening. He dropped from a charcoal hood and spun in the middle of the street as the squad buggy peeled around the corner. I got all pushy trying to move product quickly, but most everyone was both dancing and taking in the new developments, and waved to Andrés to make sure he was also on the hard sell. Kid Tippy made one last jump onto a good coupe, no head cam but of course wearing his patented camo tights and beige turtleneck tee. Things had been a little testy with him ever since our video blew up, and this, well, I hoped against all odds and made another desperate go with the merchandise. But then Tippy made a real stylish spin-stop with his arms high, right in front of the squad buggy, and then I sank as he produced some kind of identification to the cop, who immediately stood down. He was the licensed #ETT celebrity and, well, you learn something new every day about what that kind of stuff will allow somebody to get away with. It had all happened so fast that I never thought to run the wagons around the side of the building and hope I could bring them back after the smoke had cleared. But now the heat was on us, you know, to protect, I don't know, whatever. I pulled the wagons towards Andrés as the officer moved towards him too, and traded death glares with Kid Tippy before he drifted into the line with a bunch of horseshit lines about how great they all were and other nice things he probably barely ever said to his friends and family. But I wanted to get to the officer before he mistook Andrés' excitable speech for some kind of challenge to his authority.

"Hey, officer, we're just trying to get people to celebrate Mexican Independence Day with a little of this and that, maybe that'd be okay for another half an hour or so?"

"Ya you got your vendors' licenses?" He looked exactly like one of the four heads sculpted from bronze at football barn entrance, distinguished members of The 1985 Super Bowl Champions and Best Defense Ever Chicago Bears.

"Noooooo……..no, we don't."

"You need dose vendor licenses ta be out here."

"I know, I know, the waiting period is forever, and this was a spur of the moment thing…….just half an hour, please….." I turned to a guy who had run up to my wagon and taken a guacamole. "HEY!" He turned away without response, or even eye contact. I looked to the officer for a little help with that.

"You see, da vendor's license proteicts you from dat kind of stuff."

"*Please*. It's a holiday."

"#ETT."

"Mexican Independence Day."

"El Grito! El Grito!"

"Sure it is, pal. In Mexico. But right here, it's #ETT."

"Well, technically speaking, the holiday is inside. They are waiting in line for the holiday." A few more dared a grab for some food, and I was down to a depressed head shake to deal with it, before pulling the wagons between us.

"They're well within dere rights ta be out here."

"I know, but, really, the holiday is the waiting. The only reason the holiday exists is because so many people will wait, to be first. They are waiting to be first. And we're just trying to help them enjoy the wait, maybe even forget about it, maybe even a few will break their cycle of always waiting to be first."

"Well that's a real hero effort, pal. But you can't be selling out here without a license. You two haveta walk it away, or else we'll have to go through the whole show at the station."

"Fine. Okay."

Andrés and I looked at each other, and I could tell he was low about far more than lost sales, too. We pulled our wagons along, heads down, quiet. Some guy ran out of line, I saw him peripherally, and just as he was about to lunge for some food I flinched my torso at him with the arm cocked behind, and that backed him up quick. He stood away, all stupid-faced, and I tossed a tamale at him and said, 'on us', making the poor bastard sure that I felt sorry for him. But as we pulled the carts away, I kind of wished I had spiked the thing at his feet and made him pick it off the pavement if he needed a free snack that bad before dropping an inflated sum on a new charger module inside.

It just would not sit still anymore. The breezes had been moderate for a few days, giving me hope, but it was foolish hope all stemming from my growing desperation to recapture just a touch of that summer chill, where the moment I sank into that tranquil and clear water the rest of the day was easy bliss radiating through me and off me and seeming to have a calming effect on everyone and everything around. Now it seemed as if one little burp of wind a few hundred miles up sent a bunch of wrinkled plaid down the long right arm of the Great Lakes caricature, and all of the cross-hatching rolled and bounced off of shorelines, gaining dimensions with every ricochet, tireless in its unsettled roil so that a dip into the water felt like a struggle against a hundred unsettled thoughts, coming endlessly from every direction and no resolution in sight until they were weighed over by ice. Don't get me wrong, it was still better than not going into the lake. But one surprise morning of placidity would have gone a long way towards the nonsense at the #ETT falling from me, and maybe even some extremely clear thoughts about what to do about the pickle situation.

There was always the brief consideration that it could be all she wrote, just before I lowered myself in. It wasn't all tight rope over a gorge, only a healthy reminder that nature did not know and could not care if I got myself into a bad spot within its grips. It was nice that nature would tell it straight what the world, by nature, always lied about. The world at large would keep you afloat for decades in a catatonic state, adrift and senseless, selling you thermal gear and prescriptions and subscriptions and intoxicants, popcorn and data and lifecoach and vocabulary, selling you just about anything and everything besides a shitty old five-pound chunk of concrete pick axed out of infrastructure past that would be just heavy enough to drag you under with all the stuff if you didn't fight to stop buying.

I had found two rocks at the far edge of the range where I could alternate contact with the hands and feet, and have the best contingency to push off into safety if the balance became shaky. That was pretty key, having that predetermined movement that I could fall off into if the situation got sketchy. I had my hands cupped and arms extended, being tossed back and forth pretty good, and I really wanted to think that it was all bad luck that Kid Tippy drew the police to our little party, but the water was pushing at me with too much weight from every direction to dismiss the strong chance he did it all to get rid of us. I stewed on those thoughts until my palms were raw, and then dropped back onto the next stone, lowering my feet very slowly until they made contact and then letting my legs and hips go floppy so I could move with the water instead of fighting the worst of all battles. Financially, at least, our morning debacle was not a total catastrophe. And the shirts were moving, nothing major, but moving along from the video site and maybe just weird enough to be swept into a passing fad. I waved my arms about in the loosely patterned chop, somewhat worried over Andrés. Part of me hoped he'd walk in with a sweet woman with a smile and a nod which I'd know to mean he was finished with the pickle stuff.

Getting back out was the toughest part. The rocks were closer to the surface and the waves caught me in too many directions at the snap of a finger as they bounded off the wall. It was probably a ten minute ordeal, navigating the last four or five stones, bracing and holding while feeling out the next move. Finally I grabbed the ladder, all of my thoughts pumped out from the many loud heartbeats of survival alone. I toweled off my head and threw on the sweatshirt, and then bounded up the terrace beneath the thick sweep and tumble of the sky and knowing quiver of the greenery, fueled into the day with hopes that Carly would come by tanning bed later on.

Very strange that Gehri had put out a doupon for tanning bed, where doupon had all these people who followed around one doupon after another and counted up all the money they saved through doupon even if they would not have gone to any of the places anyway without the doupon, and then always posting on yak with their outstanding opinions about all the great and easy changes the places could make before they came back, if there was ever another doupon offering. Anyway, the doupons were usually for businesses low on cash and even shorter on ideas, so that's why it was weird that Gehri put one out. And, peeking at it, it had this weird verbiage about being 'a wonderfully sensual experience' and 'a retreat for the rich and famous' and it all stunk like a trio of farts from every corner of the food pyramid.

Anyway, I saw this about an hour before leaving for work, so had enough time for the irritation to wane so I could think clearly enough to grab the tee shirts and buy some green food coloring for the leftover guacamole.

Here came the thundering herd. Already two standing
outside after a pull on the front door and peeking at
their phones and then in at me, as if their clock was a
golden church key to unlock it. I gave them a dry face
after finished hanging up a sample tee and arranging
guacamole along the counter, opening at three after the
hour. All of the beds were full just a minute later, and
then what sucked is I had others sitting in both of the
chairs, waiting for the half hour to be up, but at least my
line about the guacamole, I don't even know what I said,
something like the avocado was crucial for oxidizing the
reverse fat cells beneath the bulbs, but at least that was
working, along with my inability to smile until they
transmitted a few bucks of gratuity along too.
Tomorrow I would have to buy an industrial-sized tub
of lotion and mix in some of the unused cilantro and
ancho chili flakes with an eight-dollar suggestion to rub
two-ounces of plastic cup worth on an aching joint.

There was a couple in the big chair who thought they
could use one doupon to share a bed, and threatened for
a moment to contact doupon when I said no, and I swear
the words 'get out' were steamrolling up from my gut
when something caught them in a nick of time, and out
came 'well I can break the rules just for you two if you
spend fifty on merchandise', and they went for it, but it
still was awful that there was another twenty minutes
wait and the couple was intermittently talking with a
girl, whose sitting in the weird chair didn't really count,
they were looking up from their phones every so often
to share their disappointment with last doupon at ball
pen. The house phone was ringing a lot too from
doupon holders who wanted parking recommendations,

and some still thinking of purchasing who wanted me to tell them exactly what 'sensual experience' meant, and then one guy who asked if he could bring in a dog under ten pounds, and I said fine by me but the sous chef next door might think differently, then immediately clicked off the call and ate some pickle right in front of everyone, saying it was the best diet when you couldn't afford the guacamole, which I then hit again with food coloring when no one was looking.

Brianne burst in, arms flying upward at swing of the door, and I barely had my hands up in a shrug when we shared a look of understanding, and then Brianne stood right over the couple in the big chair, and said, "Excuuuuuse me, darlings, this is my chair here, MMMMkay, *thanks*," and they got up and stood awkwardly against the wall as Brianne plopped down. "Andrés told me about your issues at the #ETT, sorry honey, if it weren't so early ole Brianne would have drawn away the sarge with the tweedle pop the badge boys all love soooo much." Brianne stood and did the one-two-three hip gyration right in front of the standing couple, then sat again.
"Ha, thanks……it was Kid Tippy's *big day* so what can you do."
Brianne noticed the guacamole on the counter and checked off the next words. "That's right. Shake it off and go home to change the setting on the shower head….."
I laughed. Bless Brianne's heart, always taking it right at the audience. "Yeah, something like that."
Another doupon holder came through the door and before I could even give the guy a forlorn greeting, Brianne just shook the head no and froze the guy in his

tracks. "No no no sweetie, you've got a long way to go still, go do some livin' and check back in a year or two……okay bye bye." The little hand wave brush off too. I'd never know how Brianne could pull this stuff off.

"But I'm……." He looked at everyone else for support. The girl in the weird chair was practically eating her phone, and the couple, I think they were halfway through the drywall. "I'm a……I already bought the doupon!"

"Sure sure, you'll have no problem trading that for some pills, or better yet a nice five-minute butt tickle…..second alley down thataway, you'll run into the right people."

"That's not……um……." He did a few double-takes before heading back to the door, probably to contact doopon.

"Too much messy! Guacamole on the floor too much messy! PHHHH…."

Oh boy. "Andrés you know how important that avocado is for the upside-down carbonation, there's been a little spilled about before….."

"Nah, man, too much dirty, I going next door, changing, finding cloths." Andrés threw an arm in the air and stomped back down the hallway.

"Okay, you two are up in Everglades, clock starts right now, don't miss the first whoosh of the crocodile tail through the marsh!"

They were all too ready to go into any other room. Another woman came in, gnawing around a direct complaint that she was supposed to be in a bed six minutes ago, and I snapped out, "well there's a bunch of spillover traffic over at Asian Pita and the food runner called off to do a puppet show, and the corporate handbook clearly spells out that Andrés has to fill in and get the dishes out hot before he comes over to clean the beds but that one general motorcycle dish over there is fantastic if you'd like to relax with a bite while you wait."

Head returning to the phone, body returning to the sidewalk……

Brianne leaned into the girl in the other chair. "Any fresh videos of water bondage going around that you'd like to share with Brianne?"

"I'm…..water balms?......I'm doing my grocery shopping right now."

"HOW DO YOU PICK OUT A *CUCUMBER* WITHOUT GOING TO THE STORE? BARRY, HOW? How *on earth* do you pick a cucumber without going in the store?"

"I don't know! I don't know! AAHAHAHAHAH! Oh shit!"

I was still laughing when another couple arrived in my face and I don't even know what they wanted because I just kept laughing, and made one tiny effort to stop but Brianne just made sure to spark it up again, so I probably just laughed in front of them for about two minutes before they just walked out.

We were barely ninety minutes into the day and Andrés had simply left spray bottles, towels, and Asian Pita margarita glasses, with 'propina' in marker, in all three rooms. I promised him more pickle for tomorrow, then picked up my phone and shouted, "Hey it's Barry, I need twenty, can meet anytime before two tomorrow, let me know, please, thank you" into Ron's voicemail, instead of dealing with whomever Brianne hadn't already scared off and happened to be in my face, Brianne's attention turned a bit to all of the juicy takes trending on yak over what a weird and horrible place tanning bed was.

It just went on forever. They came and went and for all I knew all of the madness was the best chance they'd have in there at an actual experience, if they were even looking for that, at least. It wasn't long before I met any complaints or qualms over time by just recounting the story of the video in the tights, or singing the song from martbar that one day, or simply closing my eyes and stretching until I opened them and they were gone. The phone ringer was off by six-thirty and that guy never showed up with his tiny dog, but there was a mother who pushed in a stroller and I let it slide for twenty bucks worth of guacamole and then might have heard of the mess from the next person into that room, but it was tough to say, I might have turned it all into visions of trees and grass and the lake and been swimming around behind the counter for a few minutes. And, then, it all disappeared at the snap of a finger, nine o'clock, nothing at all, and I double-checked the doupon for some hour restriction, but there wasn't one, it just seemed to be universal curfew in the consumer realm. I stood there alone, hoping like never before that Carly would stop by, I still had no other way to reach her, and it was a very long two hours of standing there alone, flinching at every form that appeared outside at the hope it was her, then walked it off like no big deal each time it was not, until the last twenty minutes reprised into dull reality, and then I locked up while not especially looking forward to dumping a bunch of cash in Ron's hands come morning.

I went under almost immediately after leaving my apartment, as everyone on the street looked like a doupon holder about to demand perfection, so I had to flail and dive and twirl in the deep to avoid all of the hassle until the inevitable stuck a hook in me later on at night two of the doupon doubleheader.

There was post-holiday lull when I surfaced at connec....tittyvity, not a customer in sight. That was not the shock of the moment. The magician was on the right, his suit blending into the wall, and three others behind the counter on the left in their usual shirts, and I spun back and forth a few times to recheck that I was facing martbar and not the street, then stood there all wobbly for a moment waiting for someone, anyone, to say, 'rearrangement' or 'redecoration', but they all just planted stoic, not even a tiny gesture from the magician, and I made one more fail at looking down towards martbar for everything to be as I'd known, but the sides were still flipped, and I fell over. I was on the floor and things weren't really spinning as much as the counters on both sides seemed to be shooting closer and then rippling back away, and still not a word from anyone as I tried to prop my forearms and hold my head and make it all stop. But there were no signs of it fading, the violent reverberations moving the walls in and out, they kept on, and I knew full well not to even try and stand, so I crawled on my hands and knees, little by little, for what seemed to be a very long and painful time, that twenty feet, until I got one hand on the first stair down and felt a touch better, but still did not dare to try and

stand until fumbling down all three stairs, as much as I didn't want to draw too much attention to my entrance.
"GOOD MORNING EVERYONE!"
There was a good deal of laughter about the room, amongst the seven or eight in the place. I looked for Karim's reaction immediately, that was most important, and saw he had a half-smile going, and that allowed me to ease into my walk, definitely light-headed but feeling okay.
"You ate two of your jerky sticks already?"
"I don't think it's breaking news that I meet others in here too Barry."
"Oh, yeah.....of course, but....."
"Did you trip over your shoelaces up there?"
"I had doupon to deal with all last night."
"Barry what you stick up your ass is your business but I certainly don't want to hear about it."
"Come on, Ron, it's a shared advertising thing. And it brought in like a hundred people who are clueless and trying to know everything the minute they spend a buck."
"Huh. That doesn't sound like Gehri."
"No it caught me off-guard."
"But he did say something to me about whether I had time and resources to help him open another location......so......."
"Really? Why?"
"I don't know. But maybe he's feeling out the demand right now."
"Well if that's gonna be the crowd at a new one you might as well save your special bulb liquids......and the prints on the walls......and the music......yeah, probably just hang some sheets from rods and public school lighting in the ceilings, that'll do....."

"Oh, Mr. Experience here, a tanning bed connoisseur from the very beginning, how quickly we forget."

"No, it's not all that Ron, really……Karim! Hey Karim, would you ever put out a doupon for martbar?"

"Most certainly not. No private events, no doupon, and of course, no chariot racing as well." Karim set down my bonus juice.

"Well unless these people clubbed your knees last night, I fail to see how they're responsible for you crawling to the stairway."

"Everything was all backwards up there when I……..never mind."

"Sure, sure, you were just making your case for why I should sell you twenty of these. Wonderful pitch, Barry. I would've gone with the incomprehensible babbling myself, but hey, that's just me."

"Well, you know, it doesn't *have* to be twenty; ten or a dozen would be fine, it was just a number I threw out in the heat of the rush last night."

Ron went for his last jerky stick, fiddled with it for a moment, and waved it under his nose. But then he set it back onto the napkin. "I don't want to get into another argument over time here, especially since I have so much less of it than you appear to. Can we agree that it was under two months ago when you first tasted a pickle?"

"Yes."

"Okay. Under two months ago. And, let's just say, give or take, somewhere around two weeks before I gave you a few more. Now, here we are, ten minutes ago you crawled like an infant to the stairs, after asking me for twenty last night."

"I'm committing to a good winter. I don't want to wake up and see snow and have none, and say to myself, well, I'll just sit here and eat canned tuna until April….."

"I'm not going anywhere."

"No, of course not. But I asked for twenty last night and am ready to pay for twenty today. I've already pocketed five or six hundred bucks between Mexican Independence Day, outside there….." I waved my hand at the street. "…..and last night at tanning bed, hell, I might match that tonight with all the stuff I have lined up for these doupon holders….."

"Wait, let's back this up a bit. Are you sitting here right now with the audacity to tell me, let along the audacity to do it…..you are telling me you've been *selling* PICKLES over the counter at tanning bed?"

"Nooo……..NO. Come on Ron……" I edited off the recollection of eating one over the counter, though. "…..tee shirts, guacamole……tonight some special lotion and some cucumber slices all dressed up with some mystical herbs and spices, you know, to rest beneath the goggles."

"Well that's……better….I suppose? What on earth are you telling them to sell all this?"

"I am telling them that I am pursuing happiness and I would like their money."

Ron and I stared at each other. His lip was jumping up again, and the mustache was covering it over, but it kept sneaking up over and over, and he definitely knew I was seeing it. His eyes though, man, they were car headlights backed in deep behind the garage roof, absolutely lit on full beam, but, like, no driver, no engine running, just lights that were always on, had always been on, had been drawing from some tiny power source buried in a corner behind some storage boxes since, like, forever ago, and no one would ever be able to dig it out, but everyone knew that it would always keep the lights on. And so, needless to say, even though Ron was most definitely suppressing a laugh, I had not a clue if it was a laugh that he was just sold on twenty, or a laugh that he was just sold on zero. And the longer we stared, the more I realized that I was not going to find that out. So, in time the headlights just kept blaring, and that was another thing about Ron, you know, he always had other places to be, but then times came when he made it very clear that he could sit and stare for a very long time to not talk next. And by the time I opened my mouth, I could remember the general gist of our conversation, but not the specifics of where we left it.

"Listen Ron, if you think you made a mistake in judgment ever giving me one of these, just say so."

"WHAT WAS THAT?"

I could see the source in his eyes now. "When you first had me run one with the cash, if you think that was a mistake to get me started in the first place, just tell me it was a mistake and I'll move on, find something else or find it from someone else……"

"Barry I hope you're not forgetting the mistake you made of letting the magician take you on that ride. Do you remember that Barry? That was after I gave you the first pickle. And also after we had a very grave discussion over the perils of it all."

"You think that was a mistake Ron. But I don't. I don't think I made a mistake at all with that. And I don't think you made a mistake giving me that first one, either. But that doesn't matter. If you think you made a mistake then I'll go by that."

"Barry you are still a long way from seeing the full complexity of the issue here."

"Maybe so. But it still seems simple for you to either think you made a mistake in judgment or not."

"Well it's not."

"So if you can't say for sure that it was a mistake, then I don't see how you don't sell to me today."

I knew pretty well when Ron was burning to just punch me dead in the nose. I never felt like he would actually do it, but maybe it was that way because I was always just a little wary of a slight chance he might. Anyway, right then he was feeling those meaty knuckles crunching in and me wobbling and then falling off my stool. I supposed the best I could draw from it was not to say the word 'mistake' again.

"I'm not taking your money today Barry. Forty, fifty or so hours of work, nothing too technical or grueling. I'll have something for you over the next few months, not on a crew, I'll be there. You and me. We'll work it around your tanning bed schedule."

"Labor? But I have the cash right here!"

"That's over thirty an hour. Or, I tell you what, I'll also give you the option of paying me two grand even, one month from today."

"A hundred a pop?"

"The shit isn't marked retail at bighome, Barry. Some work, or two grand in a month."

The clever bastard. He knew I'd have to either sell enough off myself to justify the payment, or be of wary of staying strong enough for the labor, even if he probably already forgot about my merchandise sales at tanning bed. I was frustrated and baffled right then that somehow he had all the cards again. "Alright. Labor or two grand in a month."

We shook on it.

I had gone overboard with the green food coloring. So I grabbed the blue, yellow, red, brown, and purple, it was only available in the six-pack the day before, and, well, sometimes I could get to acrylic painting and the best part of it was layering more and more on top of the abstract disaster until it eventually covered up the hacky effort to be a pro with enough carefree amateur brushes and splotches and dabbles to like it. That must have been the source of my confidence with the food coloring, no test on a little bit of the guac first, no, I just began dropping colors in the tub, dancing around and shaking my head to the music and arbitrarily grabbing four colors at once in a crazy double-fisted pass over the tub, then firing off an air guitar solo, pretty sure that one full lick at the end of it would turn everything into a perfect color, but then when it did not, I hit it again with several bottles, stirred it up real bass line, then did a few awesome ballet moves, checked and dumped again, picked up the hula hoop I'd pulled from behind the dumpster, but I couldn't do the hula hoop, it fell really quickly, something to practice over the winter, one more pass over the tub, gyrating the whole while, then super mick moves into the other room, and some really good bird wing flapping for awhile, on and on, you get the idea, until the guacamole was absolutely perfect and ready to go, not a question about it because, well, all of the food coloring bottles were empty, so that was a pretty clear stopping point. It was, um, well, sometimes in the winter there were some blades of grass shooting up through a thick clump of dead and damp leaves, maybe one or two with a few orangey veins trickling in pattern, and a few of those yellow helicopter leaves sprinkled on top and nestled against the scattered green blades, quite rustic and nostalgic, actually, but thankfully never ruined outside for me by a dousing of the blue port-o-potty liquid atop it all. So I began scouring everything in the apartment for some vocabulary for the color, even if the day before was any indication I would just be saying whatever the hell I felt like after an hour or so.

The special heat-activated lotion would definitely not require so much verbiage. The ground cilantro and ancho chili flakes, well look at that, there we were with the red, white, and green again, and I liked knowing there was something for a laugh with Andrés right from the get-go. Also, the cucumber slices, after getting about fifty pairs cut from the four veggies, I took the effort to customize the size and shapes before brushing them with banana goo so the fresh ginger and star anise and old town spice house mix would stay put on one side and most certainly activate neural recepticons and sensory browsing, oooh yeah, that's a good one, sensory browsing, that would all kick inside the bed, and if we could sell them all, some quick math revealed that six dollars worth of cucumber could be turned into four pickles, even at the full hundred a pop I'd pay Ron to prove I could ferment too, and never have to be chastened for being left-handed around the spatial properties of a fucking two-by-four.

I had to take one last look see through the cabinet. There were odd relics aplenty in the rear. Half a bottle of ketchup, yes, ketchup, seriously, a glass container of ketchup back there, the color of what had crusted around the neck such a vivid rust that I thought for a minute of scraping out a single ounce to try and fix two gallons of blue tinted guacamole. Then I got caught wondering for a moment if I had actually packed and moved that bottle of ketchup from my previous apartment a decade ago. Also, jellied cranberry. Of course. Well some kind of Thanksgiving must have not happened at the old place because the jellied cranberry expired at the end of the roaring twenties, remake. A cemented-on lid of adobo sauce, decorative icing?, a boxed bruschetta mix, oh, what the hell, what the hell. Liquid smoke, though. I liked the sound of that. Really a good looking orange label with a few Asian symbols in the corner, too. It was almost completely full, and I had plenty of two-ounce plastic cups left over to sprinkle a teaspoon's worth into a few dozen, let's say ten a pop, spill it out onto a sensitive spot and you won't be alone in there, that's for sure.

Even though I had long given up on football barn, every so often I cued up this old steel curtain soundtrack including torpedo, and raiders, and get the man, and more, and the tanning bed hallway opened to a deep gasp of crisp morning air, fog hanging in the shadowed valleys beneath the glistening beads of dew atop the blades cut to forever by the scissors of an attentive stylist, I shook out the legs and arms to some wavering flute bubbles coming from Carly's wonderful hippy belly, and then was standing atop the counter surveying the merchandise from above while Ron's bass line recited the prices real hard, and the visitors stormed from the tunnel all crazy and in-line and then formed and faced up and made these dumb and stiff left-right-left-right forward punches before Kid Tippy circled around them as the quarterback of the week who had to take the blame for the greater dope show, and the left-right punches continued to exhibit organization while Kid Tippy's posture turned into camera work, and as I stood barefoot on the counter watching the machine Thea hollered from afar, 'there's no home team today Barry you have to jump!' and I leapt down from the counter onto the dewy grass and the ten of them advanced in pattern all stiff and clenched until Brianne whipped off a flurry of loose and feeling violin lashes and all ten shimmied real goofy as I loped off to the side and the dew splashed drop by drop upon the tops of my feet, so refreshing, as Kid Tippy hung back asking questions of his jersey, but then the ten regained direction and rushed at me, flanking my wild strides and gaining ground when then the tuba section of five guys from martbar busted in huge unison with their own left-right of the giant brass hats and forced the visitors to counter with their shadow punching for just long enough for me to feel that sweet dew and the tickle of the beautiful cut along my arches, before they came again with the same old play banking alone on me tiring and slowing, eventually nearing conclusion for its own sake as they triangulated once more, but that was when Karim walloped a gigantic mallet onto the taut trampoline canvas just one time and everyone wearing shoes just straight fell over. My urge to have some fun with them became overwhelming. By the time Andrés poked his trumpet over the counter and ripped some expressive staccato, then stooped back down before rising and doing it again, I was hurdling and ducking and leapfrogging over one and then through the legs of the next, the entire orchestra in full swing of harmony and spurring me along into such a wild frenzy of unseen coordination, dodging and circling and rolling and springing with everything I had to avoid the machine.

So, yeah, it appeared I was about ready to open up, even if at first glance most of seven or eight doupon holders outside might have been doubting their willingness to enter, and some might have walked if doupon did not already have their money. I called for Andrés, as we discussed over some pickle about an hour prior, he had another covering Asian Pita, and was going to usher people down the hallway and into the rooms, doing his best to squeeze a few strangers at once into each one while nodding and smiling and pretending to understand no English whatsoever, as I concentrated on just holding out the full seventy-five dollar combo package in front of each visitor as if the beds had never before been visited without each item, and then work backwards from there with explanations if necessary. Brianne would be in soon enough to assume the big chair, lighten traffic with personal discretions, and maybe even help me send a few for a one-way stroll around the block with merchandise and thoughts.

"Let's try for four to a room man."
"¡Sí….Sí! ¡Bueno! El Grito. ¡Por supuesto! No lo comprendo."
"But I paid for a private experience, I want my own bed!"
"Sí, sí. Con ellos, la cama para üsted."
"I want a manager!"
"Sí. Soy jefe. Soy jefe."

"This is an outrage! You cannot treat us like this, because…..you cannot treat us this way!"
"Sí. ¡Guacamole! ¿Te gustaría guacamole gratís?"
"Ha ha, perfect! There's a bunch set up at the end of the hallway so no one up front can see it being given away. Let's do it!"
"No comprendo. Sí. ¡Adelante! No comprendo."
"I love it! You're gonna destroy it buddy!"
Andrés nodded, straight faced. He was fully in character, like somebody he'd been or seen along the way in full control of a tourism parade near the sea in the old country.

"Welcome to thunder….err….tanning bed. Let's get you guys started with all the gear: goggles, tee shirt, aching joint lotion, multi-dimensional cucumber slices, guacamole to re-iodize the buttocks, and of course……."
I held up a cup of the liquid smoke. "….the special sauce which made tanning bed everything it is today."
"What's this I read about the rich and famous?"
"That's Andres and I, we are rich with sharing a pair of Mexican flag wrestling tights and with any luck you guys will be rich with that too by the time you leave. Alright, seventy-five a pop for the starter kit."
"Wait, what?" I could feel this question coming spoken from three or so, and unspoken from the other five.
"You guys all read the entirety of the doupon fine print, right?………..right?"
There was a silence I had never before experienced indoors. Not any sound, but the air full of something intangible which I did not want to interrupt, but rather wanted to intensify, with my glaring. And as I met their worried and harried and angry and miffed eyes, I really believe I was concerned for quite a bit in general, even if

not for them in particular. All of the lost staring matches in martbar had come back around. I could stand silent and try to keep their eyes engaged instead of checking the doupon, I was absolutely prepared to stand quiet right there for the entire night, even if there were a hundred pushing in from the street.

"We're protected by the doctrine of reasonable consumer expectations."

Bingo. Mr. advocate had just elected himself captain.

"Of course you are. Has any restaurant, in your life, ever mandated that you have a glass of wine with dinner?" So I stood, shrugging, making a bunch of weird faces, for the first time in my life feeling the confidence of caring not a whisper of anything except for a sale I knew I was about to make. I had lost them all to their phones, but was not at all worried over them pulling up the doupon. They were all scouring their personal history, scrambling through these mazes of their own documentation, stooping into a dusty corner behind the radiator, picking underneath a dresser for a shred of lint which collected dust as its time stamp, as if their digital recollections contained a perfectly balanced scale of odds whether or not an establishment had, at some juncture, coerced them from sit, and all the way back to stand, to accept and pay for an unwanted glass of wine. I let them go on with this for a bit. Turned and smiled at Andrés, even.

"I was kind of talking about the romance and enjoyment of it all there guys."

And the tablet was alive with pay beeps.

"Okay, looks like three, three, and two, Andrés will take you in….." And with that, I turned and might as well have been on the other side of the continental divide, engaging the next four in. Brianne showed up during my next group pitch with a tinge of disappointment that there was no one to shoo from the chair. Three more arrived right behind, looked reverently to Brianne, who immediately gestured them towards my merchandise emporium. This crowd was tougher to crack, in part because they knew they had to wait for open beds, and also because one woman bought it all no questions asked so the rest could hang back and judge her reactions.

"The color of the guacamole is a trick of the lighting." The woman scooped a chip through the eerie blue dip, then bit in, running fingers through her hair and making faces and all that weird stuff done when truly judging food. It all finished with a nod and another scoop, and we went from there. I was being patient and nonchalant, turning to see if Brianne had anything to say after a moment. But Brianne had a look of shock and horror, hands up into the cheeks, eyes leading me over my right shoulder. The woman had a button undone and was dropping the cup of liquid smoke straight down into the front of her pants. I stopped short of advising that be done inside, and not fifteen seconds later she had pressed herself into the hip of the guy next to her, as introduction. I scurried for a cup of the smoke and put it in his hand while he used the other to beep payment into the tablet. The other two were not far behind. Within a minute we had four people all trying to figure out how to best give and take with another's thigh. I looked down the hallway to Andrés for his reaction to this, but he gestured his nose at the rooms on both sides. "¡Huele a la parilla! ¡Fumar!"

Oh boy. Oh boy. I gave the next three some free guacamole and asked Brianne to try and hold the attention of four more on their way in.

"¡Gritante! ¡Luchando en las camas!"

I got the gist. They only had ten minutes left in there, no, fuck it, five minutes left if there was yelling and screaming going on. I focused on showing off the four-way circus at the head of the hallway to everybody now in my face, seven or eight or so, immediately recalculating the price of the liquid smoke to forty, but still the same deal for the entire package, and would give them two lotion cups each, maybe that would calm things in there.

"Okay, those four and the next five, you're all up in three minutes!"

There were struggles and arguments over who was in the next five. "Come on now guys. Here! Drop this in your pants and figure it out! Look at those four, don't they look good with one another? Hell, of course, the next eight instead of the next five, four per bed….."

But there were just more visitors who wanted in on that next round, and we were twenty minutes in and I was simply hoping to grab most of their phones and beep through payment, because merchandise was all over the place, people too, grinding all over each other against the walls and the front window, and someone tried for a grab over the counter for a second cup of smoke, which finally drew some kind of ethical line for me as I denied the hand, think it was a man's, plus it appeared we could not run out without everyone getting a dose.

"Barry I can't take it honey. Brianne's…..ohhhh my……I can't believe it…..ohhh my……but Brianne's seen *too much* honey. Mmmmkay, bye."

"Okay see ya tomorrow!" I could barely see Brianne walking out, and certainly had no time to mull over what I had actually just heard.

I hit the sensors for the beds and hit the cold blast too for the rooms to make them all too ready to exit as I nodded to Andres to begin knocking on doors, just before hitting a few more pay beeps for indeterminable price and product, and a minute later there was all kinds of yelling and screaming at each other and at Andrés, who I could just feel nodding and smiling and probably opening one hand to guide them forward. There was so much racket from so many voices I didn't even know what was directed at me or who it was coming from....."My pubes burned off! They're fucking crawling up the walls and slinking around towards piles of guacamole! I might have lost a nipple! Who tries a *move* like that? You liked it. What is this rash? PUBES ARE CRAWLING UP THE WALLS! You're the worst! Who takes a piss in the corner? WHAT IS IN MY HAIR?!? WHAT IS IN MY HAIR?!
"Okay now, you twelve are up! There's some sanitizer in there......let's do it!"
Andrés shot me a glance over his sight of the rooms. And he had seen some messes. He led some down the hall but then a few of them stormed back up, declaring no way were they going into those conditions, and I calmly reminded them of the backup out here and that they were free to lose some layers inside but I'd have to call the cops if they were indecent out in the hallway or lobby, wagering that the liquid smoke had them in quite a bind and trying to suggest somewhere else to go and be naughty would be too risky of losing the moment. And it worked. I was pretty sure it was just a minute or

so and we had the next twelve in the rooms, for twenty-two minutes inclusive of cleaning allowance. I spun around a few times and tried to remember who had what or if anyone owed, but it was becoming helpless. Fast. Dana showed with the mail and got a week's worth of harassment in thirty seconds, the entire room spitballing right for the pension, I'd never seen people after that pension so hard before, and almost right away I started around the corner to try and pull people away from behind, Dana backing up yet surrounded from behind too and then lost the mellow and screamed CHECK IT DOWN FREAKS, and that created enough space to hit the door and move along just before there were loud thumps on the front window, it appeared there was also a doupon for cartons of eggs at the pharmacy, because a few dozen pounded into the glass and as I watched the yolks ooze on down for just a second, saw that someone had made off with Carly's weird chair, and from then on out I really tried to stay focused on all at hand, but was growing less and less sure of how well I was doing so as the depression crept in and grabbed more and more of me, another pickle only accelerating the gravity of it all.

We were just over an hour in and I was numb. The second group had gone for eggs too, it appeared there would be a scheduled shelling each half hour for the next four or so. This accumulation of goo and dissatisfaction did not exactly slow traffic in, though. Hell, I think I even talked to two different people who did not have a doupon, and wanted information for a future visit. The goals became much simpler. We were down to doing what we could to prevent unwanted contact of any sort, hoping for the best inside the rooms. It seemed that we were okay on that front, no thanks to me, absolutely not, but it appeared that they at least had a boundary where all the shades of relaxed civility were cut off by a hard line of a moral, physical, regard for others. So we had that going for us in there, and were at least free at that point to try and avoid any structural damage or theft. Once again it all became a blur. I stood there numb and careless as to whether anyone bought the merchandise or went into the beds. But they kept on buying, kept on pushing into those rooms. I had waved Andrés away to go see if anyone from Asian Pita had called Gehri yet. There was more yelling about the mess and the horror, burning and smoking, shattered expectations, all of the momentary disappointment and angst quickly becoming so many things I could not forget about my own life. So I mulled that over as the next round of eggs thudded on the windows, kind of hoping that someone would at least throw some different food eventually.

"Andrés I'll clean it up, there's two hours left and no one else is gonna show."
"I cleaning. Helping."
"Really, if you want to go home and get away from this, I can do it."
"Two for me, one for you. I cleaning two."
"Okay, thanks buddy. I'll do my best with the eggs on the glass. You know which mornings the guy comes by with the squeegee?"

"I calling. Always close. I calling him for clean tomorrow."

"You're a lifesaver. Ohh…..here, let me give you a bagful of these." I went for the pickles.

Andrés did his quick shake. It was a very assured movement. "Nah. Me no wanting." He shook again and began to turn. He wasn't even going to ask. I could tell, he really wasn't. I was really glad that for all of the things entirely unclear in my head, at least I knew for sure right then that he did not have to ask.

"I'll get all this money turned into paper as quickly as possible, before…….yeah, I'll do it later tonight."

"Splitting Barry. Me and you splitting."

"Nope. The pickles are paid for, I can work them off. This should be a pretty good haul, all told."

"I splitting with YOU."

"I've had my time with stupid money; you'll put it to much better use."

Andrés did his shake and I did my nod for a minute or so, until I acted as if we'd split but would give him all of it.

"I suppose we should try and clean up what we can before Gehri shows. There's just no way he doesn't show if he's in town. You sure you don't want to slip him for the night?"

"I cleaning two."

"Okay. Maybe he's out of town."

Vortex, oh my, Brianne's sanctuary, first sight of it was so sad and helpless that I had this crazy thought of a controlled burn where it might grow back fresh after some time. The visitors were not fibbing about the pubes, they were everywhere, wiggling and crawling and smoldering up and down the walls and over the floor, gathering about the many, many globs of lotion and blue guacamole, shivering and smoking at one end while the other acclimated to a foreign nutrient source. The bed was closed; I snapped on the long rubber gloves Andrés had set at the door, before lifting it. There were no cracks in the glass. There were no cracks in the glass. Otherwise, I had this terrible sense that if I ever painted with the acrylics again, it would all somehow assume the form of this abject nightmare. The blue and white was slathered and blotched and streaked like nature on another planet, unloaded on by a fire hose full of long tobacco strands until volcano craters billowed with smoke and green lava. Most importantly, those were all tobacco strands, Barry. Yep, I just had to wipe up a lot of tobacco strands.

I stood and looked at it until my eyes blurred at a drop of liquid smoke long enough that I could step inside of the blur itself and become a drop of liquid smoke and suck the mess all back into a singular and misplaced molecule.

It was the only hello I could have wished to hear from the front. It was a long and winding word which changed in tone from enthusiasm to perplexity to shock, and everything in between, a few times over, that one word said it all. I stripped the gloves and ran out of Vortex.

"Oh am I glad to see your face!"

"What………*happened?*"

I could tell that Carly was hiding mild amusement behind her concern. Like she only needed to hear that no one was hospitalized so she could laugh. "There was a doupon, and I tried to make a little too much of it."

"Oh no. Barry…..oh no."

I smiled and shrugged, almost begging her to laugh. But she was filled with grief.

"I swear I barely told anyone about you and me, or this place, I hardly said a word about it…….."

"But?"

"The more I stayed quiet, the urge built to just tell *someone*, like suddenly I couldn't explain myself if I didn't mention it, I had no explanation for my strangeness if I couldn't come out with it……and I was at this party, talking to a friend of a friend of a friend, BLAAAHHHH, and then found out she worked at doupon….."

"What size of rubber gloves do you wear?"

She didn't know what to say at all.

"I'm kidding! Kidding! Unless the verbiage on the doupon was an accurate quote from you, if those were your words then I'm gonna have to ask you to leave."

"What did it say?"

"It said something about 'a playground for the rich and famous' and 'sensual experience', strung together with a few sentences of gibberish."

"GROSS! NO! Barry, I'm so sorry……."

"It was the perfect storm. The duopon was just one of many pressure systems that made the seiche."

"Seiche?"

"It's the lake's version of a tidal wave."

"Oh."

"Anyway, don't worry about it. If I just did my job it would have been two mildly irritating days." I moved behind Carly and locked the door over an hour early.

"I hope you don't mind me asking……what *did* you do?"

"Made up a side business of, well, selling pretty much everything you see all over this place. But it was this liquid smoke which really lit everyone and everything into a fire. I pulled it out of the back of my cabinet, had no idea when I bought the stuff, or if I even did."

"What made you so crazy for money all of the sudden?" I stopped dead. The question nearly made me fall over. I had a thousand answers to it and not a one at the same time. Carly gave a look to show me it was just a simple little question that didn't really need an answer. But I needed one. There was just no going on with anything else without an answer.

"I exist so frugally…………." I hung there and Carly did too, patiently, as always, such a patient soul she was. "…..the lake, it's there for me less and less with each passing week right now……I suppose the price of freedom is rising big time."

"For real, or in your mind?"

"Probably for real because of my mind."

I dropped my head and had to run my hands over my face. Carly rubbed at my back. I was pretty afraid I had just said something which made her respect me more at the same moment she became more sure of limitations to our relationship. I turned back to her, mustering up a smile.

"I'd love if you kept me company while I clean Vortex."

"That'd be nice."

"I just need to wipe down the stool and we can set it by the doorway where it's…..relatively…..no so bad."

"I'll be fine."

Carly, I should not have expected different, but she did not freak out at all over first sight. Her eyes were wide and moved about the room slowly and attentively. I could tell she was imagining stories of how everything ended up where it was. I snuck over the side and watched her do this for a little while. She was making it all human on a completely different level then I had. It was a level I wanted to be on more often.

"If you'd like to clean the bed first and then lie down, I'm all for it."
"I can't. I just……..things are always going to be messy for me. I need it as a rule for myself that I'll tidy up before seeing you. You can wonder and ask all you want about what kind of mess I might have just cleaned up……but I can't draw you into it."
"You're too sweet!"
"Yeah yeah."
And, before she asked the next question, her face drew into all those true lines, her brows and lips and cheeks and eyes and forehead, what an incredible face she had, no matter what it was doing, but anyway, this one was framing the next question solely and truly with care for me, instead of us. "But why not?"
"Because I can't……..it would be like…..stealing your youth."
Carly began tearing up. I quickly stripped off the gloves and rushed over to hug her tight. And I kept on adjusting my arms along her back so I could make the hug tighter and tighter while her ribs in front told me that it still felt good for her.

After a little while Andrés showed outside the door. I was sure he gave thought to the best time to do so.
Carly and I opened up.
"Hey Andrés, this is Carly."

Carly immediately slapped her palm on the left side of her chest, ducking her head and shoulders to that side a touch. "Me encanta el vidéo del hombre loco."

Andrés was all shy and blushing and waving it off while shaking his head quick. I figured I might as well keep it going. "If you ever run into someone at a party who's ready to buck up for this guy's skills…….my favorite coworker ever. He makes me forget I'm at work a hundred different ways every day."

Andrés shook it off again and moved up the hallway. He probably thought I was just kissing his ass after immersing him in all the madness. Maybe I was. But it was always true even if the words could only come out at certain times.

After some time and sporadic and minimal, yet meaningful, talking, I walked Carly to the door.

"I'm uh….yeah, I might not be working here for…..well, after tonight. Let me give you my phone number."

"Do you want mine too?"

"I'll have it whenever you call me first."

"Barry……I……I don't…….know….."

"You'll know when it's right. You're someone who I want to always have my number."

We hugged again. The same as before, but of course, also very different.

I am not going to sit here and tell you that it was the lake which woke me up so early and unquestionably the following morning. I also am not going to sit here and tell you that it was not the lake which woke me up so early and unquestionably the following morning. I was in the woods before I could even wonder how the full coffee canister was running a hot sip all the way through. The first thing I remember hearing, after the imaginary and indescribable alarm which threw my feet onto the floor, the first sound after that was the deep and wide stereo of singular thunder, full surround pulling me into the showroom, and then two steps later each drop drumming out on the pavement so full as if every last one was the size of a golf ball, and that's when I realized there was no wind out there at all to blow at the huge drops, the wind was blowing many miles away and sending massive carpet rolls in consistent time towards the wall, and they came in at a slight diagonal, the sound and the plumes leaping up to become golf balls way off to my left, the sound building and all of it rushing past me with volume crescendo of water just before and after it contacted the wall, then rushing past and off to the right, as the next wave came in next after, well, I know I had made up some kind of recurring jingle that went through my head and then was overcome, right on cue, by the next whoosh across the audio panorama. I had snuck into quite the sound check and did not feel pressured to leave, or the pressure of anything else. The sky, it was the only time the sky ever looked like a back wall to me, but it was a wall so rich with shades and depths of charcoal and deep blue and scattered cracks letting light through, all of it so close and so still that it seemed to be telling me that the water came from further away than the sky did. Also, the water was giving off a musty scent, both warm and cold, the scent rare, and I supposed that it was the lake's annual turnover, where the three temperature layers and their relative densities were being affected by the rest of nature enough to begin mixing together, the thirty-nine degree water beginning to haul up scents of the deep. So it appeared that I might have jumped out of my bed to see that the lake was in the process of changing its sheets until they were settled for the winter and would remain that way until it changed them again in the spring. I got a good chuckle over that just as the sun crept up into the awaiting hole in the wall and burned all of the edges into funny shapes and lit a bright streak across the lake and made the flying water glow, and it all had the look of high noon and midnight at once, allowing me to stand there with my little jingle in harmony with the water's sounds, without a care of the time back outside of that eerily intimate room.

There was still not a peep from Gehri as I opened up tanning bed. I had spent a good deal of the day waiting to hear that I should never step foot on the premises again. By the time I made it to tanning bed, I had that defeated reminiscence of showing up for elementary school after the previous night held so much promise of a snow day.

It was quite possible that he was going to wait until the place was fully cleaned. We still had a lot of work to do on that front. I had walked out last night convinced it was entirely fixed, and now was standing in disbelief that I could have found a way to tell myself just that. I was at the height of my frustration with it when the

house phone rang. It must have been a flashback from the previous two days, where I took a year's worth of calls, which made me pick it up without looking at the incoming number. "The doupon expired last night take it all up with doupon ALRIGHT!!"
"Grab your friend and lock the door. We'll be out front in two minutes."
"We can't just ignore the business right before opening!"
"Grab your friend and lock the fucking door and be outside in two minutes."
Click.

I locked the door and ran over to Asian Pita and one look was all it took for Andrés to know he had to come with me, but I had to bellow nonsense back and forth with everyone else over there about how he couldn't go and about how they would just have to suck it up and clean and bus and run for one night of their damn lives. We scooted out the front of Asian Pita.
"Gehri?"
"Ron. Maybe Gehri too. I don't know."
"I no knowing Ron. No meeting never Ron."
"Another guy who sits at the big chair during the meetings. He'll love you. You'll be one of his favorites right away."
Andrés reconsidered. "Me not going without Gehri! No way, man. I no knowing Ron."
"Yes you do."
"Nah, me no knowing!"
"Well if you are gonna think that way, then please trust me that he will get to know you one way or another and your best start is not running back into Asian Pita."
He was not happy about it, but understood, and parked there, frustrated, making his stunted noises of

displeasure until this huge crimson van burned down the block like a sore throat popping good coupe lozenges, and then jarred to a busted shock halt with a stomp on brakes that felt the foot and then relayed the force of it through chassis and cabin. The sliding side door flung open with the rumble of two interlocking iron wheels reeling haywire. "GET IN!"

I barely saw Ron's face before he returned to the driver's seat. I slid myself across the serrated metal floor to the other windowless wall. Karim was in the passenger seat, eyes forward. Brianne was in the singular chair in the rear, a ways behind Karim. Andrés settled in front of Brianne and slid the door forward, surely giving it enough momentum to latch if Ron had not jumped on the gas and sent the van's low gears into a tiger roaring over its own hiccups. So I fell back and grabbed with my left hand at the side pile of rods and boards and Andrés had to gather himself and get the door shut on his second attempt. The engine was really shaking the ridged metal floor and vibrating up my spine from the raw bang of tailbone contact. I met Brianne's eyes and had no idea what was going on. It was somewhat dark in there, no light from the rear either, but still I thought Brianne would give me something. We were in a different room now, though. And Karim, for Karim to leave martbar at this time of day, well, yeah. Brianne rubbed on Andrés' shoulders and it seemed he was regarding the touch with uncertainty to what it might signify. The van's swerve snapped off an untipped lefty curveball, which then dove back low and right, clattering my head against the side and registering my radar gun digits at one rather aggressive pass of a singular good coupe. No one was going to talk. It was time for me to open the floor again.

I decided to get up and try to sneak in behind Ron and get a look at the odometer reading, and then I could just scream out the odometer reading and get back to the floor for Ron to get going at me over something. The very moment my ass left the floor and I got into a catcher stoop directly behind Ron's chair, he slammed on the brakes, and my shoulder flew into the vinyl and springs. He knew I was up to something, somehow. Always. Somehow. I clutched my hands, shoulder wide, over two ridges and then threw my legs back to Brianne's left, and got myself into a plank, ready to bluff a move a few times to see if he'd sense it and try to throw me again. The van grumbled consistent through a reach to the front with my right hand and also me pulling up my right leg into a bend so I was one hand release from a jump forward. So I got myself into a sideways, one arm plank, raising my left arm straight up all zen and perfect for something that Ron could bark, or Karim laugh, over. Ron yanked the van right and my left hand flew into the side for a brace while I wondered how that swerve did not run the van over a curb or something, then immediately it felt like he just ripped the steering wheel clean off and smashed it through the glass of his door window for the swerve back left, which pulled my left hand from the wall and rolled me over, along with the pipes, so I was facing the roof, and Ron double-stomped the brakes to send me sliding on my back up towards the console, and I was able to get my hands up and grab the back of both Ron and Karim's chairs to upside-down swim-fling myself back to the rear just enough to avoid any good contact of Ron's attempted right hand hammer down on my chest or ribs. I sat again.

"How many miles are on this legend Ron?"

"Seven hundred and twelve, and I can see the three, two, and one on the tenth-dial. It has been out of the garage on twenty-six separate occasions in thirty-eight years. Eight of those instances were within a two-year span. I bought it with sixty-five miles on it for twelve thousand dollars, cash. One-hundred and seventy nine of the miles are from a trip to northern Indiana. Three-hundred and four miles back and forth to Sheboygan."

"What was up in Sheboygan?"

"A good bratwurst."

I laughed. Karim looked off to his right, still silent.

"You've taken it out twenty-six times total, no joke, twenty-six times ever, and, like, half of the miles are from a trip to Sheboygan for a brat."

"Yes."

The van came to an easy halt. "Oh man this must be a great one if you're stopping the van to tell us….."

"No Barry, I'm waiting for the light so we can leave the bighome parking lot."

I got to my feet, knowing he was going to allow me a peek. It was one of the most shocking things I had ever seen in my life. The exit from the bighome parking lot, I mean, there was just no way the bighome parking lot had stretches that long where he never needed to fully turn the van and could blow it out like that with the swerves and such like it was a runway. I turned back around and nodded at Andrés to let him know it was true. He gave me the eye raise and nod, real big, like, yeah, Barry, I walked across bighome parking lot when the sanitizer was not delivered, and when some of the Asian Pita chairs needed new pads on the legs, and when......

I sat. "Well this has been a fun learning experience.
Let's get that tanning bed opened and such!"
"We're just loosening up here Barry."
"For?"
"For railroading your fucking asses up and down three-
train yard."
"THREE-TRAIN YARD?!?!?"
"Yes."
"Ron.....I'm not going to have that cash, soooo.....you
know, you'll want me good and fit for the labor of
course."
"We'll see how this goes Barry. Maybe you'll get off on
that front. No more from you for now. You'll have your
chances to talk when we get there."
"¡NO HABLO INGLÉS! ¡SOLAMENTE ESPAÑOL!"
"Nice try Andy."
I spoke up. "Andrés."
"How about accomplice? Let's just go with accomplice.
Thank you Barry."
"Gehri! Me speaking with Gehri. Gehri, he knows. Me
speaking with him."
"Gehri will be there to watch."
I nodded at Andrés like everything would be okay. I
did not know how much of my doubt in that nod was
attributable to his sudden doubt in me. I had given him
that nod so many times, and he always trusted it, and
now here we were, on our way to some place called
three-train yard, and Gehri would be there to watch.

Everyone remained silent. Brianne's eyes were closed
and had been for some time, hands still on Andrés'
shoulders, which nevertheless seemed to continue a rise
up to his ears, the very top of his back arched forward,
and all I could hope was that he had not forgotten that

the way his head was one with his shoulders, and anyone who smacked the back of it would not feel a neck snap forward but rather their hand and arm reverberating from the blow, as if they were blindfolded at a boxing gym and thought they were getting a swing at the speed bag when they were actually standing in front of the heavy bag.

I fiddled my hands about the metal rods and wooden boards beneath me. There were all kinds of different lengths and widths. I began to consider that, all told, Ron may well have set them in there not as forewarning to what he might do at three-train yard, but rather to give me full chance to do it first. So that settled me a touch. But still, the back of my own neck probably had too much cartilage in between the vertebrae. Someone with mitts like Ron could swat the back of my head and then watch it bounce and wobble in every direction for awhile.

One gear of the van's transmission spoke the most and the others got in a few words after a stop. If we were somehow in that bighome parking lot again then Ron was doing a really good job of imitating the norms of the road.

I saw Karim's open left hand reach into the open center, and for an instant I thought it was for Ron to plop something in his hand, but then the hand crept forward towards the console, and then the index finger extending for a touch at a button.
"Not tonight Karim."
"I'm shotgun Ron."
"Not tonight."

I did not like how Ron was saying tonight when it was still afternoon.

"I've never before known you to overrule the code of shotgun."

"Karim you cannot turn that on right now." Oh boy, here we went again with a touching-it lecture. "It's not the time to become comfortably numb or hear the second-hand news."

I waited for him to explain. But that was it, it seemed.

"I'm your second-hand news I'm your SECOND-HAND NEEEEEEWWWSS YEEAHHAHAAAAa!"

Karim leaned out and turned quickly with both of his palms down to settle Brianne before Ron could.

"Thank you Karim."

"You're welcome. However......."

"Karim, dammit, every time you say 'however' it's followed by something too kind."

"We could offer them a chance to double-down on the peace train."

"I'm listening....."

Those bastards, I knew nothing and everything about what was going on. They were about to offer me a sketchy wager.

"If I press that button and the peace train is coming through, then you and I will share a pickle before all of this. If it does not......"

"Yes?"

"I'm thinking."

The silence was long and heavy.

"If I press that button and the peace train is not coming through, then you and I will utilize a double-sweep at some juncture while at three-train yard."

"I like it. You know how I enjoy a quality double-sweep too. Barry? Do you like it?"

I did not like it. But that did not mean I would not ask a few questions about it. "First of all, what the hell is the peace train coming through, or a double-sweep?"

"They are the uncertainties you must accept if you wish for a chance of Ron and I sharing a pickle before all of this."

"I'd put your odds at one-in-fifty. Karim, do those odds seem like a fair estimate to you?"

"Indeed. Most certainly no better than one-in-thirty, and no longer than one-in-one hundred."

"There you have it Barry. How about one push on the button to see if the peace train is coming through for you two?"

"Do I get to push it?"

"No. If you accept the bet, Karim pushes the button."

"I think I should be able to push the button. No disrespect to Karim's shotgun, but for a one-in-fifty chance I think I, or Andrés, either myself or Andrés should get to push it."

"No. Karim pushes it."

"Why?"

"Because you, and maybe Andrés too but we're short on time to find out, but certainly you, you will snake your ass up here and close your eyes for an eternity and make all kinds of stupid dramatic faces as you act as if you can somehow sense when the peace train….even though you don't *even know* the peace train, or anything about it--it might as well be the matching cherries on a slot machine for all you care—you will still close your eyes and act as if you can sense when it's coming through the frequency. And we would have to sit around wanting to poke our own eyes out as you make it into an opportunity to stall, and also, of course, be the center of fucking attention. We're getting close and are short on time. Ten seconds to say yes to the wager and Karim pushes the button. Ten."

"Full pickle for each of you."

"Fine. Eight….."

"And I want an explanation of the double-sweep from each of you."

"It's a crossing maneuver."

"It's a crossing maneuver."

"Four, three….."

"You both said the exact same thing!"

"Indeed. Two, one…."

"No way, no way, I am not taking fifty-to-one odds to risk you two cracking at my legs…..or Andrés' legs…..no, not from both sides, no way. Take the double-sweep off the table, none of that."

"Absolutely. You have our word."

"You have chosen wisely."

I shrugged at Andrés, hoping he could at least use the whole what-to-do to get a better sense of these guys and the situation. I had very little idea if I was doing a lot, or nothing, with regard to both efforts and results, for his sake.

The van stopped gently. Then it jerked as Ron thrust the lever up the column. I tried once more to initiate some conversation. "Hey, just for shits and giggles…….?"

"No, we're not pushing it without consequences. It's time to get serious now."

"Oh."

"You two stay in the van. Brianne, come up here to step out in front. I don't want to open the sliding door yet."
Brianne gave us both a pat on the shoulder and stooped through to the front. I thought it was a given that Brianne would slip out on Karim's side.

The doors shut firmly, one-two.

Andrés plopped himself hard on Brianne's chair and crossed his arms. I was restless as all hell. I shifted back and forth, stood up halfway then sat again, tossed my arms over my knees and then set my hands on the floor. I had zero to say to Andrés. All I wanted right then was to have zero to say to Andrés outside of that van. I wanted to step outside and stretch, or balance, or try for a few loose strides across the yard, no matter what kind of yard it was, I mean, I knew full well there was nowhere to go, we weren't going to scurry off and never show our faces again, I was pretty sure we had that in common, even if our reasons were very different, other than pride, the pride was probably holding similar weight, but anyway, we weren't going to scurry off or anything and the others seemed to know it too, but still, when there was nothing to say it would be nice to be out in the yard.

But the time had come to sit still in my discomfort until someone else opened the door. Or, you know, maybe to just take a look out from the front. I stood up and stepped forward to see that we were double-parked along a residential street, nothing at all out of the ordinary as far as the homes or sidewalks or volume of foot traffic, just a street in the city where if we were actually getting out there, I couldn't imagine going anywhere besides into someone's home. I turned back and shrugged at Andrés. He nodded and stayed in his chair. I thought that we were as good as we could be with each other at that moment.
"I wanting to see Gehri."

"I want to see Gehri too."

The handle on the outside popped and the door slid
open. Ron and Karim were there, but not Brianne.
Andrés jumped out with no hesitation and, really,
without further prompt from those guys. I rattled my
butt over the serrations and set my feet on the
pavement. The way Ron and Karim stood there, we
might as well have been at martbar, waiting for a stool
to open up.
"You're going to leave the van double-parked?"
"It's fine here."
"It just sucks when someone is double-parked and then
whoever comes out to their car blocked in starts laying
on the horn."
"Well Barry, sooner or later that someone will check to
see that the van's door is unlocked and the key in the
ignition, and then they will move the van forward
twenty feet, set it back in park, cut the engine, and then
maybe wave their fist skyward in all directions to show
frustration with having to go through all of that to get
out."
I shook my head down at the pavement.
"You two missed your chance for a nice spin."
I waved it off, like, whatever, I didn't want to stomp on
the gas and push the button of that big stupid van
anyway.
"Okay, let's not keep everyone waiting."
Ron and Karim broke towards the rear of the van as if it
was lunch break and time for Italian beefs. We walked.
On the opposite side of the street, three homes behind
the van was a single lot interruption of development,
and a good number of people in white tee shirts
huddled and scattered along the sidewalk. We crossed

the street diagonal, no worry of traffic. The open plot gained depth in brick and benches and more people in white tees. A few steps more and the el tracks became visible at the rear of the park. People noticed us approaching and gave quick looks before leaving the center and moving towards the buildings on each side. Fifty or sixty total, there was Gehri, and almost everyone else familiar too, guys from martbar, repeat customers from tanning bed, people who had been around here and there over the years, the ones I didn't recognize, well, I could feel Andrés next to me taking them in, and was pretty sure that they were from the part of his circle that had not yet overlapped with mine. Each and every one of them was wearing the tee shirts we made up for the #ETT morning.

Everyone began forming into an arena, clearing a living room of space in the center, as we walked between the benches and towards the crusty beige and peeled corners of fence wiring beneath the tracks. Brianne left the crowd and joined us again. A train clacked from right to left, jammed to the gills, a few curious eyes, too far off to see but not too far to sense, there were a few curious eyes taking in what they could during the momentary window.

"You guys are getting off easy, being that it's rush hour. I wanted to do it much later, with more time in between the trains passing. Take it away Karim…."

"It is quite simple. Of the five of us, two will be out in the center, engaged, if you will, at all times. Those two will remain engaged until the next train passes. If the train happens to come from the left, then first person up, on the left, comes out, taps one of the two in the center to exit to the right, and then begins with the person they wished to remain in the center, that is, after the person exiting makes a gesture of their wishing at the passing train. And the process repeats as the trains continue to pass from each direction. If, and this does happen, if all three people not in the center end up on the same side, then second in line will hustle around to stand and wait on the other side. We will give you a nudge or a nod if you are unclear that it is your time to run out into the center. That will all fall into place easily enough.......”

"Any kind fighting? The fighting any kind lucha? ¿Patadas en las bolas?" Andrés made a duck and cover, then a one-two of jabs, then kicked a leg forward. Karim was tallest and Ron the heaviest and on average they probably had a foot and a hundred pounds on Andrés.

"No, no, my friend.......I hope not to let you down, but it will be mostly talking.”

"Talking......PHHHHH. Shittt. I talking with Gehri.”

"Gehri is over there......" Karim motioned to the audience. "....if you wish to speak only to Gehri, you may do so. But you must do so through whomever you are engaging, out in the middle.”

"I walking over there. With Gehri, talking. No making sense, trains, left, right, running, no making sense. I walking over there by Gehri.”

"Gehri wants you here with us. If you are at all worried at the prospect of losing your job, Gehri has made it no secret that your job is safe. Please trust that you have the ability to say more good things to Gehri through us, than over there with him.”

"PHHHH. No making sense........”

"So we're all cool at tanning bed then, yeah?”

"Shut it Barry. You know full well Karim was not speaking to you.”

"So I'm going out there to fight for my job?"

"Cut the act over caring about your job."

"But I like to see Andrés and Brianne."

"Well then, you'll have to dream up good reason to be able to keep seeing them at work, or dream up good reason to see them some other way."

Brianne leaned in from my right. "That was sweet honey."

I smiled at Brianne. Then I simply considered myself fired from tanning bed, like, for the best of whatever we were about to do, and everything else too, I was not going to fight or worry over that job for another second. Karim motioned to the hovering crowd to indicate that we were almost ready. "Back to the rules for one moment. This is the most important one of all. As I mentioned, we'll all be able to guide each other as to who runs out when a train passes. But if you are out in the center, and, let's say, for instance, I run out and tag the other person to leave, then you must go along with what I suggest, with how I begin the engagement. Please trust that we have no interest in making this any more complicated than it must be. Andrés, if you and Barry are in the center, and then I come out and tag Barry, he walks the other way, and then I might call you a majestic rhinoceros. What happens if I call you a majestic rhino?"

"I charging you! Like rhino I charging you!"

Damn that Karim, he picked the perfect animal.

"There you go. Now would you rather charge me like a rhino, or go talk to Gehri?"

"You call me a rhino I charging you!"

"I like it. Remember though, we're simply playing here. No real punches and kicks, okay killer?"

"Charging only. Rhino." Andrés leaned his head and shoulders forward, a few slow head-butts.

"Karim can I have an animal now too?"

"Barry it is my opinion that you have run around free and wild for long enough."

"Oh. Well, give me something good when you come out there. I don't want to be some dope stuck in the back of the van, sulking and being chastised."

Ron cut in. "Why not Barry?"

"Well……." I looked at the crowd. "…..I mean, damn…." I flung my hand off at everyone in our tee shirts.

"I think you're onto something here. I might as well state the obvious that Karim, Brianne, and myself don't want to disappoint the audience either, so we're sure as hell…."

A train passed.

We waited.

"….sure as hell not aiming to take away your chances of captivating them. This is a big deal that they came out here. All in less than twelve hours notice. For most of them, it's the only entertainment they can count on."

"Oh. Yeah. I can be dolphin drone. EEK!"

"Sure."

Karim turned to the audience once more. They had filled in the center of the park, making a u-shape, still open to the rear, the train side. "Welcome everyone! Thank you for coming out this evening. By a show of hands, has anyone been into the pickle before?"

There might have been three or four who did not throw up an arm.

"Thank you! We will draw straws now and begin. It is likely unnecessary to state this, but please refrain from talking during the show."

We sauntered out into the center of the round room of tee shirts and big eyes. A few pedestrians moved past on the sidewalk, and they must really have had somewhere to be to not even break stride. Karim pulled out a fistful of straws. "Ron and myself will perform an opening scene until the second train pass. After this, the shortest straw will initiate the engagement with second-shortest. So if either of you two pull the shortest straw, you will have a few moments to know who your scene partner will be, and how to begin. After this everything will move much faster, and the luxury of thinking will diminish considerably."

The four of us picked straws, and then Karim opened his hand to show the one left for him. Brianne was going to start something with me, after Ron and Karim did their thing. I was very nervous.

Brianne and I split sides, and Andrés came with me. As the tail end of a train clattered past, Karim began making gestures with his hands, as if he was pouring drinks and moving glassware at martbar.

"Karim they nearly destroyed several years of research and development in a few hours."

"I do not care for that vicious scented-candle lobby."

"Me neither. But this was a pair of fifth-graders starting a food fight with my protein-free pizza......" There was scattered laughter from the audience. But not Gehri.

"......they started a viral uproar over the dangers of protein-free pizza."

"Do we need to pay off the cafeteria workers to hand them nothing but canned peaches for the rest of the year?"

"I like your thinking, but no. We need them to start a bigger food fight with the old pizza."

"We'll make up an exchange program and send them to a different school for a day."

The first train passed. Karim acted out the glassware movement and Ron pretended to fiddle with a jerky stick.

"That sounds perfect. We'll need to send a horde of their enablers too. I'm not sure they have the guts to start a food fight alone, in a strange crowd."

I think that the guts statement got Andrés' attention.

"One classroom full of kids for one day, coming right up. I suppose I could throw in a bonus juice on the house…." More laughter.

"Don't mind if I do, thank you."

Karim spread his thumb and pinkie as if he had a phone to his ear. "The noise while I'm on hold is rather disconcerting."

"An insurance jingle?"

"I wish. It is four voices screaming out their own job titles repeatedly."

The second train arrived. Ron turned towards it and did a very proper bow, one arm in front and one behind. He did it slow and consistent. Then Karim, he made this totally alien move where he brought up his knee and hopped with the other foot, bringing his arm out and upwards, following the momentum of his raised knee, and then when his arm was at its peak, like, way up in the air, he opened his hand as if he was a sorcerer lobbing something at the train. I didn't know if he made it up or not but I had never seen anything like it before.

Brianne and I were up. I stepped out, tight. Brianne hooked a thumb into the waistline, then, turned over pinched thumb and forefinger, dumping a pretend cup of the liquid smoke into the tights. I stood. Brianne ran in heels, stunted quick steps, jumped, and wrapped both legs around the side of my hip. I staggered for a few steps but kept my feet. "Brianne we can't do this at football barn!"

"But I want you *now* baby, you're my fave man lesbian!" We were making circles. "My fantasy matchup is still up in the air!"

"Let's see what *else* is in the air!" Brianne released an arm from around my shoulders and smacked my belly. "I NEED MY FOOTBALL TEAM TO WIN FIRST!" A train came. The crowd erupted. It took me a second to process that Andrés was about to come out, reminded by Karim of what to do, and that Ron was muttering dammit that he didn't get a piece of me just after Brianne. Andrés stomped out all boss and Brianne, feet back on the ground, made a welcoming gesture to Andrés to show him a softer tone if he tagged me out. Andrés brushed Brianne's arm though, and Brianne planted, and did the one-two-three with the hips, the tweedle-pop I think it was called.

"I tell you the gringos no liking your guacamole! Throwing everywhere, chips all gone no chip mess, guacamole they throwing!" Andrés made a heaving gesture with his hand from mouth.

I smiled. "No-name food here, get your no-name food! It's food.....you get to name yourself!"

I held out both hands as if I had a bowl. Andrés did his head shake while pretending to swipe a chip. "Which faraway planet is that from sir?"

"The one with the rings." I nodded. "¡Saturno! Coming from the one with the rings!"

"Did it grow underwater? Or fall from the sky?"

"From the blue ring…..falling from the blue ring…..too much raining….SPLAT!.....too much messy!"

A train came and there was so much going on that I looked in both directions and Ron, Brianne, and Karim stood out so clearly in front of the consistent backdrop of the audience, and they all nodded that we got another train, and I had never been happier.

"But sir it is the *cleanest* and *tastiest* thing on this faraway planet and it only falls….well, how often does this fall sir?"

"El Grito! Every El Grito falling, raining!"

"Well now that has been some time…….is it coming down differently than it did during the last El Grito?"

"Last time more green. More green last El Grito!"

"Yes of course. Did it fall from a different ring?"

"Green ring! Roja too! Before green red!"

"A miracle of nature! What a holiday! Please, take a taste……."

I held the bowl out again and Andrés waved a chip. The silence and stillness of the park was amazing. He knew it too and held them, and me, there. He chewed and rubbed the patchy whiskers on his chin. I think he somehow knew to pause until the next train came. When it did, he smiled huge while shaking his head, and a giggle snuck out two notes just before he said:

"Nah….too much smoky!"

The crowd's huddled eruption shook the yard and the train was passing like a snake in the distant weeds, minding its own business.

Andrés and I were bathing in it when Ron came out and dropped his mitts on Andrés' shoulders. Andrés did a head-forward, arms back rhino charge towards the train, the crowd was still his, and then settled behind Karim, and I was spinning like a top and the crowd was just feet away and very noisy until Ron said, "Son......" And everything immediately went quiet. ".......that was a great home run, but you have to sit down now for the next at-bat."

"Oh, yeah....of course."

"Do you see that 'no pepper' sign behind home plate? The white letters on the green wall?"

"Sure. Is it warning for the hot dogs?"

"Pepper is a warm up game, and this park is the last one with a sign that says 'no pepper'. The sign used to be up in all of the parks. What do you think son? Are the players warming up with pepper again in the other parks, because the signs were taken down? Or were the signs up for so long that by now they see no need to play it?"

"What do the new signs say?"

Ron's brows moved in a twitch of frustration that I had responded with another question. "How do you know there are new signs?"

"You said it yourself when you were driving me to practice. I noticed that the clown billboard was gone, and it was bare, and you said there would be a different sign soon, and then something like how there would always be more and more signs than before......."

"I did say that. I'm proud of you for listening. So, what do you think the new sign says in the Los Angeles ballpark?"

"I don't know……no boobs?"

He did a finger wag. "Don't say that around your mother."

"But it's true! No boobs……"

"How about talking over what the signs say in the Boston ballpark with your mother."

It leapt out of the deep, like so much else. "No hokey pokey?"

Ron's mustache twitched. "You don't want to go to the roller skating rink?"

"It closed down! It's a bbbb….." I laughed just before it came out. "……bighome parking lot now."

I thought that was gonna get him. "You can roller skate in the bighome parking lot you know…."

"Are you kidding me?!? THERE'S GIGANTIC RED VANS HAVING DEMOLITION DERBIES OUT THERE!!!" I was waving both arms all crazy and spinning at the mock horror of being on skates as all these vans closed in. It got a pretty good laugh from the audience as the train came to bring out Karim.

Karim planted and flung an arm forward to get my collar with his index finger. It was strange when he did because, like, three trains ago I had a quick thought of being tagged out and able to stand aside, and now when it happened I was a little bummed that I did not get to stay out with Karim. But I was still so happy, so……well, everything, that when I planted my feet together and had my arms straight at my sides, bent my knees and then sent flops up my legs and through my hips and midsection, then shoulders and head, flopping through and rising slowly until I was on my tip toes, my head and shoulders back, still wavering some and still rising slowly, and as I was doing this and blowing bubbles at the train from so far under to let it know how amazing it was down there, I did not know if I was doing it because of the rules, or everything besides them.

I settled besides Brianne, grinning like a loon. Brianne was smiling too and sifting hair over the ear. I pretend dropped a cup of the liquid smoke in my jeans and made a few more flopping motions against Brianne's hip, to retaliate. Brianne laughed, folding over a touch, and smacked me in the belly.

Karim was beginning with the glassware in his hands again. He shook it so that I thought that the clacks were coming from a shaker of ice in his hands, instead of the last train car. "I just got a call from the principal. There are still two periods before lunch break, and legend has spread throughout the school of those two blowing out a window in the science lab."
"How did they do it?"
"It already does not matter how they did it. Even if it was nuclear fusion, to the kids two classrooms over, it was a rock."
"Well they should have no problem disparaging the old pizza to the world at lunch."
"Pizza? You still believe the cafeteria will be there in two hours? It is a riot over there and getting more severe by the minute. We have to go."
"Grab me three jerky sticks. My van's outside."
A train came for Brianne. Brianne waved it off. Andrés was across the way, brimming with confidence from his

last exit, and I could tell by the way he stood that he had decided on his opening when it was his turn.

Ron clutched the steering wheel. "Sorry about the mess. And the two bulldogs in the rear."
Karim turned his head for a look. "What type of music do they like?"
"I don't think they hear anything when they lie on their backs and roll about on the floor."
"Should we take them into the school?"
"Buster and Lilac don't like to walk on tile. I'm pretty sure they picked out the carpet at home."
I caught a peek of Gehri chuckling and could tell it was not the first one of the night for him.
"Maybe they can lie in the grass outside and all the kids will come out and pet their bellies."
"I was thinking more along the lines of you and me double-sweeping the hallways." Ron snapped his right arm out and then back in really fast.
"The National Guard is in the hallways."
"Are they trying to get everyone out or keep everyone in?"
"The peace train may know, let me see if it picks up."
Karim snuck a finger forward and pushed the button.
Ron slammed a palm on the steering wheel. "Fucking eh! We're on the highway to hell AGAIN?!?"
Everyone roared over the scene as the train came for Andrés. I was glad I just got to stand aside and be stupefied over all of this. Andrés, ohhhh, he was really loaded up with something. For whom, I had no idea. He did his rhino charge, and bumped a shoulder into Karim's forearm just right. Karim had to make one step to keep his balance, and turned back to Andrés, smiling big, and I think also to make sure that Andrés wanted

Ron. Which he did. So Karim, once more, did his strange move of bringing up one knee and hopping and swinging the arm over and releasing his hand way up high, and I was not for sure but it seemed that he did it with the opposite leg and arm the first time. All three of us were on the same side now, and I thought I remembered that I was supposed to fill in the other side, but there was a minute for that and Brianne and Karim did not seem in a hurry to usher me over there either.

"YOUR MOUSSTACHE!" A five-octave giggle fluttered high from Andrés. "Your mousstache, it looking like the PUBES!" Another three-noter. "It looking like the cooorly hairs, crawling, burning, everywhere crawling the PUBES!"
I saw a twitch, from distance. "Well thank you. I do get it waxed and never knew what happened to the ones that were pulled off."
"Crawling up the walls the PUBES. Into the blue guacamole from the rings, SHAKING, PUBES, heheHeHEEHe, they say too much smoky, the coorly hairs they crawling, heheHEHEEHe, looking like your mousstache!"
Ron, I swear he tried to get the first syllable out all the way through the next train pass. That was it. There was not a peep or a flinch from the audience, or the three of us. Only Ron, spitting a 'b' sound after every four clacks of the train. Clack, clack, clack, clack, BUH, clack, clack, clack, clack, BUH. It seemed he was trying to get out the word 'but' to regain his feet. It was not going to happen though. We knew it and Ron did too. Andrés stood about two feet from Ron, eyes huge and mouth agape, maybe even a bit in shock that he was, so suddenly, about to be a heavyweight champ at three-train yard.

He stood still and quiet through Ron's attempts, with his elbows and knees slightly bent. The tail car made its clacks; and Ron one more BUH. Andrés raised an index finger gradually. When it was finally extended up and out, to Ron's slight stoop, he whispered it so soft, but everyone could hear. He whispered 'pubes', so feint but so clear, and the word inched his index finger forward, he did not touch it, but I will always remember it as the moment when the peace train came through. Ron's dam broke. It sounded like santa claus' brother mocking his sibling. "BOOOOOOHOHOHOHOho! BOOOOOOHOHOHOHOho!" Karim slapped the back of his hand on my arm and then rested it on his forehead. Everyone was quiet and stunned and probably saying to themselves, damn, that's how Ron laughs? Andrés, still planted there in front of Ron's slow bend forward, began giggling. "BOOOOOOOHOHOHOHOhoheheHEHEEEEHeBOO OOOHOHOHOHOHOhoheheHEHEEEEEHeBOOOOO OHOHOHOHOHO."

The chain reaction from there was a beautiful explosion of sound and gesture. The entire yard fell apart very quickly. It was not going to be a lonely winter.